PRAISE FOR MICHAEL RAY EWING

…an intricate, well-detailed, compelling, action-packed story that grips from the first page and doesn't let go.

— DIANE DONOVAN FOR MIDWEST BOOK REVIEW

A cleverly plotted techno-thriller populated with complex and wonderfully original characters. Highly recommended.

— THE WISHING SHELF

. . . a thrilling story full of adventure, conflict, and characters who largely look after themselves and those they care about in the midst of a world of corruption and greed .

— THE BOOK REVIEW DIRECTORY

An intelligent high-tech financial thriller!

— DAN LAWTON, AWARD-WINNING THRILLER, MYSTERY, AND SUSPENSE AUTHOR

The fast pace and consistent shots of adrenaline kept me on edge . . . fans of the Jason Bourne series will find *Satan's Gold* highly entertaining. Every single page of *Satan's Gold* is a quicken-your-pulse and "hold on for the ride" experience.

— PIKASHO DEKA FOR READERS' FAVORITE

Lovers of crime novels will enjoy the storyline and fascinating characters as they are transported into the world of internet crime.

— KAT KENNEDY FOR THE US REVIEW

Fascinating, a very recommendable read...

— THE PRAIRIES BOOK REVIEW

The fast pace and consistent shots of adrenaline kept me on edge . . . fans of the Jason Bourne series will find *Satan's Gold* highly entertaining.

— JENNIFER IBIAM FOR READERS' FAVORITE

SATAN'S GOLD

SATAN'S GOLD

MICHAEL RAY EWING

Grand Canyon Press

Tempe, Arizona

Grand Canyon Press
Tempe, AZ 85282
www.grandcanyonpress.com

Cover Design © www.tatlin.net

Title: Satan's gold : money makes the world go 'round, or stop / Michael Ray Ewing.

Description: First edition. | Tempe, AZ : Grand Canyon Press, [2021]

Identifiers: ISBN: 978-1-951479-36-7 (paperback) | 978-1-951479-69-5 (epub) | 978-1-951479-50-3 (kindle) | 978-1-951479-49-7 (ipub) | 978-1-951479-38-1 (pdf) | 978-1-951479-37-4 (ePIB) | 978-1-951479-52-7 (audio) | 978-1-951479-51-0 (audio)

Subjects: LCSH: International finance--Fiction. | Robbery--Fiction. | Money laundering--Fiction. | Hackers--Fiction. | Computer networks--Access control--Fiction. | Banks and banking-- Computer networks--Security measures--United States--Fiction. | Federal Reserve banks-- Computer networks--Security measures--Fiction. | LCGFT: Thrillers (Fiction) | Detective and mystery fiction.

Classification: LCC: PS3605.W554 S38 2020 | DDC: 813/.6--dc23

To my long-time editor, Donna Hoagkemp,
and to my family for giving me time to write

CONTENTS

The idea of money being something physical is almost entirely a fiction. Sure, you can go to your ATM and pull out cash. And you can feel cash in your back pocket and have some tangible comfort there — but in reality, the majority of your money is a number on a screen.
— TYLER WINKLEVOSS, American investor

Storms always reminded Tyler Jackson of Suzanne.

The last time they'd been happy, before she'd ground up his house key in the disposal and FedExed the repair bill, they had been in the White Mountains of Arizona, with heavy black clouds throwing bolts of lightning across the roiling sky. A cool breeze drifted through the open window, bringing with it the sweet scent of rain on ponderosa pine. It had been a wonderful night, one of the best he could remember since Daemon's two slugs tore through his chest.

Standing at the Peninsula Hotel's window, Tyler Jackson watched the flashes of lightning beyond the Water Tower and out over Lake Michigan. Some made the mistake of calling Chicago America's Second City, but even Suzanne, a country girl at heart, would have loved this view.

His cell phone buzzed. He removed it from his pocket. "What's up?"

"Sorry to bother ya, Ty," Dixie Stevens's soft, Texas twang whispered over the connection, "but six more zeros just moved out of Daemon's account in the Cayman Islands. They went through the same maze of offshore corporate shell accounts. I can get more on each hop, but I don't want to spook whoever's at the other end."

Two paths. One goal. Getting his life back.

"Where's the money going this time?"

"That's why I called. Ferguson's transferrin' the funds to the dummy corporation he set up last week in Nassau."

"The money's landing in Nassau? Not another bitcoin account that leads nowhere?"

"Yes, sir. This one's as simple as it gets. Another thing. His cell phone just started movin'."

"Now?"

"Yes."

He stared at the black steel skeleton of the Hancock Building. He had been stuck in Chicago watching Todd Ferguson for two weeks, and every minute of that time had run together in a blur of boredom, greasy food, lack of sleep, rain, more rain, and endless *when is it ever gonna stop raining.*

"All right." He massaged his forehead. "I'll take care of it."

"Be careful, Ty. You're not in the show anymore, and we both know what happened the last time you tried to corral Daemon."

The connection dropped.

Tyler went to the closet and yanked open the three cases inside. The first held his Colt automatic and two hundred rounds of ammunition. The second had a 12-gauge Browning automatic shotgun with fifty rounds of custom-load steel shot. The third contained three prepaid cell phones, his laptop, an Ethernet packet sniffer, Kevlar vest, electric razor, toothbrush, twenty-thousand in emergency cash, and a medical kit. All the comforts of home—if home was a war zone.

He scooped his good luck charm from the nightstand and put the chain over his head. After Daemon's bullet had flattened it, the tiny silver owl was barely recognizable. Suzanne had given him the owl after he graduated from Quantico. Money had been tight, and he hadn't been happy about getting man-jewelry as a gift, but now, five years later, it was one of the few things he had salvaged from his previous life.

Trying not to think about how tired he was, he ran down the stairs to the Peninsula's lobby. His eyes stung from lack of sleep. Dixie had a point: he wasn't in any kind of shape. Despite the bulky vest, his windbreaker looked a size too large. The months of recovery had cost him muscle, and lately, he hadn't been eating right. Never knowing if death was looking over his shoulder made for an excellent diet.

He threw his equipment into his rental sedan, started the engine, and squealed out of the parking garage. He started up the GPS tracker on his phone. A map of Chicago popped onto the screen, with Ferguson's cell phone's location blinking red and his own position in green. The red dot moved west, so he accelerated onto the Kennedy Expressway. The freeway had cleared out from rush hour, but it still had a lot of traffic. Chicago, like most large cities, never slept; brake lights flashed, a chain reaction of red slowing the car ahead.

He shouldn't panic or get his hopes up. He'd gone through this before. If Daemon was involved, it would be stupid to go after him without help. The last time he had flown solo had cost him his career and nearly his life. To be on the safe side, he could leave an anonymous tip for Chicago's finest, call in a robbery in progress. Or he could phone Bruce Lambert in New York. His old partner wouldn't be happy to hear from him, but Lambert might be able to call in a favor. Or he could turn the car around, go back to the hotel, and do nothing.

Listen to Suzanne for once. *Ty, it's not your problem. Let someone else deal with it.*

She was right, of course. The problem was him. He was not a good listener. He passed a tow truck pulling a car away from the guardrail, and the traffic broke free.

Trying to look everywhere at once through the humidity-fogged windows, Jackson sped west away from Lake Michigan, following Ferguson's signal onto Grand Avenue.

Ferguson turned onto Canal Street, and eventually into the Kinzie Park Warehousing District, the brick buildings blackened by decades of soot. The Chicago River was only two blocks away, and the swampy air smelled of diesel exhaust.

He slowed the sedan, turned off his lights, and crept through the rain until he saw Ferguson's car parked in front of a derelict warehouse. Jackson pulled to the curb, got out, and jogged up the street, trying not to worry that his phone was getting wet. The red dot had stopped.

As he halted by the door of the warehouse, uneasiness tickled the back of his neck. He tried the knob and the door creaked open. The interior was a jumbled gloom of rusted metal and water spilling through a leaky roof. The only illumination came from a weak security light hanging from the rafters and swinging back and forth. Gusts of wind switched it on, and seconds later, it swung the other way and clicked off. The light had an electrical short in the cord.

Why had Ferguson stopped here of all places? Could this be a setup? Jackson let go of the knob. He could turn and walk away, but then he would never know why Ferguson had gotten the money from Daemon. Not an option. Holding the Colt in both hands, he shouldered the door. An ungodly stench rose from the slippery cement. Something had died nearby. He searched the gloom, carefully placing each foot before shifting his weight. A prowling cat hissed and slunk away.

Rain smacked the metal roof and his ears rang. He had almost reached the swinging light when he noticed a white glimmer at the far end of the building. Blinking the rain out of his eyes, he carefully skirted the light. As he drew closer, he saw something swinging gently back and forth, something so heavy it made the rafters creak. The light switched off, closing everything down to just beyond the tip of his nose.

Turn around, his instincts demanded. *Get out.* With a barely audible click, the light switched back on.

He took another step. A section of the metal roof crashed

to the floor behind him. Spinning left, he looked up, shading his eyes against the rain. More metal fell, this time in front of him. He backed away and bumped into something soft. Scrambling the other way, he came face-to-face with Todd Ferguson.

Light off.

An eternity went by before the light switched on again.

Two men had been hung by their ankles from the rafters. The first man's throat had been torn open. Blood had run down his neck into his hair and eyes. His mouth had twisted into a scream.

The second man, Todd Ferguson, was still alive. He had dirty blond hair and a face swollen from hanging upside down. Though he approached his mid-twenties, he didn't look much older than fourteen. White lettering on a black T-shirt said BUFF ME TILL I SHINE. A CanAm Labs security swipecard dangled from his sleeve.

Jackson pinched off the narrow plumes of steam emerging from Ferguson's nose. The kid's eyes opened.

"Shh! I'm here to help. Who did this to you?"

The engineer blinked. "Daemon...." he began, and then started to cough.

Jackson stiffened. "What did you say?"

Ferguson shivered, the fear plain to see in his face. He looked up past his feet. Jackson followed his eyes and stumbled backward.

The rafters were full of hanging bodies.

The first bullet snapped at Jackson's coat collar. The second slammed into his vest. The darkness spun. He fell to the floor and water splashed his face. He elbowed the cement and started to crawl. Ferguson screamed and thrashed like a puppet snarled in its strings. An approaching shadow became man-shaped. A bullet skipped off the cement and wailed away.

Jackson's shoulder struck a support post. He grasped at the metal, rust crumbling under his fingers, and lurched to his feet. The door was nearby. He could make it.

The cat darted toward a hole in the wall. Jackson veered after the animal and smashed through into the alley. Wiping rain from his face, he put the Colt's sight on the jagged hole behind him and emptied the clip, aiming each shot towards the back of the building, but knowing he wasn't even coming close.

From down the block, an engine roared to life. Tires squealed, headlights stabbing through the rain. The vehicle barreled out of sight. Jackson, bruised chest heaving, watched it disappear.

Holding his ribs, he limped back into the building. There was no hurry. The shooter had gotten away. Ferguson had been shot. Blood dripped from his forehead.

Jackson looked up. The bodies up in the rafters were only tattered sheets of plastic. He picked up a spool of networking fiber, wondering what Daemon would want with a network engineer. He checked his watch. He had been here far too long. The police could show up at any second.

Leaving through the alley door, he limped to his car and called Dixie.

"This doesn't make sense," she snapped. "Why would Daemon go after a geek like Ferguson? The government could have followed the money like we did. Why take the risk?"

"I don't know." Every word wheezed out of him as he unlocked the car. The bullet had hit him in the lower floating ribs. "I'm just tired of being late all the time. Every lead we follow ends in a dead body."

She sighed, the sound hard to hear over the rain on the car's roof. "When are you flyin' back to New York?"

"I'm headed to the hotel now. I'll let you know my schedule."

"You sound horrible. Get some sleep."

Thinking through every step that had led him to Ferguson and what he had done since arriving in Chicago, he drove through the empty streets. Had Daemon known he was being followed? Had the entire evening been a setup of some kind?

Disturbed, he stepped on the gas.

Twenty minutes later he skidded into the Peninsula's parking garage, parked illegally in a loading zone, and, ignoring the hotel staff's stares, lurched inside the marble lobby to the elevators. He was a grimy mess.

The elevator opened. He punched the button to the twenty-eighth floor. The car started up, barely seeming to move. The doors finally opened and he staggered down the hall. Fingers fumbling, he swiped the card and snatched open the door. The suite was empty. Nothing had been touched. *Thank god.*

Behind him, the door swung shut. Was killing Daemon worth losing everything? Was Daemon worth the frustration, the gnawing fear, always a hair's breadth away, that he would die again? If he didn't stop, he was going to need a good shrink or a hole in the ground.

He removed his coat. The first bullet had gone through his collar. The second had hit him in the ribs. There was a pucker in the Kevlar where it had turned the bullet. But the hole through his collar bothered him the most. Another inch to the left, and that would have been it. His hands shook.

He glanced longingly at the bed but checked available flights on his phone as he headed for the bathroom. With Ferguson dead, there was no reason to stay in Chicago. He could sleep on the flight back to New York.

He peeled off his muddy clothing and was about to step into the shower but stopped and went back to search the room.

Bad luck.

The owl was gone.

2

ALEC JANNÉ PULLED his BMW into a parking space off an alley. Even though real estate was pricey on Chicago's Near North Side, no other buyers had wanted the boarded-up brownstone—too much noise from the dance club next door. But the building had suited his purposes. His men had done their jackhammering after dark. He shouldered aside the back gate. Construction debris—a bankrupt developer's failed attempt to do a quick rehab and flip—littered the backyard. The developer had left sections of rusty scaffolding, rolls of roofing paper, a cast-iron bathtub, and even a small cement mixer. A few more chunks of concrete hadn't even been noticed.

An angled steel storm door kept rainwater from flooding the basement, and that had been important because he needed a building with a dry basement. He grabbed the rusty storm door's handle and heaved the door open. It fell behind him with a thunk. He trotted down the crumbling concrete steps. An old girlfriend had once told him he moved like a bouncer—shouldering through a crowd with his chest thrust forward. Actually, come to think of it, he was probably better at muscling his way through computer code. In crowds, he didn't have to push his way through. People shied away from his pale eyes.

He kicked open the basement door and went inside. Powerful lights were strung across the basement's ceiling. Fiber-optic cable looped across the floor and linked the computers to the network switches. Servers hummed. A cloud of cement dust hung in the air, and particles fell like snow.

He stopped at the hole his men had jackhammered through the basement floor. The hole opened to an electrical service tunnel, and the tunnel led to a manhole at the corner of Erie and Franklin. Planning was everything. If the FBI staged a raid, he and his crew could escape like Jean Valjean running through the Paris sewers. But that wouldn't happen. Now that he had Todd Ferguson's case, everything would work out.

Spikes of rebar secured an aluminum extension ladder. If they had to escape this way, the lightweight ladder would be easy to pull into the hole. Down in the tunnel, they had a six-foot wooden painter's ladder and flashlights, both purchased when they'd bought the jackhammer. Today would be the reward for all the hard work.

He turned and descended. Clamped to an overhead pipe, a halogen spotlight glared. With no working shower in the building, he saw that his two techs, Hassan Tarazi and Carl Jester, were still covered in dust. Tarazi was thin with bony arms, an angular face, and long black hair, while Jester was short, with a face as bumpy as a sausage lover's pizza. Jester always smiled, showing teeth stained from the chocolate bars that seemed to grow from the lint in his pockets.

When Janné's foot touched the damp clay bottom, he heard the click of metal. Catalina Sing flicked the straight razor in her hand. With thick black hair, a dusty complexion, and dark eyes, Sing was a striking, muscular woman of mixed French Caribbean descent. She pressed against him, the fingers of her free hand slipping inside his suit and caressing his chest.

"Did you get it, *amoureux*?"

"Yes." Janné put the case down carefully on the tunnel's damp clay floor.

"So it begins," she whispered.

Janné nodded. "Or ends."

The case was locked, but Todd Ferguson had given him the key. Janné swung the lid aside.

Jester leaned in for a better look. "You sure this will work? Splitting light off live fiber is impossible."

Janné glanced at the hacker's heavy face. "I was very specific in my questions."

Ferguson had built the optical coupler from a gutted, standard 19-inch network switch. The case was missing the top plate, but it didn't need to look pretty. Processor boards, cooling fans, and wires jammed the interior. The RJ-45 jacks on the face plate had been replaced with small, centimeter-square optical ports. The prototype had no identifiable logos or model numbers.

Shielding his eyes from the light, Janné looked up at the numbered plastic industrial conduits running along the tunnel's ceiling. One of the conduits had been cut open, revealing dozens of slender fiber-optic strands. A strand of the spliced glass dangled from one of the cables. On the strands of the exposed cable were tiny stenciled numbers.

Janné removed a sheet of paper from his pocket. "Tarazi, unfold the ladder and separate the strands."

"I can do it," Jester said.

"Your weight will break the ladder," Sing said.

Unfolding the ladder, Tarazi gave Sing a wary glance. The only thing predictable about Sing was her unpredictability.

While Tarazi separated the strands, Janné carefully matched the numbers on the paper to the numbers on the strands. Then, he ordered Jester to extract the coupler from the case and its sheltering acoustical foam. "Don't drop it, whatever you do."

"I'm just fat," Jester said, "not clumsy." He lifted the coupler and held it so that Tarazi could slide it into the angle-iron bracket they had lag-bolted to the tunnel's ceiling. After Tarazi had screwed the case's rack rails into place, Jester plugged in a power cable and then picked up the optical cable.

"If this doesn't work," Jester said, "it'll take down their entire network, and we won't get another chance."

"I know," Janné said.

Jester pushed the connector into the input jack. The coupler's lights flickered to life.

"I'll be damned," he whispered.

"How long will you need?" Janné asked Tarazi.

Tarazi stepped into the light. The cement had turned his black hair gray. "Two minutes to route the traffic through our systems, another minute to start my code. Once we're connected, you'll need to break their encryption. The theoretical permutations of a gigabit crypt key may as well be infinity."

"It is infinity!" Jester insisted under his breath. "Even a billion processors running for a million years couldn't crack that key!"

Janné put a hand on the ladder. "Get me connected. I will handle the encryption." He motioned to Sing. "Are you ready to wish *Directeur* Byrnes a happy birthday?"

A smile lit her dark, bottomless eyes and she put the razor away.

Janné followed Sing, Jester, and Tarazi up the ladder. Then he sat in front of his computer and brought up their software. Sing handed him a list of TOR gateways and slipped her fingers into his hair. It didn't matter where they were or when, she was always touching him.

"I have something for you." He withdrew the bit of silver from his pocket and dropped it into her palm. "Another puzzle, I believe."

She lifted the broken owl to the light. Her eyes widened. "Where did you get this?"

"It was on the floor of the warehouse. I believe he dropped it."

"Then that would mean—"

"It had to be the money. You were careless to use that account."

"But after all this time!"

Janné nodded. "And still the Owl hunts."

After turning back to the computer, he picked an anonymous gateway and used it to open an encrypted video cam link.

"*Bonjour, Directeur*," Janné greeted his former employer. "Another year has passed. What is the term you Americans use —ah, time moves quickly when I'm having fun, yes?"

CIA Assistant Deputy Director of Special Operations Marcus Byrnes was a big-boned Texan with a head large enough to mount horns on, a heavy frame, and surprisingly delicate hands that could cradle a cocktail glass as easily as break it. A shock of regal salt-and-pepper hair covered his head, the part on the side straighter than an ethics line. He sat at his desk, the Great Seal of the United States on the wall behind him.

If Byrnes was surprised by the call, he did not show it. "Alec Janné and Catalina Sing," he growled. "I wondered if you two were going to call."

"I have not yet missed one of your birthdays, *Directeur*. I do not see a reason to begin now. Years of preparation have come down to this exquisite day."

A resigned look crossed Byrnes's heavy face. "Don't do this, Alec. I have resources at my disposal. Return my money, and I will try my best to accommodate you."

Janné noted the worry in Byrnes's gravelly voice. For as long as Janné had known him, Byrnes had always been at the top of his game. Now he sounded tired.

"It is a bit late for compromises, *Monsieur*. Five years is but a moment since your betrayal of me. I have not forgotten. I will not forget."

"I'll find you, Alec. It's only a matter of time."

"Yes, all good things must end, *Directeur*. Even you and I."

"So, this is the end then?"

Janné nodded. "Or the beginning."

The connection dropped.

Janné reached into his suit pocket and removed a slender red and blue metal card. A long LCD window split the card in half, displaying a string of sixteen integers. As he watched, the numbers changed. He held the time encryption card up to the light so that Jester and Tarazi could see it.

"Do you know what this is?" he asked.

Jester licked his grimy lips. "Infinity."

Janné handed the card to Tarazi, and the long-haired bony tech carefully typed in the sixteen numbers on his computer. A pop-up window opened—a map of the United States. The twelve Federal Reserve District banks blinked brightly on the map; a single, encrypted strand connected them.

Janné smiled. "*Joyeux anniversaire, Directeur* Byrnes."

3

WITH A SHRIEK, the bullet screamed through the snowflakes falling on the lake and tore through his heart. Tyler Jackson started awake. The nightmare had never been this bad before, not even in the hospital when the dream had caused him to claw at his bandages. Beyond the blinds, he saw Riverside Tower's broken sign. Day already. He had thrown himself on the bed fully dressed.

Dixie Stevens glanced up from her computer, pulled out her ear buds, and pushed her keyboard away. She was slender, young, and looked more like a college coed in her varsity sweatshirt and tattered jeans than one of the best hackers in the world. He accepted the offered glass of water and took a sip, half expecting water to spurt from his chest.

"Same dream?" she asked, Texas twang bending around the vowels. "Can you remember it this time?"

"No."

She touched his hand, her dark hair falling from her shoulders to brush his cheek.

"Find the key and unlock the memory," she said. "It's the only way you're ever gonna find your way out. Did you see his face this time?"

Jackson shivered again, wisps of the nightmare already dissolving. "No. Just the snow on the lake. Same as always."

Her computer beeped. She turned to her keyboard, fingers flying as she traversed the electronic highways crisscrossing the North Atlantic seaboard.

"How ya feelin'?"

"Fine," he lied.

She glanced at him, frowned, then went back to the screen. "Before I forget, Pavak called with another of his so-called jokes."

Jackson sat up. "What'd he say?"

"Why do you always make me tell them?" she protested. "If you want to hear it, call him."

He motioned for her to continue.

She rolled her eyes. "I'm at the doctor. He walks in and asks me what's wrong. I tell him I need help because I'm a moth."

"You're a moth?"

"Do you mind? It's bad enough tellin' it in the first person."

"Sorry. You tell him you're a moth —"

"—and he tells me he can't help me because he's a general practitioner. What I need is a psychiatrist."

"And then?"

She gave him another eye-roll. "I tell him I was on my way to see a psychiatrist but stopped when I noticed his light was on."

Wincing, Jackson swung his feet off the bed and laughed.

"I thought your ribs were fine," she said.

"Did Pavak say why he wanted me to call him back?"

"No. Of course, he knows I despise him, so our conversations leave a lot to be desired. If he looks at me one more time like I'm not wearin' anythin', I'm going to get out a pair of very sharp scissors and do nature's majority a favor."

Jackson limped slowly into the bathroom. "How long was I asleep?"

"Three hours."

She plucked up the yellow sticky he had left her before going to sleep. "I got your note about looking at ImTech's 911 network monitorin' software. You really think they're using one of the monitors to move Daemon's money? Hackin' the accountin' software makes more sense."

In the bathroom, he looked at himself in the dirty mirror and rubbed his bristled chin. No time for a shave. He settled for splashing water on his face.

"They could have changed the alerts," he said, toweling off and grabbing clean boxers from his suitcase. He turned his back as he dressed. "Besides, we've gone through every line of their accounting code. It must be somewhere else. Accounting is too obvious. That's the first place an auditor would look. Nobody would think of examining their monitoring tools."

She grumbled something about wasting her time then cocked an eye at him. "Is this one of your crazy hunches?"

"There's nothing crazy about my hunches—especially since most of them turn out to be correct." He slipped a shirt over his head. "Go on. I want to hear you admit it."

"I will not! The last time I listened to one of your nutty ideas, I ended up soakin' wet at a bachelor party at one in the mornin' with some pervert named Sal and his three musketeers. Yes, that is what they called themselves, and no, I will not tell you why!"

He tried not to laugh. "That was an honest mistake on the address."

"Oh, brother! You, sir, are a horrible liar."

"I am not!"

She scooted the desk chair back from the computer and propped her feet on the bed. "How many of these hunches did you get through before you fell asleep?"

"I got through most of the database monitors. You should probably start there."

He picked up his jacket from a chair and holstered his Colt.

"I keep thinking about what happened to Ferguson last night. What would Daemon want with a network engineer?"

She shrugged. "The entire world is networked. Everythin' from the financial centers to about a billion miles of world-wide packet-switched nets. Ferguson has over forty optical communication patents. Maybe Daemon was after something he's workin' on."

"The more I think about this, the more my head aches."

"Speaking of headaches," she noted, "I glanced at Todd Ferguson's code while you were sleepin'. CanAm Labs's boy-genius really goes out of his way to make his code unreadable. I don't think he uses a single variable name over three characters in length. You should probably take a look after you meet with Lambert. You're better with iterative algorithms than I am." Her brown eyes flicked over him and her syrupy voice dropped. "You sure you're up for this? You look terrible."

"I'm just frustrated. Every time we get close, Daemon disappears."

"Wall Street is near the Federal Building. Maybe you should mention Ferguson to Bruce Lambert."

Jackson snorted. "Yeah, I'll do that. I haven't been arrested lately."

Opening the door, he limped down the hall. Even with the nap, he felt tired.

NEW YORK in late August was a steam room. Humidity blanketed the city in a suffocating haze. Normally Jackson hated the heat, but today he didn't mind it. Compared to the nightmare of being shot, heat was no big deal. He just wished he could sleep through one entire night. The six weeks they had been trying to crack ImTech felt like six years. Promises made. Promises broken. All he wanted was to get back to the life he'd had. In the last few months, he had worked around the clock more than he cared to think about, with more of the same coming.

The sidewalk led away from the Hudson River, but even though he grimaced at the pain in his bruised ribs, no one bothered to look him in the eyes. The stress of living in the city had robbed their faces of kindness. His, too, he supposed, stopping at an ATM to check his cash. He pulled out his wallet. Six twenties and change. Just to be on the safe side, he'd better withdraw another six hundred. And there, behind his debit card, was Suzanne's tattered picture: golden hair and hazel eyes. Man, that girl had a smile, sparkling and off kilter. He had taken the picture at his parents' ranch in Arizona a few days after the corn had started showing in the fields. They had just finished riding his father's quarter horses, and her hair had blown back from her face in a nest of wind-tangled curls. She hadn't wanted him to take the picture, but he had, and now, almost four years later, it was the only thing he had linking who he had been to who he was now.

Why did he keep chasing Daemon? The FBI didn't need his help. The only reason they hadn't thrown him in jail was because he stayed out of their way. On the good side, he had made a lot of money tracking down the accounts Daemon had stolen, but was it worth getting killed? Was his life worth the damned eighteen percent of whatever he found?

He removed a new prepaid cell phone and called Suzanne. A pair of skateboarders did rails off a broken bicycle rack in front of a corner grocery store. A portable stereo spat out a steady stream of rap so fast it sounded like gibberish.

"Hello?"

"Suzanne? This is Tyler. Please don't hang up."

"What do you want?"

Her soft, sweet, irritated voice knifed through him. He rubbed his eyes and turned. East Manhattan was only a few miles away, but it might as well have been on another planet.

"Are you free for lunch?"

"No."

"Why not?"

"We've already gone over this."

A snake coiled in his gut. He took a deep breath.

"I'm hoping you and I could take a few weeks off and go home. I'm trying to move on. I really am. I don't want the rest of my life to be like this. I know that. But I'm getting close. I almost got him last night."

"Tyler, an engagement isn't supposed to be this hard! You're never here, and when you are, I wake up in the middle of the night and find you gone. This isn't a relationship. I don't know what it is, but it isn't two people planning a life together."

"I love you, Suzanne. Please."

Except for the rap music, it was very quiet.

"Suzanne? Are you there?"

"Yes," she said. "Yes, I'm still here." She sighed. "Ty, can you answer a question?"

"I'll try."

"Remember when we used to laugh all the time? I used to complain to my friends that all we had were these nonsensical conversations where I would try to discuss our future and you would spring some inane joke on me. At the time I felt like throttling you because you were so frustrating, but after a while, and lots of therapy, I got used to you, well, being you. Tell me, when was the last time you laughed? I keep trying to remember and I can't. I'm not sure you're the same man I fell in love with."

He took a breath and crossed his fingers. "Yesterday, I went to the doctor's office and said, 'Doc, I think I'm a moth.'"

He finished the joke and waited. For a few seconds she didn't say anything.

"I had to ask," she finally said. "Like a fool, I had to ask..."

He closed his eyes and released his breath.

She sighed. "Lord knows I shouldn't, but I'm willing to

give you one last chance. I have to meet with a client at six, but I'm free for dinner afterwards. Meet me down at the Hat and we'll talk."

His soaring spirits plummeted. He tried to speak, but the words wouldn't come.

"Ty? Are you there? I hear music, but—"

"I can't tonight," he said, voice lifeless even to himself.

"You can't?"

"No."

There was a click and the call ended.

4

JACKSON CAUGHT another cab and rode it deep into the
concrete and steel canyons of upper Manhattan. Crowds in
their business suits and dresses, all in a hurry, rushed past as if
he were a rock on a stream. He couldn't really blame Suzanne
for hanging up. At least she had been willing to talk. Anything
was better than the night she had ground up his key.

The cab dropped him off at a hotel. At a pay phone in the
lobby, he called Lambert at his office in the Federal Building.

"Hello?"

"Is this the Met's ticket office?" Jackson asked. "I need
tickets."

There was a slight pause. "You have the wrong number."

Jackson hung up and leaned against the wall to wait. Ten
minutes later, the phone rang.

"I have something you'll want to look into," Jackson said.
"Something you'll have to be careful about. Wilkens won't
like it."

"That's nothing new," Lambert replied. "Your name's come
up a lot lately, and he's not happy."

"Me? Why?"

"We were watching one of the accounts you tracked down

for the Russians. Moscow moved on it, and it caused problems."

"It's their money. They're entitled to it."

"Yeah, but they weren't happy to find out we haven't been as forthcoming as we could have been about their stolen funds. The Russian Ambassador is demanding to know all of Daemon's other accounts, at least the ones we know about."

"That's not my fault."

"That's not how Wilkens sees it. He doesn't like flushing an investigation because you keep getting involved. Just talking to you right now could get me fired."

"I'm careful. I didn't leave anything behind on the account."

"That you know about."

The call dropped.

Going over what his friend had said and especially what he hadn't, Jackson stared at the receiver before putting it back gently in its cradle. If the government had proof of how Jackson had tracked down the missing money, that could lead to serious problems. The last thing he wanted was for the FBI to be looking closely at his activities. They didn't have to hack, and they didn't have to break the law to get ahead. Every phone call and every data packet on the internet went through their taps. Years ago, they had gotten a lot of bad publicity for doing warrantless surveillance, but they hadn't stopped. If anything, they had started tracking even more. The NSA had just opened a new high-performance computing center in the Utah desert. Every packet on every public network on the planet went through that center. There was a reason why it was located so far from the oversight hounds in Washington.

He'd survived by staying out of sight. If the government had any idea how many laws he had broken tracking Daemon, they'd lock him away. He took a careful look up and down the street, then caught another cab to where Quentin Pavak had parked his van in the shadow of Melissa Nigrovic's uptown condo complex. The van's engine rumbled quietly, with condensation puddling on the asphalt. Jackson slid open the door. Pavak sat in the back of the van typing on his laptop and talking on his cell. As Jackson got in, Pavak looked up, grunted something into the phone, and snapped it shut.

"Yo, Tyler, 'bout time, man. How's the ribs feeling?" His nasal Jersey accent sounded like a head cold.

"I've been better. What's up?"

Pavak grinned. "Well, that all depends on if Debra's in the mood, if you get my drift."

Jackson groaned and found a spare chair. Racks of surveillance and communications equipment filled the van. It was hard to fit himself, Pavak, and all the equipment inside. For some reason, the van smelled of fish.

Wrinkling his nose, Jackson took a Snickers bar — his "go to" meal — from a sack on the floor. Maybe nuts and chocolate would overwhelm the fishy smell.

Debra, Pavak's girlfriend, was an organic herbalist with odd ideas about nutrition. Jackson never knew what Pavak was going to bring for lunch. A week ago, she'd fed him broccoli, avocado, and rose petal nutritional shakes, leaving Pavak with a lethal case of gas.

"Did Dixie give you my message?" Pavak said.

"All she told me was you'd called."

Pavak gave him his penetrating cop stare and scowled. "I comment on her rack a couple of months ago, and she never lets me forget it. I could reach a hundred and still not understand how a dame's mind works."

Jackson looked out the window. A dreadlocked street artist was setting up an easel. Innocent enough.

Quinten Pavak was easily twice as big as Jackson, most of it muscle. He had carefully combed dark hair, a handsome face, and a bleached, glittering smile that always reminded Jackson of an insurance salesman's. He was a former New York City police detective who had quit the public sector after his wife had enough of the sewer he crawled through each working day and had left him for a man who sold advertising space in women's magazines.

Money had been tight during his divorce, and Pavak gradually lost sight of the difference between his personal life and the evil he found himself mired in. One day ran into another until, one cold winter afternoon, two detectives from Internal Affairs paid his apartment, his safe deposit box, and even Debra's garden shed an untimely visit.

It had taken every favor he had collected over the years not to get charged for possession of stolen property. He found himself busted loose and penniless at the age of thirty-nine. All he had were the clothes on his back, but he had survived over fifteen years of policing the Big Apple's rotting core, and a lot of people owed him favors. That had been over four years ago —more than enough time to exact a full measure of revenge.

"Was that Debra on the phone?" Jackson asked, sniffing the air.

"Yeah. She was just calling to see what I thought of the fish oil smoothie she packed me."

"Fish oil smoothie?"

"Non-fat yogurt, sunflower seeds, blueberries, organic cream, and fish oil blended together." Pavak poured himself another shot from the thermos.

The shake had a stomach-turning yellowish tinge. "She must have you by the balls," Jackson said.

"Yeah, she does, but I'm not the only one. I have some news about Vaccaro," Pavak said after taking a sip. "You're gonna love it." He turned back to his laptop and typed awkwardly on the cramped keyboard. One of the monitors bolted to the side of the van's wall came to life. The monitor showed a grainy black-and-white video of Joseph Vaccaro, the chief financial officer of ImTech Technology, walking into a building. Vaccaro was clearly nervous and kept running his right hand across his bald, shiny head.

It had been a month since Jackson had traced a maze of financial transactions to ImTech. Daemon's holding accounts in the Caribbean had moved through multiple offshore companies before bouncing off a closed account in ImTech's receivables — which was peculiar since money was only of use if it could be spent. Considering all the accounts the money had traveled through, letting ImTech's software bounce the transfer as an error that didn't make sense.

Jackson squinted at the display. "Is that a bank?"

Pavak nodded. "The first of three. Vaccaro started pulling funds from his safe deposit boxes just before lunchtime. You should see the pile of gym bags in the trunk of his Mercedes. He's even wearing his ImTech golf shirt, if you can believe it. For the CFO of a major tech company, he really isn't all that bright. He may as well walk in with his company badge clipped to his shirt pocket. I'm surprised his wife hasn't realized he's been spreading his DNA elsewhere."

"Is he upstairs?"

"Yeah. The love birds have been celebrating for the last hour. Once I realized they were going to be there awhile, I planted a camera in the building across the street from her condo. It's the second window from the left, eight floors up." Pavak clicked his mouse. "Take a look."

Jackson unfolded a canvas stool. At first, he could see very little, but then Melissa Nigrovic, carrying an armload of clothes, walked across the condo. The windows had blinds, but they were partially open, and Pavak had gotten the wireless camera's angle exactly right. She was young, had thick, luxurious blond hair and, as always, looked like she belonged on a magazine cover. As a bonus, she was dressed only in her lacy underwear.

"Is she packing a suitcase?"

"Yes."

Jackson's cell beeped. He noted the number and hit the button. It was Dixie.

"I really hate to say it, so I won't," Dixie grumbled.

He blinked. "What won't you say?"

"I know how Daemon's movin' the money and how Vaccaro's gettin' his cut."

Jackson stood up so fast he hit his knee on the van's desk.

Over the phone, he heard the clicks of her keyboard. "As you know, the two most important questions with ImTech have always been why Daemon's money keeps bouncin' off a closed account, and how Vaccaro has been movin' his percentage into his growth funds in South America. As far as we know, nothin' has ever moved in or out of ImTech since the destination account is closed. Every time the sendin' computer tries to transfer the funds to ImTech, the transfer bounces because it has nowhere to go. It's the perfect cover. They have thousands of rejections as proof of their innocence."

"So how is Vaccaro moving the transactions through a closed account?"

"After our conversation about the alert monitoring, I started watchin' the process tables on the accountin' server. About an hour ago, I noticed that every time the 911 client-error-monitor process would cycle, Vaccaro's investment accounts in South America would populate."

"I was right!"

"You and your hunches," she groused.

He smiled. "How does it work?"

"Inside the 911 client error monitor is a small include snippet of Perl code that intercepts the money before it hits the closed receivables account. The snippet transfers the money, clears the logs, and then reverses the operation the next cycle —all of it at millisecond speeds. Vaccaro dumps his cut offshore into some Mexican and Brazilian growth funds. ImTech's accountin' software times out the transaction and bounces the transaction back to the Caymans as an error where it sits in a log file as a dead end. Unless someone was insanely gifted," she said, typing again, "or knew what to look for, chances are they would miss it."

Jackson flashed Pavak a grin. "Hey, Q, do you think I'm insanely gifted?"

"Only with the women, boss."

Dixie snorted.

"So where does the transfer go after Vaccaro takes his cut?" Jackson asked.

"You're not gonna like it. The destination is a bank on the island of Madeira off the coast of Portugal. As you know, the Madeirans are notoriously, ah, lax with their bankin' standards."

Jackson swore. Would he ever catch a break?

"But at least we're one step closer to the end of the rainbow," Dixie said.

"How much money has been moved this way?"

"Hundreds of millions. Probably a lot more."

Shouting about Jesus, God, the end of world, and how hellfire would soon be raining down, a homeless man staggered past the van.

"There's one more thing, Ty," she said. "Something about this doesn't make sense. You pay me a lot of money to get you access where you need to go. Most of the time, we're chasing overseas, which is logical. If I was Daemon, I wouldn't want the FBI involved unless it was absolutely necessary."

"So?"

"The money in Madeira is movin' to accounts here in New York."

Jackson sat up. "Why would Daemon do that? There's more scrutiny here than anywhere in the world."

"I know. It doesn't make sense. Maybe you should call Agent Lambert again and see if the Feds know anything."

Jackson grimaced. "Well, about that. I spoke with him earlier and he's not happy. We tripped over one of the accounts the FBI was watching. Moscow's angry the FBI was sitting on it and demanded all the money and accounts they know about. As you can guess, Wilkens is upset. He wants me thrown down a hole."

"Your old boss always wants you thrown somewhere."

Jackson sighed. "Just another perk of being me. We'll talk about it later. Right now, Vaccaro's taken the day off to visit his safe deposit boxes around town. He's at the lovely Ms. Nigrovic's condo where she's busy packing suitcases."

"What!" Dixie started to type furiously. "Should I empty Vaccaro's account? He won't be able to go anywhere without the money."

"Not yet. Pull the money and he'll disappear."

"What should we do then?"

Jackson watched Melissa carry another armload of clothes. "My guess is if Vaccaro knew he was under surveillance, he wouldn't be letting his girlfriend parade around the condo in her underwear with the blinds open. We have enough to hand him off to Moscow. Vaccaro will probably tell all to avoid being extradited. Maybe the FBI will find something we missed."

She sniffed. "I'll believe it when I see it."

"Shut everything down. Once the Bureau starts digging, I don't want to be anywhere nearby. How much is in Vaccaro's investment account?"

"It'll probably break eight million sometime this weekend. Why?"

"What are the odds Vaccaro could code the account transfer into the monitors?"

She thought for a second. "If you're askin' me if the guy who changed the company monitorin' system is the same fool who keeps his criminal to-do list on his phone where anyone could see it, I would have to say no."

"He would need help." Jackson rubbed his face, thinking. "I'm going to call Lambert again and arrange a meeting. Some advance warning on Vaccaro might calm the waters. Keep an eye on the money, and let me know if Vaccaro pulls anything out and where it goes. Where's Doc?"

"Eating lunch."

"Text his cell and let him know Lambert's on his way so he can make sure the meet is clean. I know Wilkens. Once he gets angry, he doesn't give up. I wouldn't be surprised if he has people looking for us right now."

"Tyler, one more thing," Dixie said. "How did you know to investigate ImTech? Was it one of your crazy hunches, or was it somethin' else? Most people would look at the transactions bouncin' off the closed account and move on. You didn't."

He paused. "I wish I knew. How does a cop know to call in a license plate on the freeway? How does a mother know her kid's broken his arm at school before she's told? I can't explain it. I kept asking myself why Daemon would go to all the effort of moving the money all over the world just to let it error out at the end. It has to go somewhere to be of use."

"With your instincts, you should still be at the FBI. Wilkens is an idiot. I don't know how Bruce Lambert stands workin' for him."

"My time at the Bureau is long over, Dixie."

She sighed. "We need a vacation. Someplace warm and sunny where we can sleep for a month."

"You'd go nuts after a day."

Jackson returned his phone to his pocket and sat back to think about Vaccaro's visits to the three banks. Had Vaccaro started to suspect somebody was after him, or had he decided to simply call it good at a round number? Eight million was more than enough money to take his mistress and start another life. His wife and kids would get the shaft, but judging by the surveillance they had of the man and his family, only a fool would think he had a happy home life. Jackson was surprised Vaccaro had stayed around this long. He almost felt bad about what was going to happen to him. Not only would he lose his nasty wife and spoiled kids, but his mistress and the money, too.

He got out of the van into the hot sunshine.

"Sometimes Dixie really pisses me off," Pavak said, following him.

"Only sometimes? Not to get in the middle of your little war, but it would help if you didn't hit on her every time you saw her. You and Debra are a couple."

"A man can look around, can't he? Besides, Dixie should consider it a compliment."

"What did you say this time?"

Pavak smirked. "I just told her she had me at a disadvantage. She could kiss my ass while I couldn't." Pavak laughed it up.

"No wonder she gets tired of you." Jackson spotted a cab driving by and started to wave it over, then stopped. He elbowed Pavak and tipped his head toward a man at the other end of the block. There was nothing about the man that would normally draw attention, except he was the only person in sight wearing a baggy windbreaker in the heat, and he was talking on his phone. Jackson scanned the street.

"Q, see that white Ford at the far end of the block? What kind of tires does it have?"

Pavak squinted at the car then stiffened. "BSW pursuit-rated, police issue Firestones. Let's get out of here." He ran around to the driver's side.

Jackson jumped into the van and slammed the door. Throwing the chairs out of the way, he opened a rectangular metal case sitting on the floor, grabbed the three laptops, and flipped them on their sides. Fingers clawing at the eject buttons, he ripped the drives out of their bays. All three laptops, tiny speakers screeching, started spitting out errors.

"Three black and whites just turned the corner!" Pavak yelled from the front seat. "I can see at least one more unmarked Ford behind them! Damn it! A Navistar truck just pulled behind the Ford! A hundred bucks says it's SWAT! This does not look good!"

Jackson dropped the drives into the metal case on the floor and slammed the lid. Trying to find the power cord, he groped frantically around in the dark.

"Turn on the lights back here!"

"What?"

"Turn on the lights!"

Pavak bent forward and twisted the knob on the dash. The back of the van flooded with light. Outside the van, a siren chirped. The first police cruiser skidded to a stop in front of the van; the next pinned the van from behind. Red and white lights flashed outside the windows. Risking a quick look, Jackson saw a dozen heavily armed men running up the sidewalk.

Squirming under the desk, he located the elusive cord, plugged it in, and hit the switch on the side. There was a whining hum as the inside of the case was magnetized. The lights dimmed for a few seconds before he turned the case off.

He got to his feet, cut the power to the laptops, and had just sat down when the side door was yanked open by a half dozen police in full riot gear. An ugly old man stood behind them, his bony face split by a smile.

"Tyler 'Wild West' Jackson," FBI Field Supervisor Ralph Wilkens said. "How time has flown since our last visit."

5

WHY HAD he even bothered to wear a suit? Alec Janné was in a bad mood, and the hot Chicago morning, combined with his pending visit to see his half-brother Adrian, only worsened it. Loosening his tie and undoing the top button of his shirt, he guided his BMW north along the winding road bisecting the Illinois Elgin Mental Health Center's grounds. Through clumps of drooping trees, he caught his first glimpse of the abandoned Old Center building. Above it and to the west rose two brick boiler stacks from the facility's coal-fired power plant.

Old Center always reminded Janné of something from a Dracula flick. The windows were smashed, the roof had fallen in, and rust riddled the protective wrought-iron window screens. Thick patches of ivy smothered the crumbling foundations and crept through empty doorways like cold fingers looking for something to choke.

The building had originally been designed in the late eighteen hundreds by an architect from Pennsylvania named Kirkbride. He died around the turn of the century, and his dream of creating a model mental hospital had died with him. The decorative lakes and ponds were filled in, grass replaced the flower gardens, and only the wind and rats moved through a building that had once housed more than a thousand patients. Since Janné's visit a month ago, the wind had carried off a few more slate shingles, but the peaked roofs and chimneys still reared into the white ozone-laced sky.

The road cut through a grove of maples, the leaves brown from lack of rain, and ended in front of the blood-colored brick-and-glass building housing the Center's criminally insane. There was a small sign out front that couldn't be seen from the road, but Janné didn't need a sign. He'd been coming to see Adrian for five months. After the first visit, there was no forgetting the way.

He parked under the oaks and walked up the cracked cement sidewalk to the only glass door in sight. Fluorescent lights lit the lobby. A handful of cheap plastic chairs were bolted to one wall, and above them hung an abstract painting. It looked like the artist had gulped a quart of chocolate milk, stuck a finger down his throat, and framed the dried mess. Two security guards watched from in front of a white reinforced steel door thick enough to stop an armor-piercing bullet. A large red sign informed all visitors they must be escorted.

Except for the rattle of an air conditioner, the lobby was silent.

"Good morning. I have an appointment with Dr. Rice," Janné told the guard on the right, handing across his old CIA-supplied government identification.

The guard lowered his eyes to check the ID against his sheet and gave Janné a red visitor's badge. Janné clipped it to his lapel and followed the second guard, who wore squeaky rubber-soled shoes, through a door and down a hall. The door of a cramped office stood open. A window looked out on the Fox River Valley's rolling hills, but the psychiatrist in charge of the criminally insane sat with his back to the view.

Dr. Rice was a tall, middle-aged man with thinning black hair, skin the color of Elmer's Glue, and a mole the size of a rabbit pellet near his left nostril. He looked up from his patient charts and stood to shake Janné's hand.

"Agent Janné? I'm Dr. Glen Rice. I spoke with you earlier."

Rice was almost seven feet tall, but he had a permanent stoop. The security guard closed the door. Janné took the offered chair and glanced at a sign proclaiming that mental health was a partnership between the doctor and patient. *That and dancing the tango*, Janne thought.

Rice folded his tall frame into his chair and opened Adrian's patient chart.

"From my review of his records," he murmured, "I see that Adrian Laroque was found comatose in January with a gunshot wound to the head. Fortunately, there's a great deal of bone above the right eye. Other than losing a lot of blood, he was very lucky."

Rice bent over the page. "He emerged from the coma six weeks later and began exhibiting delusions, hallucinations, and severe mood swings, all of which suggested an organic psychotic disorder. Five months ago, he was transferred from Cook County Hospital and has been under the care and supervision of Dr. Sorenson, but last week Dr. Sorenson went on medical leave. You've been the patient's only visitor."

Rice looked up from reading and inspected Janné's wide face and peppercorn eyes. "Why do you keep coming back?"

Janné blinked at the unexpected question. "Excuse me?"

"Security has you visiting him the last Tuesday of every month. Why do you keep coming back?"

"The man who shot Adrian has not yet been apprehended."

"So far you've been wasting your time. You've been coming out here for months and haven't learned anything."

Janné glanced at his watch. "My time is mine to waste."

"And mine also, now that Dr. Sorenson's on indefinite leave," Rice replied, an impatient edge entering his dry voice. "The last time you were here, Adrian attacked one of the staff.

It took six men to take him down. For someone who lies around on the floor all day, his muscle reflexes are quite impressive. If one of the nurses hadn't gotten a needle in him, six men wouldn't have been enough."

"Did you try and clean up his cell?" Janné asked.

"We call them rooms, not cells."

"Dr. Rice, I do not mean to agitate Adrian, but my options are extremely limited." Janné glanced at the sign on the wall and allowed annoyance to enter his voice. "Mental health is a partnership, yes? I do not have a degree in psychiatry, but Adrian and I make a pair if my addition is correct?"

Rice's jaw clamped shut, making the rabbit pellet jump. "Practicing psychology bears little similarity to a spy interrogation, Agent. You cannot demand or expect answers from someone this ill. With acute psychotic conditions, one person's fantasy is another person's reality. What my patient perceives is his reality, not ours. He may never be coherent again, especially with an underlying brain injury."

Janné noticed a fly that had somehow circumvented the building's locked windows and doors; the fly bobbed back and forth along the grimy glass. Like the fly, Adrian must want to get out of here.

Rice pushed back his chair. "You may visit this time, but when you get back to your office, please fax me a document that can prove these visits are warranted for reasons of national security."

"I meant to do that after my last visit," Janné said, "but it slipped my mind."

"Don't let it slip again." Rice opened the door to the hallway. A large male psych tech with stitches under one eye stood waiting. His starched white shirt made his muscled arms stand out.

"*Bonjour*, Elden," Janné said. "What happened to your cheek?"

"Adrien had one of his episodes last night. The only reason

he didn't get my eye is I'm up too high. I've never seen anybody move so fast."

They rode the elevator to the fifth floor, where a uniformed security guard sat to one side of an electronically locked double steel door. Above their heads, a wide-angle security camera recorded their presence. The guard turned the visitors' log around. Janné signed in, wondering how many pages had been filled since Adrien had arrived.

The guard buzzed them in. Two more psych techs and a nurse joined them on the other side. The door clanged shut. A single long hallway stretched ahead, interrupted only by numbered doorways. As they marched down the hall, no one spoke. In one room, a patient stared dreamily at the light. In another, a heavyset man had difficulty negotiating an invisible maze. A steady stream of expletives burst from his mouth as he tried to find his way out. In room seventeen, a naked man stood admiring himself in front of a dented stainless steel mirror.

Janné ignored the patients and dropped his eyes to the floor. The vomit-green tile had been polished to a high luster.

Rice stopped in front of Adrian's room.

"You have three minutes," Rice said. "If he shows the slightest violent tendency, you are to leave the room immediately. Do you understand?"

"He will not harm me," Janné said.

Elden gave him an appraising look. "Then maybe we should give you a mop."

Rice withdrew his keys and unlocked the door. The tumblers clicked. He pushed the heavy steel aside. Janné took a deep breath and followed Elden's burly figure through the doorway.

Even though Janné had been there before, it was always a shock to enter the cell.

Using chalk, Adrian had turned his room into his own private tropical paradise. The room's light fixture glowed like the sun. Against the far wall and halfway down each sidewall, a beach rolled toward a powder-blue sky. At one end of the beach, a vendor hawked cold drinks under a palm tree. Janné read the neatly lettered sign:

COROLAS Del Mar BEACH RESTRICTIONS
NO GLASS BOTTLES

Drawn across the middle of the floor, a narrow reef and a band of surf split the cell in half. From the edge of the water to as far as Adrian could scratch under the door when it was locked—including the walls, the ceiling, and the door itself—the cell was black. The only part that wasn't black was where the janitor had started mopping, and he hadn't cleaned up much of it—just enough to make Adrian violent.

"One of the techs Adrian put in the medical ward said Adrian pounced on him like a cat," Elden said, cracking his big knuckles.

The taste in Janné's mouth turned bitter. Of course Adrian pounced. He wanted out.

"Three minutes," Rice told him flatly.

Janné used the reef to cross the water. Adrian, muttering up at the clouds, lay on the floor. When Adrian saw Janné, he sat up. At one time Adrian had been one of the meanest men Janné had ever known, but now his half-brother's brown eyes were empty. He wore gray cotton pants, a thin shirt that hadn't been white for a long time, and enough chalk dust to stir up a cloud when he moved. He was barefoot. Where the bullet had entered, a thumb-shaped scar puckered his right eyebrow. At the sight of Dr. Rice, a smile that did not reach his eyes split his dirty face. Adrian's lips moved, but Janné could not make out the words.

"What is he mumbling?" Janné asked Rice.

"He probably wants out of here," Elden said. "I know I do."

Adrian lay back down. His eyes went to the clouds on the ceiling. Janné took off his suit coat and tossed it to the male nurse. Elden caught it, but nearly dropped the tranquilizer.

"*Comment allez-vous ce matin,* Adrian?"

Adrian moved his head slightly toward Janné's voice. His eyes were unfocused, as if he were staring at Janné from the bottom of a swimming pool.

Janné glanced around him at the drawings and switched to English. "You have gotten Corolas Del Mar exactly right, my friend. Remember the times we spent drinking cocktails on this beach?"

Adrian didn't answer.

Janné crouched and touched his brother's scar. "Who did this to you, *mon ami*? Tell me his name, and you and I will take *un avion* to Corolas tomorrow."

"Two minutes," Rice said.

Janné felt a surge of anger. Removing a piece of chalk from a small box by the mattress, he drew a crude picture of an owl on the floor.

"You know who this is, yes?"

Recognition stirred in Adrian's eyes.

Janné tapped the owl. "Give me his name, and I will remove you from here."

Adrian examined the bird, and then his head rolled to one side. Janné followed his eyes to a tree on the wall. Near the top, and almost invisible in the branches, perched a white owl.

"*Qui est-il, mon ami*?" Janné coaxed. "You found him eight months ago. Tell me his name."

A thin line of saliva trickled from the corner of Adrian's mouth, cut a furrow through the filth, and plopped onto the chalky floor. His body started to shake.

"You know who he is," Janné urged. "Give me his name."

Rocking back and forth, arms around his knees, Adrian gulped for air.

"You're pushing him too hard," Elden warned.

Janné glared up. "I must know who shot him."

"Back off or you will never come back," Rice said.

Janné threw the chalk against the wall and stood. Elden stepped forward. Janné patted Adrian's arm.

"I must leave now, Adrian. I will visit again soon. *Au revoir.*"

Adrian sprang up, but instead of attacking them, he grabbed black chalk and obliterated the owl.

Rice leapt for the door. Elden clamped onto Janné's shoulder and dragged him out of the cell. The door clanged shut.

"What's with the owl?" Rice said.

Janné ignored him and walked away.

6

RALPH WILKENS WAS GAUNT, wrinkled, and had silver hair that looked as if it had been riveted to his bony skull. Three years earlier he had weighed almost three hundred pounds, but a heart attack and triple bypass had carved away half his weight. He glanced distastefully at the fast food wrappers, empty soda cans, and discarded newspapers.

"Nice place you have here, Jackson."

"Why thanks," Pavak answered from the front. "I like that lived-in look."

Wilkens glanced at Pavak as if the former cop was something that had ended up on the bottom of his Florsheims. "I need a word with Jackson. Get out."

Pavak left, following two agents over to a waiting police cruiser. Wilkens ducked inside and took the other chair.

"What insanity would possess you to work with that scum?" Wilkens demanded. "You realize he's under investigation in the disappearance of three government witnesses?"

"If memory serves, weren't all three under indictment?"

"Two were. The third was cooperating against the other two—and your friend. Only the Grand Jury knew who was talking and who wasn't."

"I guess the point is moot now," Jackson said.

Wilkens looked like he had bitten into a lemon. "I'm disappointed. It wasn't that long ago when you first arrived here in jeans and cowboy boots. Top of your class at University of Arizona Law. Passed the bar your first time through. Nothing but good things from your superiors. Now look at you."

"I guess it'd be pointless to ask if you have a warrant," Jackson said.

"Relax. This is a social call. I just want to ask you a couple of questions and maybe enlist your services toward the greater cause."

"I'm not going to re-up if that's what you're thinking."

Wilkens shrugged and sat down. "You haven't heard what I have to say yet. You could change your mind."

Jackson glanced at the men on the sidewalk staring at him from under their Kevlar helmets. "I would feel more comfortable without all the hardware."

"I'll need your weapon first."

Jackson removed his pistol, thumbed out the clip, and handed both across. Wilkens inspected the .10 mm. "Not a lot of these cannons around. What do you use it for, killing cattle rustlers on your parents' ranch?"

Jackson ignored the question. "What's this about?"

Wilkens gestured to the police and they stepped back from the van. "Right to the point, I see. I like that a lot better than the fishy smell in here. You guys gut a carp for breakfast?" He glanced at the disassembled laptops on the table, his old eyes missing nothing. "I heard you're helping the Russians track down Daemon. I'm glad to hear you moved on."

"So you decided to drop by and congratulate me. You should have called first. We would have cleaned the place up."

Wilkens snorted.

"My people tell me you've made a lot of money finding the money Daemon stole," he said. "What are the Russians paying for each dollar you find?"

"I would rather not comment on percentages."

"Maybe you'd prefer to comment in front of a grand jury? All it would take is a phone call."

Jackson shrugged. "I perform a service for a customer who feels they have been underserved by the authorities of this country. I have a letter of understanding from the Russian Federation if you wish to review it."

The old man smiled. "We can do that later if necessary. I didn't come here to lean on you. I really don't care about the Russians. I just wanted to ask if you know a man named Hugh Dobrowski?"

"Should I?"

"Judging by the number of questions he's asking about you, I thought you two were acquainted."

"I haven't had the pleasure."

Wilkens stared, sharp eyes unblinking, before he leaned back. "See, there's the problem. I believe you, but that doesn't help me."

"I take it you know him?"

"Of course I do. I've known Hugh for years. We go back a long time."

"So you want to know why your good friend is asking about me. Maybe I'm missing something here, but wouldn't it be easier to ask him?"

"We're not that kind of friends."

Jackson relaxed slightly. "Ah, a typical government urinary contest—which, by the way, is one of the truly excellent benefits of not having to worry about a pension. Thank you very much."

Wilkens ignored the barb. "There are a lot of things going on right now, Jackson. Hugh Dobrowski is just one more question among many that have me concerned. Daemon's moving a lot of money through a handful of accounts we know about. He's moving assets into the States. We could close the accounts, but we think they're the tip of the iceberg. That kind of money has a lot of people worried."

"What does this have to do with me?"

"Quite a lot, actually. I may have made a mistake three years ago in kicking you out of the Bureau, but that doesn't mean I'm stupid." He glanced around again. "I was hoping Dixie Stevens would be here. I have a warrant in my pocket with her name on it. Arresting her would have made my day. You realize aiding and abetting a felon is a criminal offense?"

"You have a funny way of asking for cooperation."

Wilkens's droopy face flushed. "We've been after Daemon for years, and we're no closer to finding him than you were when you got shot. Every time I take a step forward, doors slam in my face. Who does he work for? Who's protecting him? And most of all, why can't we get close?"

"I seem to remember asking those same questions."

Wilkens lifted his homely face. For the first time, Jackson saw worry in the old man's eyes. "Every hacker and terrorist and foreign government wants into the financial district. We've known for years that Daemon's wanted to go after the financial district. Think about the kinds of numbers that go through those systems. Billions of dollars cross those networks every day. Computer automation has gotten so tightly integrated into our lives that a computer hiccup can easily become a global disaster at mainframe speeds. A butterfly beating its wings on Wall Street really can start a financial hurricane in China. I don't even want to think about what would happen if Daemon were to gain access."

Jackson started to protest, but Wilkens held up a veined hand. "The financial markets are built on trust every bit as much as actual currency. For high-speed electronic systems to work, you and I and everyone else must trust the automation. Billions of transactions happen every day—all of them networked through tens of thousands of routers and switches pushing packets across electronic highways. Our networks have gotten so sophisticated and reliable that moving currency has become routine—so routine, in fact, that no one thinks about it anymore."

Wilkens held up his phone. "With this, I can walk into a store and instantly purchase anything. With nothing more than the touch of a finger, I can buy a new car or even a house. Think about the trust, Jackson. Then think about what will happen if it stops."

A car backfired nearby. The team on the sidewalk jumped as if a bomb had gone off. Jackson had a very bad feeling.

"Why are you here?"

Wilkens smiled. "That's the one good piece of news I have. I'm here to offer you your job back. I might not agree with your approach, but you get results. We both want the same thing. Find Daemon while there's still time to stop him."

Jackson's heart skipped a beat. If he took Wilkens's offer, he and Lambert would be partners again. He could reconcile with Suzanne and work normal hours. Instead of risking his life every time he stepped onto the street, he'd have someone to go home to every night. He would have the government helping him instead of always wondering if they were going to crush him like a bug. He would have paid time off, medical benefits, and an office where he could put up pictures of his family. Everything he had dreamed about would come true.

But then he noticed Wilkens's sneer. He had seen that look on the old shark before. Something else was going on.

"You don't need me. You have a decent team. Bruce Lambert's a good agent. The CIA and NSA are tapped into the world's financial and communication networks. You'll get him eventually."

"Your former partner has talent, but he doesn't have your instincts. Nobody's better at following money than you are. I want the two of you back together again." Wilkens leaned forward, voice dropping into a leaky hiss. "What would you say if I could get you unrestricted access to the NSA's PRISM data? Think about it. Every phone call, every e-mail, every dime that moves worldwide, all of it will be at your fingertips."

"But what happens after we get him?" Jackson asked. "PRISM data isn't admissible in court. Without probable cause, a judge will throw the evidence out. Daemon will walk."

A leer twisted the corner of Wilkens's mouth. "All those rules are out the window, boy. There won't be a conviction. Find him, and someone else will figure out what to do with him."

Jackson stared at Wilkens. "No insult intended, but I just can't seem to get past nearly dying for nothing. I'm sorry."

"I don't see you having a choice in the matter."

Jackson stiffened. "Don't make this ugly. I'm grateful for the market tip, but I'll never work for you again."

"Then you give me no choice."

Wilkens removed a folded sheet of paper from his shirt pocket and handed it over. On the paper were three typed columns listing bank names, account numbers, and balances. Jackson scanned the list and stiffened.

"My accountants tell me that is most of what you have, Jackson. Quite an astonishing sum, I must say. You've been very busy. As of five minutes ago, every cent has been locked down, pending government investigation for wire fraud, tax evasion, and whatever I care to dream up."

He leaned forward, eyes shining. "I want Daemon, and you're going to gift wrap him in paper and a red bow. Anything else, and the Treasury Department will take every dollar you have. Then they'll move on to your parents' home in Arizona. After that, they'll target your fiancée and your brother. I'll make sure your family will be in tax court for years. Your parents will end up bankrupt and broke—which is not how I would like to be going into my golden years. And while all of that is happening, I will send Dixie Stevens down the deepest, darkest hole I can find in the Federal penal system. And finally, I will go after you. You think getting two slugs through the lungs was fun? Just wait. I will make you my career."

"You can't do this."

The old man snickered. "You and the rabble you work with exist because I allow it, boy. You have one week before I have the pleasure of destroying your life. Or give me what I want, and everything will quietly go away. Your choice."

He beckoned to the waiting men on the sidewalk. With weapons trained on Jackson, they shuffled forward. "Now get out. I don't know if you would be stupid enough to leave anything of interest in this wreck, but I'm not going to chance it. You have a lot to do and a long way to go to get there."

Holding his ribs, Jackson stumbled into the sunshine.

Wilkens held out the Colt. "Welcome back to the show."

JACKSON HAILED A CAB. Pavak got in. Downtown, standing in the cool air of an office building's lobby, Pavak watched the street through the window while Jackson called Dixie. Wilkens hadn't gotten all their money, but she confirmed that most of their funds were locked.

"I can't believe I didn't see them comin'!" she snapped, her syrupy voice so angry that her words ran together. "We must have gotten careless!"

"We were too busy watching Vaccaro to see if anyone was watching us."

"Do you think Wilkens got our information from Lambert?"

Jackson frowned. "I don't think so, but I'll find out." He pinched the bridge of his nose. "It's times like this I ask myself why I didn't just give up and go home after Wilkens forced me out. Now I don't have anything to go back to."

"You don't believe Wilkens will keep his end of the bargain?" she asked.

"Of course not. He's never done a good deed in his miserable life. Pack everything up. As soon as I finish meeting with Lambert, we need to get out of the city. If we can't get Daemon, I want Wilkens instead. Something where we can put an apple in his mouth and serve him up like the pig he is."

"Ah, yes, a challenge. I like that. What about Vaccaro? With our accounts locked down, we're gonna need funds."

"Good point."

He put his cell away and motioned for Pavak to come over.

"Q, shake the love bird. I'm going to empty his account, so he should be eager to chat. Get everything you can on where Daemon's money came from—account numbers, transaction amounts, dates, names, places. If he cooperates, I'll return seven digits. Anything else, and I'll burn him. That kind of money is more than enough to run off with his mistress in style. He'll sing."

"And if the threat doesn't work?"

"Find a way to convince him."

Pavak smiled around his perfect teeth.

7

JACKSON HAD a taxi drop him off a few blocks from where he had asked Lambert to meet him. Running late, Jackson limped up the walk. What should he do? His options were extremely limited. The old man had known exactly how to hit him.

He found the alley. Something sticky had been dumped onto the asphalt, and every step stirred up clouds of flies. Halfway down the alley, past an overflowing dumpster, Tracy O'Connell waited by an open freight door. O'Connell had a linebacker's build and flame-colored hair cut close to the skull, making his rough features look even bigger than they were. He had been a military combat medic for twenty years and held a .9 mm automatic in his left hand.

"Hey, Doc, what's with the weapon?" Jackson asked.

"We have a visitor. Showed up about ten minutes ago. White male about sixty. No identification, and he won't say anything except Lambert isn't coming."

Jackson stopped. "Did he give a reason?"

"No."

"Is he armed?"

"Revolver in his right pocket. Spare shells in his left. No

wire. Some pocket change, and a pack of gum. He didn't like the wait."

"One of Wilkens's men?" Jackson asked.

"He doesn't fit the type."

Jackson looked left and right and nodded. Jackson unzipped his windbreaker and tightened the straps of his vest. "I'll see what he wants."

"Just to be safe, I'm going to see if he brought company," O'Connell said, stepping aside so that Jackson could enter.

The building had once housed New York Paint & Pigment until a vengeful employee had doused the sales floor with lacquer thinner and torched the place. The owner had taken the insurance money, put the building up for sale, and retired to Florida. It had never been sold, and now there was nothing left but the empty shell of a once-thriving business. Even after a decade, the heavy odor of smoke hung in the air. The charred studs that surrounded three blackened oak desks had once boxed off an office. After his look around, O'Connell returned and took up a position by the door.

In the darkened interior, an old man with a broken nose, white hair, and flat gray eyes stood puffing a cigarette. Despite the heat he wore a stained black raincoat, a Brooks Brothers suit, and soft-soled Doc Martens that looked older than he was.

"Hey," Jackson said.

"It's about time." The man took a last drag and flipped his cigarette onto the ash-covered floor. "Waiting for you is worse than standing in line at the DMV."

Jackson eased his butterfly knife from the sleeve of his windbreaker. He snapped his wrist, letting the knife's steel catch the light. The blade made a pleasant click.

"Looks like you've gotten a bit more cautious than you used to be," the stranger added, nodding at the weapon. "'Course, most people aren't all that willing to crawl headfirst down a hole after a snake more than once—especially after they got bit the first time."

"Who are you?"

"My name is Hugh Dobrowski, and I'm looking for Tyler Jackson. He used to work for Ralph Wilkens in the Bureau's New York office until he took two of Daemon's slugs through the chest."

"What do you want?"

"Daemon's head. Same as him."

"The day my walking papers came in was the day I left. One way, without looking back."

"Good story. Too bad it's not true."

"Believe what you want."

"Even if I can give you a better than even chance of getting him?"

Jackson scowled. "Tell it to the FBI. Wilkens isn't much to look at, but he has decent people working for him."

"You're better. You came closer than anybody ever has."

"You still haven't told me exactly what you want."

Dobrowski loosened his tie and unbuttoned his shirt to reveal a bloodstained bandage taped high on his shoulder.

"A few days ago, I made a career move. Let's just say that instead of a gold watch, I got this."

He removed a rumpled pack of cigarettes from his pocket, then seemed to realize what he was doing and put them back.

"Do you know how Daemon got his name?" Dobrowski asked.

"No."

"Your client, the Russians, gave it to him. Daemons are divine beings. Half mortal, half god. Their knowledge and power make them almost untouchable. The Russkies gave him that moniker because he was so good at cracking their banks. His specialty was currency manipulation. He drove them nuts until he vanished with over four billion US. Nobody's seen him or the money since — which is quite a feat since Moscow has a sizeable reward on his head."

Dobrowski coughed, the sound low and deep in his lungs. Although his chest moved, very little noise escaped. He opened the cigarettes and withdrew one. As he lit it and inhaled, the tip glowed a fiery red. His voice regained its gravelly strength.

"Across the Atlantic, just off the coast of Portugal, is the island of Madeira. About ten years ago, the Portuguese government started selling off pieces of their banks and eventually got out of finance altogether. Coincidentally, this was about the time Daemon went to ground. The major player on the island now is a company called the Espírito Santo Group, which is mostly made up of relatives and friends of the local politicians. They're big into short- and medium-term credit with anyone or anything that breathes. They don't care where the money comes from, and they care even less about where it goes. Best of all, every cent is exempt from taxes and capital gains until the next century. That means none of their transactions need to be accounted for publicly, and with no external audit, they're almost impossible to track. They're big with the Mexican cartels."

Dobrowski glanced over at the door. O'Connell, apparently seeing something he didn't like, pulled the door almost shut and raised his weapon. Looking through the charred studs, Jackson saw nothing but mixing equipment, steel drums, and scattered cans. If Dobrowski had brought anyone with him, they would have made their move by now.

"So it's a money laundering operation?"

"Not exactly," Dobrowski said. "For the past few months, a lot of money has been bouncing from Madeira into the States. The accounts change day-to-day, but the pattern is the same. Sort of makes you wonder what Daemon is doing with all that money, doesn't it?"

"Get to the point. I'm a busy man."

Dobrowski chuckled, the sound more of a rasp than a

laugh. "I see hanging it up hasn't helped your sense of humor. 'Course, I'd be pissed too if somebody told me I was chasing the wrong end of the tiger."

"You're getting on my nerves, old man. If you're trying to say something, then say it."

Anger flashed in the back of Dobrowski's eyes before he took another hit of nicotine. "I need your help."

Smoke wheezed in and out of Dobrowski's lungs.

"Why me?" Jackson said.

"Have you ever stopped to wonder why the Feds have never gotten Daemon?" Dobrowski asked. "You'd think he'd be pretty high up on their list. The last time anyone got close was you, and that was right before Wilkens decided you didn't fit the mold and cut you loose. Did he really have you go through a complete psych evaluation before you got out of the hospital? It must have been tough to return to work for him with all that in your file. You guys don't like each other too much, do you?"

Jackson thought about the day he'd packed up his office and said goodbye to friends and coworkers. It had been a good day until Wilkens had him searched on the way out of the building, and then had New York's finest pull him over and ransack his car on the way home.

"I don't plan on inviting him over for dinner anytime soon, if that's what you're saying."

"What does Bruce Lambert think about working for Wilkens?"

Jackson shrugged. "He puts up with him—the same as anyone who has to look at him every day."

Dobrowski smiled and slid a hand into his raincoat, but stopped when O'Connell, guarding the door, whistled a warning. Dobrowski eased his hand into the inside pocket of the coat and withdrew a folded yellow piece of paper. On it, Jackson saw a handwritten IP address.

"When in doubt, follow the money. That's where Daemon

is pushing it from. You wouldn't believe how much work went into finding that number. Just be careful because it isn't a pot of gold, but a beehive, and those bitches can sting."

Jackson took the paper and unfolded a street map ripped from a phone book. The map was crinkled, but the roads were still readable, as was the IP address written on the back.

"How do you know Daemon's there?" Jackson asked.

Before Dobrowski could answer, a chunk of ceiling plaster broke free and landed on a rusty barrel. A pencil-thin ray of sunshine fell on the floor.

Dobrowski swore, pulled out a Smith & Wesson .38 revolver, and rushed over to O'Connell. "I need to get out of here," Dobrowski said.

O'Connell put a hand on Dobrowski's chest. "Wait a sec."

Dobrowski looked back at Jackson. "You have thirty-six hours until I go to the Bureau in Chicago!" he hissed. "The agent there is Dan Harris. If he moves on Daemon, then you'll know you've run out of time." With that, he pushed past O'Connell and darted from the building.

After closing the door behind Dobrowski and throwing the slide bolt, O'Connell put a finger to his lips, grabbed Jackson's elbow, and pointed up. Another chunk of plaster fell from the ceiling and puffed into the ash.

"Two minimum. Probably more. Use the back exit. I'll stay here." He disappeared behind a tangle of galvanized water pipes.

Jackson moved along the blackened walls and passed mounds of heat-mangled paint cans. Ahead, he saw a large ill-fitting double freight door secured by a rusty deadbolt. Just as he reached the doors, they creaked slightly apart, and a pair of bolt cutters slid through. The cutters settled on the bolt and bit down. There was a quiet *snap* of breaking metal. The broken bolt fell to the floor.

Jackson looked for a hiding place. The interior walls had collapsed long ago, and the stub walls that remained wouldn't hide him. His eyes fell on the frame of a metal stairwell. He moved behind it just as the door scraped the ground.

Three men wearing body armor and carrying silenced assault carbines slipped through. Eyes moving back and forth, they separated without a word. The closest man looked directly at the broken stairs. Jackson froze and held his breath. The human eye, like that of most predators, is attracted to movement. If he stayed where he was, his dark windbreaker and the gloom of the building would conceal him.

The leader made a hand signal, and the men advanced slowly into the darkness. Jackson released the air in his chest. Were they Wilkens's men? Had they followed him to the building, or had Dobrowski brought them?

He slid through the open door into the back alley, the sunshine blinding after the darkness. No one shot at him or sounded the alarm. He waited for O'Connell, but the other man did not appear. Should he go back and try to help? At least two were on the roof, and three had come in through the rear. He didn't want to get into a fight. That bordered on suicide. But he wasn't willing to leave O'Connell either.

"C'mon, Doc!" he whispered through the door. "We have to get out of here!"

No answer.

Jackson switched off the safety on his Colt and started to go back inside when a man stepped around the alley's corner. Chin down and talking into a radio on the shoulder of his vest, the man had a government-issue SIG automatic on his hip. Their eyes met, neither moving, before the man went for his gun.

Jackson dove sideways against the alley wall. The Sig boomed. A bullet tore past. The Colt kicked twice in Jackson's hand. The first bullet caught the man in the hip, the second under his armored vest. The man spun backwards, catching at the brick with his free hand. The Sig barked, bullets ricocheting off the pavement. He lost his grip on the brick and fell face down on the pavement.

Jackson scrambled to his feet, and, Colt on the fallen man, scooped up his shell casings. Who had he just shot? What was going on? Running footsteps sounded in the warehouse, and O'Connell grabbed him by the back of his vest.

"Move! There are three behind us. Two on the roof and four out front!"

Jackson lurched into a run. Crashing against the wall hadn't helped his ribs. They turned into another alley, sped by a dumpster, dodged through a broken gate, and ran past an empty loading dock.

Five blocks later, he gasped for O'Connell to stop. His ribs were on fire. He sagged against the corner of a building to catch his breath.

"What just happened?" Jackson said. "Who were they, and what did they want?"

"They're some kind of covert unit. If they were SWAT or FBI, they would have locked down the block and had NYPD standing by in case we got past their perimeter. So far we haven't seen any police."

"Did we bring them or did Dobrowski?"

"Since we've never had trouble there before, my guess is Dobrowski. Funny how we show up for a face-to-face with Lambert and get Dobrowski instead. You think your partner's changing the rules without telling us?"

"I spoke with Lambert an hour ago. Wilkens is angry. My name's come up a lot."

"In a good way, I'm sure."

Jackson snorted. "Do you think Dobrowski got away?"

"No way to tell. But I don't think he ran very far. He's only a few steps shy of a nursing home."

Jackson unfolded Dobrowski's map. "Does any of this look familiar to you?"

O'Connell examined the circled spot on the map. A rare

smile creased his dirty face. "How many places do you know about has a river named after the city of Chicago?"

～

BY THE TIME Jackson reached the Riverside Tower Hotel, the adrenaline had long since worn off. The wind had changed direction and blew off the Hudson River, bringing with it the smell of mold, oil, and garbage. He turned the lock to his room, limped inside, and shut the door. His suitcase lay open on the floor, and next to it sat a brown cardboard banker's box, perfect for carrying cable. Equipment and clothing covered the bed. Behind him, he heard a metallic click and froze.

Dixie lowered her pistol and stepped forward to give him a hug. She was shaking, but his arms felt too leaden to hug her back.

"You could've let me know you were okay," she said.

"I broke my phone diving into a wall."

She knelt and went back to stuffing cable into the box. "What a terrible day."

Jackson scooted one of the room's chairs next to her. He told her about Dobrowski and the unexpected visitors. "I don't know if this means anything or not," he said, taking the map out of his pocket and putting it on the desk, "but maybe it's the break we've been waiting for."

Dixie put a lid on the box and, holding the arm of his chair, stood. She fingered the bullet hole in his windbreaker and gave him a doubtful look.

8

THE PAINT WAREHOUSE stank of chemicals and made CIA
Assistant Deputy Director Marcus Byrnes's nose run. One of
his men lay outside. Scott Crosby's body armor had been
removed, exposing the bullet wound in his lower left side.
Byrnes looked for a wedding ring and tried to recall if Crosby
had a family. It didn't really matter. He wouldn't be getting a
gold star on the wall at Langley.

Roger Blume, his operations assistant, stepped forward.
"Director, you shouldn't be here. If local law enforcement
shows up, it could get awkward."

Byrnes ignored the concern. "Who shot him?"

"We don't know, sir. But whoever they were, they knew
what they were doing."

"How do you know?"

"They picked up their brass."

"Any sign of Dobrowski?"

"No, but we're sweeping the area. He probably had transportation waiting."

"Keep looking. I don't need to tell you how important this
is. And I want to know who Dobrowski came here to meet."

"Yes, Director."

Trying not to think about Scott Crosby and the others who had died on his watch, Byrnes left the warehouse and walked down the alley. He slid gratefully into the air-conditioned car and ran his fingers across the seat's soft leather. These things couldn't be helped.

"Do you know what we used to call these kinds of ops back in the day?" Byrnes asked.

His driver, Steve Farris, glanced in the rearview mirror. "No, sir."

"We'd say we were out 'six-packing'. That way our superiors wouldn't ask questions."

"I never heard that."

"It was a long time ago."

So many years, and, if he didn't find Alec Janné and Hugh Dobrowski, so much wasted effort. He had been the Assistant Deputy Director of the CIA's Special Operations Group for the past sixteen years and a player in the congressional power circuit for almost a quarter of a century. Forty years was a lifetime in Washington's bureaucratic mire of committees, delegations, and commissions. He had learned long ago that politics was a matter of professional survival, especially if one was ambitious. Politics was not about truth, but rather about the interpretation thereof. It wasn't necessary to legislate truth because there was nothing to dicker over. Politicians needed a line drawn in the sand. Debate meant space to maneuver, a reason to give or gather favors, or, as one of his aides accurately put it, room to troll. Information might make the throne, but deals made the politician king.

There were a lot of people claiming the government had gone to hell and that the CIA had led the way. Gloom and doom about the state of the nation wasn't news, but the extent of the mess was. Southeast Asia was an intelligence and political nightmare. Iran, North Korea, China, and Russia spent billions annually on defense. Al-Qaeda and the Islamic State were trying to turn the world into a fundamentalist Muslim caliphate. Paying lip service to the executive branch over the weapons-of-mass-destruction mess in Iraq had only been one mistake. The CIA had a long list of mistakes starting long before nineteen terrorists slammed jets into the World Trade Center, the Pentagon, and the field in Pennsylvania. He had spent decades fighting the nation's covert, quiet battles, and he'd be damned if he was going to let the enemy win.

"Why did you pick now to run, Dobrowski?" he wondered aloud. "What are you hoping to accomplish?"

"Sir?" Farris said. "Your appointment is here."

"Let him in."

The door opened abruptly, and Joe Tresher got in. Farris exited into the heat and headed for a patch of shade in the alley.

"Thanks for coming on such short notice, Joe," Brynes said.

His dark eyes unreadable, Tresher nodded. He was slender, with brown weather-streaked hair over the emptiest eyes Byrnes had ever seen. His face and hands were the color of sand and looked like they had spent most of their time under the sun. He wore a pair of dusty boots, a khaki cotton work shirt, faded jeans, a Stetson cowboy hat, and a belt with the word RODEO spider-scripted across the buckle.

Byrnes pulled a manila envelope out of his briefcase and handed it across.

His eyes never leaving Byrnes, Tresher took the envelope with his left hand. His movements were as silky as warm oil.

"I need you to find someone," Byrnes said. "His name is Hugh Dobrowski. Last Friday, he called my office and left a message on my private line telling me he was going fishing. No reason why—just goodbye and good luck. Fortunately, I was working late and got his message before I left for the weekend. I tried calling him at home and drove over to see if I could catch him, but he was gone by the time I arrived."

"Why did he leave?"

"That's an awkward question."

Tresher shrugged. "Not for me."

Byrnes removed a cigarette, lit it with a gold 1976 Republican National Convention lighter, and took a hit.

"For the past few years, Dobrowski has handled delicate issues for me and my associates. Everything from intel case files to messy situations that are sensitive to those you and I represent. For the last few months, Dobrowski has been acting erratic. He stopped returning messages, or would call back long after we didn't need him anymore."

"Family problems?" Tresher asked.

"I don't believe so. He's been divorced for as long as I can remember. His ex's name and address are in the envelope."

"Who else is involved?"

"Just my people. They've almost gotten him twice, but came up empty both times. Dobrowski has a knack for knowing when to run."

Tresher dusted off his hat. "Why call me, Director? Finding one man, even an ex-agent, shouldn't be that hard for someone with your resources."

Byrnes pulled on his cigarette. "In all the years I've known him, Dobrowski's only failed me twice. The first was not being able to locate an ex-agent of mine named Alec Janné. The second was finding the identity of a man known as the Owl."

"The Owl?"

Byrnes nodded. "That's what he calls himself, if you can believe it. Nobody knows who he is, who his contacts are, or how to get hold of him. The only thing we know for sure is he sometimes works with the FBI. Most of the time though, he runs solo."

"How are Janné and the Owl related?"

"For the past three years, I've been trying to locate Alec Janné. His code name when he worked for me was Daemon. His specialty was destabilizing currencies. He used to be a French operative. What the French, and whoever else is looking for him, don't know is that he worked for me. Having a few hounds sniffing about was good for his cover, so I didn't care if they kept looking until about four years ago. Then the FBI's counterterrorism division got involved."

"Why is the FBI involved?"

"Janné is here in the States."

Tresher blinked. "Who's he working for now?"

"As far as I know, just himself."

"And he's an expert in destabilizing currencies?"

Byrnes nodded. "I believe you see my dilemma."

Neither of them said anything for a few quiet seconds.

"And the Owl?"

Byrnes handed across a clear plastic bag holding a nature postcard with the picture of an owl on the front. The back was signed with Dobrowski's signature.

"This arrived at my office on Monday. Dobrowski mailed it over the weekend in Virginia."

"You believe Dobrowski has identified the Owl?"

"Given the postcard and his actions, yes."

Byrnes removed another envelope from his briefcase and handed it across. "The only real lead I have for you on Janné is the name and address of a woman he used to date. She lives in Chicago. Her name is Sara Branson. She has a place on the Chicago lakefront. Her address is in the envelope. As far as the Owl, I know he has worked in the past with the FBI in New York. Ralph Wilkens runs the office, but he doesn't know who the Owl is—I have a source inside who has confirmed it. My guess is one of Wilkens's agents quietly works with the Owl outside official channels. Inside the envelope is a list of the major cases that have broken through Wilkens's office in the past two years. Maybe you'll see something I've missed."

"I understand why you'd want to find Janné," Tresher said. "What you haven't told me is why Janné left."

Byrnes closed his briefcase. "Janné's first assignment with the French was cracking Iraqi banks. He was just a young kid then, but he was very good at what he did. That's why we recruited him. After the Russians invaded Ukraine, I put Janné to work hacking the Russian Federation's Central Bank."

"You sent a French agent after the Russians?"

"The quiet war we fight needs funding, Joe. For obvious reasons, we can't go to Congress."

"How much did he get?"

"Five billion US."

Tresher whistled softly.

Byrnes nodded. "If word gets out a foreign agent operating in the United States was recruited and trained by the CIA to attack the Russians, they could declare war. That can't happen, not because one of my fish got away."

"What do you want me to do when I find Janné or Dobrowski?" Tresher asked.

Byrnes smiled coldly. "Have you ever seen the cover ripped off a baseball? I cut one off once as a kid. Just to see what was inside."

Tresher nodded and got out of the car into the bright, humid air. To the southwest, a dark line of clouds marched towards the island.

Something told Byrnes the storm was only beginning.

9

JACKSON DROPPED the connection to the router he had hacked and pushed the laptop away. The motel room's shades were down, and he hadn't bothered to turn on the lights. Even so, he could still make out Dixie's dark hair, spread across her pillow. Jaw cracking, he yawned. He tried to remember the last time he'd gotten enough sleep. The nightmares hadn't left him alone for months.

Using the chair as a crutch, he got to his feet. He was stiff. The room's worn furniture swam. Earlier that day, they had relocated to a motel in north Jersey about a mile from the Newark airport. There was a beer bottling plant nearby, and the stench of cooking yeast made him wish they were back in New York. Over time, all the cheap accommodations ran together in a blur.

He limped into the bathroom. The tile was cracked, and rust stained the sink, but it was as clean as eighty dollars a night and three decades of neglect could make it. He turned on the shower. The plumbing banged, and, finally, the water warmed.

When he finished showering, he got dressed and returned to the computer.

Dixie groaned and rolled over on the bed. "What time is it?"

"A little before one."

"Morning or afternoon?"

"Afternoon."

She rolled out of bed and leaned over his shoulder to squint at the screen. Heat radiated off her, and he could smell her strawberry shampoo.

"You should've woken me two hours ago," she said.

"You needed your sleep. I've made progress on the IP address I got from Dobrowski. You're not going to like it."

"I haven't liked anythin' about this for months."

He tapped the keyboard. The screen cleared, showing a red thread woven through Manhattan's communications grid to a fiber gateway heading west. Reaching up with his finger, he tapped the blinking yellow square at the end.

"That's the router of the server Dobrowski gave us. It's registered to Verizon Business Communication Services. It's located on Chicago's Near North Side about a mile from downtown. The server behind it is a primitive store-and-forward Linux machine. At first, I thought it was some kind of hack, but the more I look around, the more convinced I am that whoever wrote the code knew exactly what they were doing. Everything's encrypted, even the kernel."

"Did you try strippin' a bit on one of the transmissions and catchin' the crypt key after it forced a NAK?"

He shook his head. "Didn't work. The protocol didn't care that the target was hashed. The other side just kept sending."

"What happened when the gate tried to read the corrupted header?"

"It polled a few times before the queue timed out and died. Without the header, the gate had no way of knowing where to send."

Her eyes widened. "Then nothin' else can go through the gate! They're gonna take one look —"

"I added the bit," he said, "and manually kicked off the transmission."

She still wasn't convinced. "What about the logs syncing up?"

"I made a copy before I kicked off the transmission, and I moved the copy on top of the original after it finished."

"But the file and the log won't have the same time stamps! If they're as good as we both know they are, they'll notice!"

"There's over a gig of logged transmissions in the queue. By the time they track down the problem, it won't matter."

She gave the motel door a worried look. "What if this whole thing was somethin' Daemon dreamed up to keep you logged in! We could be dead!"

"I was careful, Dixie."

Her brown eyes flashed, but before she could respond, Jackson's phone beeped. He checked the caller ID and hit the button.

"I hope you have some good news for me, Q."

"I have some news, but I don't know if I would go so far as to call it good," Pavak answered. "I just finished meeting with Joseph Vaccaro. He was cooperative, but not overly so. I kept wondering if he was going to break down and cry. He must really love his mistress, the fool. How much do you want to bet that whatever we let him have will end up in her pocket?"

"What did you get?"

"Vaccaro was approached by a man who paid him to change ImTech's monitoring system. He was given a hundred thou in cash to change the code, plus a small percentage of every transaction routed through the company."

"How were the code changes passed?"

"The man e-mailed him the source accounts and told him how to change the 911 monitoring so the money could be moved," he said.

"Any idea when the transfers started?"

"Back in August," Pavak said.

"How did Vaccaro look when he was telling you all of this?" Jackson asked.

"I think he was telling the truth. Once he started telling his story, it all came spilling out like he was finally glad to talk to somebody."

Jackson thought for a second. "Okay, here's what we're going to do. Dixie will send you some money. Take it over to Vaccaro. It's not enough for him to run, but he'll feel better with something in his pocket. It will give him hope. Just make sure you give it to him personally. Tell him this bump-in-the-road will be over soon. Give him a reason to stay for the rest."

"And then?"

"I'm going to go through ImTech's logs again. Now that we know when Vaccaro started, we should be able to find when Daemon first accessed their systems. Hopefully, he wasn't as careful early on as he is now."

He hung up and caught Dixie looking at him. "You really think Daemon left the logs intact? If it was me, I would make sure nothin' was left behind. Besides, we've already been through the logs."

"It's worth another try. Besides," he cocked a grin at her, "I have a hunch."

She groaned, putting her face in her hands. "God help us all."

He logged into ImTech and, beginning with the previous August, copied the logs to a scratch file.

"This could take forever without somethin' more definite, and we don't have forever," Dixie said. "Dobrowski is going to give Daemon to the Chicago FBI tomorrow night."

"If you have a better idea, I'm open to suggestions."

Jackson counted the number of columns in the log and wrote down the column numbers of the incoming date, the incoming IP address, the unique hardware MAC address of the source computer's network card, and the ImTech user ID. Popping up another window, he started scripting in AWK.

When Dixie saw what he was doing, she made a face. "I don't know how you can stand that language. It operates backwards."

"Do you know anything better at stripping text?"

"A database would work."

"This is faster. Most AWK scripts are less than five lines for a reason. It's extremely powerful."

"And extremely annoyin'," Dixie added.

He finished the script and executed it. The other screen cleared, showing four columns: the date the firewall had logged the incoming connection, the originating IP address, the originating hardware MAC address of the computer's network card, and the user's login ID. He ran the script against all the log files for the past twelve months and piped each of the modified log files' originating IP addresses through a graphical network trace-route tool.

The other window cleared, showing a rapidly expanding spider web of routes. Most of the access points were from the New York area, but thousands of other routes outside the New York area flashed across the screen.

"We could be here for years trackin' all of these down," Dixie said.

"This is where Dobrowski can help us."

Jackson clicked on the Midwest part of the map, clicked on Illinois, and then finally on Chicago. The tens of thousands of routes disappeared, replaced by a web of a hundred or so. Glancing at Dobrowski's map, Jackson traced his finger over the laptop's screen until he found the Chicago River. Moving the mouse slightly north of downtown, he clicked again, then turned Dobrowski's map over and typed in the IP address. A blinking red dot appeared on the screen. Jackson clicked on the dot, and as the screen refreshed, he counted each of the origination points.

"ImTech was accessed by fifteen different IP addresses in the past year that were in the same geographic area as the IP address Dobrowski gave us today. How much do you want to bet they all came from the same router?"

He clicked on the IP address. The registration information came up.

"Starbucks!" In the light from the screen, Dixie's eyes looked enormous. "Daemon hacked ImTech from a Starbucks!"

Jackson stared, suddenly unable to breathe. Could it be that easy?

Dixie stood, went to the closet, and jerked out her garment bag. "When do we leave?"

10

THINKING it would be better if they weren't seen together, Dixie let Jackson order two cabs, twenty minutes apart, for the short cab ride to Newark International. By the time she arrived and checked their bags, Jackson had cleared security. Groups of Japanese and South Korean tourists were intent on filming the departure lines with their cell phones while their tour guides tried to keep them together. Non-profit organizations hustled the crowd for donations while young thieves dressed respectably in silk ties stole wallets and purses from the unwary.

The more Dixie traveled, the more she was convinced the transportation industry was right. People were cattle, or as one flight attendant had remarked, lemmings with luggage.

After holding her arms up in the metal detector, she followed the signs to their gate and boarded the plane, the last one on. Jackson started rifling through the magazine in the seat pocket.

"Why don't you get some sleep?" she said. "You look terrible."

"Do you know what it feels like to be afraid to close your eyes?"

"Unlock the memory and step inside. It's the—"

"—only way to find my way out," he said. "Spare me the psych eval, okay?"

She reached up without answering, switched on his reading light, and looked pointedly out the window. Jackson sighed and plucked at her sleeve.

"Hey, I'm sorry. I didn't mean it. I can't remember the last time I didn't feel tired."

"Don't worry about it."

He closed his eyes and fell asleep.

She stared out the window and wished, as she always did, that she were going home. Two long years had passed since she had seen her family, and she missed them terribly. Her sister Jenny had gotten married in May, and the closest she had gotten to the wedding was an invitation. Her brother Greg had had his second child a month later in June, and she hadn't been there to croon admiringly over the new member, although she had heard him squall a few precious times over the phone.

Greg continued to send pictures to the blind post office box Dixie had set up in El Paso, but by the time the photos arrived, they were weeks old. Worst of all were the letters from her parents. They were full of the little things that would bore anyone else to death, but almost always brought tears to her eyes.

The only time she ever got to talk to her family was from prepaid cell phones, and never for more than a few minutes. A simple forty-minute call last Christmas had nearly gotten her arrested. Jackson had dragged her out of the New Jersey South Holland bus terminal just as two heavily armed federal agents came through the door.

That had been a lesson she had never forgotten. Even after jumping through a maze of corporate switches, gateways, and routers, the government had been able to track her down on a day when the national call volume exceeded a hundred million connections for a given second. Dixie had been running scared ever since, hiding in Jackson's shadow and lying to herself that she wasn't.

Last Christmas, she hadn't even called home. Her present to her parents had been to pay off their mortgage, but an electronic transfer was as close to Texas as she had gotten that year.

She'd spent the holidays camped out in Las Vegas hotel room, where she'd stared at the phone and tried not to cry. On New Year's Eve, she'd gone to a liquor store and calmly filled up two grocery bags.

Three days into the New Year, she woke up to find Jackson, with eyes as sharp as the broken vodka bottle on the carpet, sitting on the foot of her bed. She staggered into the bathroom and threw up.

"Some party, Dixie," he said. "You really know how to bring in a new year. Ever think about a career as a frat house party coordinator?"

She rinsed her mouth and brushed her teeth. "Leave me alone."

He stood up. "Sorry. I haven't given you your Christmas present yet. Time to go."

"I don't care. Get out."

She had known Jackson for a long time, but she hadn't known how strong he was. Before she could protest, he grabbed her by the back of her neck and dragged her out. She fought him, but he had this funny way of being in three places at the same time, so she didn't know which one of him to hurt. He dumped her in the back of a cab and hauled her to a gym where an old man with a broken nose tried to kill her with a murderous regimen of vitamin C, B-complex, and sparring.

"When you can lick me," he grinned, "you can git."

Later that day she went looking for Jackson with premeditative intent to do just that, only she found him chatting with her parents at the hotel. Seeing her folks had been the best Christmas present she had ever received.

A stewardess asked if she wanted something to drink. Dixie ordered for them both in case Jackson woke up. She took a sip of her soda and watched him twitch while he dreamed. He had dark hair, a strong jaw, and a pleasant, almost boyish, face when he was asleep. Dark bags sat under his eyes, but they would go away if only the nightmares would fade. He was the best friend she had, and it pained her to see him taken advantage of. Dixie had been there for him when Suzanne first tossed him out, and when Suzanne had changed her mind, Dixie had warned him not to go back. He went anyway.

It was only much later that Dixie realized she had other reasons for objecting. She cared a great deal about Jackson, and the emotion went so deep that, crazy as it was, she would gladly kill for him.

If Daemon didn't kill them both first.

11

WITH THE SEDAN'S air conditioner on full blast, Alec Janné took the Kennedy Expressway to Lake Shore Drive. He smelled of disinfectant from the Elgin Mental Health Center and needed a shower. The late afternoon rush hour shouldn't have been this bad, but an accident south of the Loop had snarled the roads. The further he traveled toward the lakefront, the worse the traffic became. Despite using secondary roads, it took him two hours of stop-and-go driving before he arrived at his condominium.

A shower and a bourbon took his temper down a notch. Naked, he padded over to the living room window to look at the tour boats inching through the locks. History recorded the Chicago River as flowing east into Lake Michigan, but the Army Corps of Engineers had changed that decades ago, making the river flow backward to the Mississippi. Today, he would do much the same: change the flow of money.

Everything in America revolved around money. The country had no culture and no history—only dollars with which to dominate the world. The longer he lived here, the more he was convinced Americans cared about only two things: shopping for bargains and buying cheap Chinese goods. If not for Byrnes, he would have left long ago.

Tossing his towel into a hamper, he stepped into his closet and ran his fingers along the row of hand-tailored suits. To celebrate the start of the next chapter in his life, he decided on a silk, double-breasted jacket. No point rushing. He could take his time getting dressed. He had spent years preparing, and now all he had to do was put on his shoes and execute the plan.

TRAFFIC GOING NORTH on Lake Shore was still bumper-to-bumper, but at least it moved. He took the Randolph exit west to Clark. The sun was on its way down. Granite skyscrapers turned the financial district into a canyon. Men with briefcases and corporate women who'd changed into tennis shoes headed for the Metra station and the suburban trains.

In the next few days, their world would disappear.

He drove under the El, listening as he always did for the screech of metal wheels. As he headed north, the corporate skyscrapers quickly give way to martini bars, sports pubs, wrought-iron fences, and historic apartment buildings. It always amazed him how quickly Chicago exchanged its business suit for the classy informality of the Near North Side.

He pulled into his parking space behind the brownstone. If the Owl was on his trail again—and he must be because, otherwise, why would he have been tailing Todd Ferguson—it would be wise to take extra precautions. Better not park behind the building. There was a 24-hour parking garage half a block from the manhole at Erie and Franklin. From now on, he'd leave the car there, and warn Sing to stop making her Starbuck's runs. The fewer people going in and out, the better.

He dropped the car at the garage and walked back to alley. Shouldering open the gate, Janné looked from the security camera, mounted under the eaves, to the storm door that allowed access to the basement. The storm door was the one weak link in his security system. After he'd paid cash for this crumbling ruin of a building, he hadn't wanted to disturb its appearance of neglect. Besides, he wouldn't be in Chicago that much longer.

In the basement, dust hung in the air. Tarazi and Jester sat in front of a row of Linux workstations. Faces intent on their screens, they sipped Starbucks lattes. Janné wondered if the coffee even tasted good in such moldy-smelling air.

He sat down at the workstation next to Tarazi's. "How much have you pushed through the Fed?"

"Three hundred and thirty-one billion US. We'll keep going until the financial markets open tomorrow in New York."

Janné turned to Jester. "Are you ready?"

"Yes, sir." The hacker clicked his mouse. A new graphical window flashed up and showed a computational grid of thousands of computers. The word IDLE blinked next to each.

"The grid's ready," Jester said. "Once you tell me to start, I'll turn off logging and start moving the money. I'll start small, maybe a few thousand transactions, and then grow it exponentially. With any luck, they won't realize what's happening until it's too late. The senior UNIX admin at the Chicago Fed is Manny Rodriguez. He's very good. I worked with him while I was there. He'll eventually realize that something's wrong and kill our programs. When he does, one of my process watchers will crash all the storage arrays system-wide. All of their high-availability clusters will fail."

He grinned and tossed a cookie in his mouth. "It'll be hours before they'll be able to rebuild their systems, only to find that there's no way to replay the transaction logs. Can you imagine unraveling hundreds of millions of transactions as they split through random accounts all over the world without a log? It'll be a nightmare. By then, we'll be down south sipping cold drinks on a beach."

A kick made the basement door screech open, and Catalina Sing, carrying two coffees, stepped into the basement.

Seeing Janné's suit, she asked, "Are you going somewhere?"

"Brossard sent word he would like to speak with me. I will not be long."

She handed him a cup and sat down. Dust coated her hair, and she smelled as if she'd gone swimming in a sewer. He sniffed the beverage cautiously.

"Tarazi and I were betting what this place smells like," Jester said. "Tarazi thinks it smells like a dead fish. I think it smells like a dead fish's ass. What do you think?"

Janné put his cup back on the table.

"Was it something I said?" Jester inquired innocently.

Janné ignored him and turned to Sing. "Is there anything new on Byrnes?"

She nodded, sitting forward. "There's a rumor circulating that Byrnes's attack dog, Hugh Dobrowski, quit, and Byrnes is ripping Washington apart trying to find him."

"Why would Dobrowski quit?" Janné said. "Byrnes owns Dobrowski. Dobrowski will kill him."

"No one knows. I'm going to really enjoy finding out though."

She said this in such a quiet, matter-of-fact way that Tarazi eyed her warily.

Setting down her cup, she used Janné's keyboard to pull information from the file server's directory-services software. A personal query window appeared, and she typed in Dobrowski's name. His round, worn face appeared on the screen.

"Has he placed any calls from his office in the past couple of days?" Janné asked Tarazi.

"Nothing the building's exchange knows about," Tarazi said, his long face looking even more gaunt than normal in the dusty light. "He hasn't talked to anybody in three weeks. His e-mail and voicemail have been cleaned out."

"He's probably using a cell phone."

"No way of telling," Sing said. "Breaking into a telephone central office is a different world than hacking a corporate switch."

Jester ran a filthy yellow fingernail along her finely toned arm. "Maybe for you darlin'," he purred. "But if you wear a certain little black nothing I have tucked away at home, I'll be happy to give you a helping hand."

"Know where I'd like to stick your hand?" she asked, grabbing it and twisting his arm into an *aikido* joint lock.

Jester yelped in pain.

"Why did Dobrowski choose now to leave?" Janné asked. "Byrnes will bury him. It makes no sense."

Sing let go of Jester's arm. "It might if Dobrowski thought he had enough to make an arrangement."

Reaching over, she moved Janné's mouse to the last folder on his screen and clicked. A list of files appeared. She pulled down the OPTIONS menu and selected SEARCH.

"Type 'Daemon,'" she instructed.

Janné entered the parameter. Text scrolled and stopped with the word "Daemon" highlighted in the middle of the screen. He continued to read until he reached the bottom. There wasn't much that pertained to them, and what information did pertain was carefully inaccurate, out of date, and completely useless. As usual, Director Byrnes's technicians had been very careful to make it look like he and Brynes had no connection.

"A few months ago," she summarized as Janné backed up and started reading the file from the beginning, "Dobrowski sent two requests to the National Criminal Information Center in D.C. This is what he got back."

"There is nothing here."

"The second request was more interesting."

She clicked, and another document appeared on the screen.

At the top was a picture of an owl. Janné swore and sent a chair careening across the floor.

Sing watched his outburst with her dark, expressionless eyes. "Of course, there is no way of knowing whether Dobrowski has figured out the identity of the Owl."

"There is also no way of knowing he has not. This is news I could have done without."

He turned to Jester. "As soon as the markets close, start it. The Fed, Wall Street, the major banks, the currency exchanges, every bit of bastardized culture this country exports, I want it gone."

12

LATE THURSDAY AFTERNOON, Jackson and Dixie landed at O'Hare and took the El into Chicago. They exited the train just south of downtown and hailed a cab. Their motel was south of Midway, and the driver sped through traffic with a bored ruthlessness that made Jackson hold on with both hands. At stoplights, homeless men with cardboard signs stood on the median. Hanging out on the corner by a boarded-up Travelodge, a posse of teenagers eyed the cab.

"Sorry," he told Dixie.

"Oh, sure you are," she said.

She was right. He wasn't sorry. Wilkens would never find her here. The neighborhood was even worse than the one in Jersey, and the motel, with its dirty windows and sagging drapes, looked like one of those rent-by-the-hour places.

Jackson dropped his overnight case in their room and told Dixie to see if Cook County had archived their blueprints and building permits. "Their system's outdated, so it shouldn't take long."

Before she could argue, he ducked out of the room and flagged a cab. Traffic was horrible, but an extra twenty got him to Chicago's Near North Side in thirty-five minutes. A block from the Starbucks Daemon had used to crack ImTech, Tracy O'Connell had paid cash for a short-term lease on a rundown storefront. Across the street were six brownstones with narrow breezeways in between. Two had been gutted by fire and were boarded up. A third had yellow police tape across the front. An old man wearing surplus army fatigues and swinging a hammer was the only person in sight, and he was headed for the corner.

When Jackson knocked, O'Connell opened the storefront's back door. Inside, late afternoon sunshine glared through the broken blinds. His laptop sat on an old desk. A slender strand of cable connected it to a digital video camera taped to the upper right corner of the window. A directional microphone sat by the wall next to a heat scope and a case of spare electronics.

"What's that smell?" Jackson asked, wrinkling his nose.

"Dead rats in the walls. There's a box of poison in the other room."

Jackson shut the door. Of all the terrible places they'd had to work in the past two years, this took the cake.

"What did you find?"

O'Connell ran a hand through his buzz cut. "I'm not sure, to be honest. I spent most of the morning going through the neighborhood near Starbucks. Nothing leapt out at me, but then the meter picked up some ultrasonic in the wreck across the street." He spread the blinds and pointed across the road to the brownstone with the plywood-covered windows. "Look close at the right second-story window, the one with the ripped screen. See that piece of new gray wire? A hundred bucks says it's live. For an abandoned building, someone's very serious about their hardware."

There was no chair, so Jackson crouched in front of the computer on the desk and used the mouse to pan the video camera back and forth. He zoomed in on the heavy sheets of industrial plywood nailed over the front door and each of the first-floor windows. "Anybody inside?"

"I don't know yet. I planted a camera around back earlier and waited to see if anybody would care. So far, nobody has, which makes me think the place is deserted, or someone has worked very hard to make it appear that way."

"Is the alarm ultrasonic multiple-frequency or fixed?"

"Fixed — so far."

"All three floors?"

"No, just the first."

Jackson switched the feed to the wireless camera O'Connell had placed behind the brownstone. The video camera only transmitted forty images a minute, so it wasn't full-motion, but the tiny camera's size, ultra-high-definition resolution, and portability more than made up for its lack of speed. Inside the back fence sat a one-person cement mixer and sections of rusty steel scaffolding. Piles of asphalt and concrete covered the lot.

"Any surveillance out back?" Jackson asked.

O'Connell pointed to a spot high on the northeast wall just under the roof. Jackson took the camera in for a closer look and squinted through the glare.

"Is that a camera under the gutter?"

"Yes."

"Why would they put a camera way up there? What's below it?"

"A metal storm door. You can't see it from our angle because of the weeds."

"Do you have binoculars?"

O'Connell pointed. "In the case."

Jackson fished out the binoculars. Starting at the curb, he carefully examined the front of the building, the second- and third-story windows, the two video cameras, the roof, and, finally, the fire escape. Ducking under the window, he moved to the other side and raised the binoculars. The building on the far left looked almost identical to the abandoned one, but the windows had glass, the roof was in good repair, and the brick had been sandblasted clean. It faced the other street.

"What's on the corner?"

"Medusa's Nightclub. It was closed when I walked by earlier, so I didn't get a look inside. It opens at eleven."

Jackson tried to gauge the distance between the two buildings. "How far apart do you think the fire escapes are?"

"Close enough to jump, but I wouldn't recommend it. They're old."

"Was there a camera on that side?"

"I didn't see one."

Jackson returned the binoculars to the case and found the listing for the club on his phone. Dialing the number, he got a static-filled recording of how to get there, the hours they were open, and the evening's events. He called Dixie.

"Did you get into the county database?" he asked.

She snorted. "Please! I had a harder time figurin' out how to navigate than get in. Their mainframes are so slow I'm gonna die of boredom. How IBM keeps sellin' these billion-dollar snails is beyond me."

"We have an address. You ready?"

He waited as she brought it up.

"It's in the database, but the blueprints are in sad shape. I think they were microfilmed first. The cracks in the film are darker than the drawings. How old is this place?"

"Can you get the prints for the buildings on both sides? Going in straight doesn't look good."

"Is it hot?"

"Three cameras, ultrasonic, and wire."

She whistled. "Wire and noise? You sure?"

"All I'm telling you is what I see."

He hung up and returned to O'Connell's laptop, continuously updating the images sent from the mobile camera. The air above the pavement shimmered with heat.

"If you had to get inside, how would you do it?" Jackson asked.

O'Connell picked up a sweating fountain cup, took a swallow, and spat the ice into the dust.

"First, I'd cut the power and phone lines. Then I'd sit and wait to see if anybody objected. If no one came running, I'd go around back after the club closed, pop the plywood off one of the smaller windows with a crowbar, and let myself in."

"What if the building is on alternate power?"

"Then I'd let you do it." He took another drink of his soda. By the time he'd finished, the humor had left his face. "We need to be very careful with this, boss," O'Connell said. "First off, we have no idea what's inside. If Daemon caught Dobrowski in New York, the building could be wired with explosives. Or we could have the wrong place. We just don't know enough, and I don't like that."

"What do you suggest?"

The big man shrugged. "We could tell Agent Lambert about Dobrowski and what we've found. If Lambert can cut a deal with Wilkens, we're out."

"Wilkens won't do it. If Lambert sticks his neck out, Wilkens will chop it off."

"Then call Wilkens and negotiate a way out where we get access to their information. Wilkens knows who Dobrowski is. He'll know how to get more answers."

"I don't trust him," Jackson said. "No matter what we do, he'll find a way to nail us to the wall. There are no good options."

"If this was easy," O'Connell said, "I suppose the Russians wouldn't be paying us to get their money back."

Jackson checked the time. "I'm going to help Dixie. Call me if you see anything."

He left the smell behind and got lucky on a passing cab. Traffic going south wasn't as bad as it had been earlier, and he made good time. He swiped a newspaper off the cab's floor as he rode. A lot was going on, most of it bad. Partisan politics had polarized the country, the Russians were trying to hack the election, seasonal road construction had Chicago tied up in knots, and the Cubs were in a three-game slide.

When he got back to the motel, Dixie had the brownstone's blueprints up on her screen. She had used a filter to heighten the contrast, but the white lines of the building's footprint were still faint.

"The prints were scanned into the system back in the eighties," she said. "This is as good as I can make it."

He examined the prints, and then went to the window and cracked the blinds to look outside at the shattered buildings, glass-strewn lots, and leaning firetraps the underprivileged called home. Billboards advertising hard liquor, cigarettes, and contraceptives glowed in fluorescent pinks and yellows.

"If the brownstone is all boarded up, how does Daemon get inside?" he asked.

"Maybe they tunneled in from next door," Dixie said, "or maybe there's a basement door. The blueprints are older than I am. There's no way of knowin' for sure without going inside. You do realize if Daemon caught Dobrowski in New York, then he could be sittin' inside waitin' for us."

"O'Connell made the same point earlier."

"Sometimes you just have to take what's offered."

He frowned. "That's what I told myself the night I got shot."

13

THE LAST TIME Joe Tresher had been to Chicago, a blizzard had pounded the city with a foot of snow. Now, seven months later, September was very different from February. Fall wasn't officially due for another few weeks, and it was hot and humid by the lake. Tresher's cowboy boots stuck to the asphalt.

The only people who didn't seem to mind the heat were the shoppers. Carrying their bags and parcels, they bustled up and down Michigan Avenue. Christmas was still months away, but the mood under the shining glass buildings was festive.

Tresher bought an ice cream and ate it as he reviewed everything the CIA had on Alec Janné. Until Deputy Director Byrnes had recruited Janné, the Frenchman had been working for French DGSE as a financial systems programmer. Using the French as a cover, Byrnes had sent Janné after the Russians' primitive financial networks. Billions of rubles disappeared. Byrnes leaked Alec Janné, a French intelligence agent, as the thief and tried to have him killed.

Janné saw the double-cross coming and bolted with the money. For months, Byrnes had tried everything he could to find Janné, and then, three months after Janné disappeared, the FBI had uncovered a sophisticated money laundering operation at the Bank of New York. Three small companies were moving large sums from hidden accounts in Russia into the United States and back out again to dozens of foreign banks. Two of the companies were based in the US, while the third, the company that had arranged for the initial electronic transfers, was London-based.

Once outside the US, the money moved into bitcoin. An entire department of the FBI mobilized to follow the money-maze. Three years later, they had unraveled only a fraction of the laundered money. One veteran agent called it an enigma wrapped in a riddle that had been smashed into a million pieces and thrown off the Empire State Building on a windy day.

The only person who really understood it all was Byrnes — and only because he had seen this kind of operation before. The scheme had Janné's name all over it. Tresher shook his head, wondering how Byrnes slept at night. If the truth ever got out that Janné had worked for Byrnes, it could destroy the CIA.

Tresher went inside a corner bar. Seated with his back to the wall, he took an empty booth and watched the street. Five minutes later, Ned Davis lumbered inside. The private detective was a hulking, square man who looked like he had been outlined by someone who could only draw straight lines. His gray hair was cut close to his skull, showing every wrinkle in his skin. He hadn't shaved since that morning, and his cheeks were stiff with bristles. The vinyl seat hissed under his weight.

Without being asked, the bartender brought him an Anchor Steam on draft. Davis took a sip, pushed an envelope across the table, and ducked his head. A normal person might have thought him anti-social, but Tresher knew better. Davis was one of the most careful men Tresher had ever worked with. Even though the bar wasn't busy, Davis didn't want to be observed.

"Janné's girlfriend, Sara Branson, is listed on the lease, but

I haven't seen her," Davis murmured. "The condo staff tells me she's been around, but they can't remember when. Her schedule is unpredictable. They see her one day. Then a month goes by before they see her again."

Tresher slipped the envelope into the folder Director Byrnes had given him in New York. "Did you get inside?"

"The bug is under her couch." Davis removed a cell phone from his pocket and handed it over. "You can listen in on that. When you're done, throw it away. So far, all I've heard is her refrigerator."

"No sign of Janné?"

"No. But I was quiet like you wanted. I didn't want to spook him if he was around."

"Utility bills?"

"Inside the envelope. The bank pays her bills electronically —which makes sense. Her schedule's erratic."

"Anything bother you about the place?"

Davis didn't answer. With his head down, gravity made his eyelids droop. He appeared to be falling asleep.

"I wasn't in there long," he finally said. "Maybe three minutes—just enough time to plant the bug and get out. I didn't see anything unusual, but I didn't see anything that was usual either, if you get my drift. Once you get past the furniture, there isn't a lot there. No pictures on the fridge, no hobbies. The bathroom's cleaner than any bathroom I've ever seen. You know women, Joe. They smear so much stuff on themselves, they can't help but make a mess. Hairspray gets all over the place—even if they're careful. Her bathroom's spotless. I don't think it's been used lately."

"Does she have a maid?"

Davis nodded. "The bills are in the envelope. But unless the maid is better at cleaning than any maid I've ever seen, I don't think Sara has lived there for a while."

"What's the rent?"

"Three large a month if you include utilities."

"She works as an international model. She can afford it."

David nodded but looked unconvinced.

"I don't want to know what this is about, Joe. Your business is your business, which is none of my business, I always say. However, I do have one piece of advice. Something about this bothers me. Watch your back."

Nodding politely, he stood up and left.

14

MEDUSA'S NIGHTCLUB, once a theater, had reopened as a dance club. The drapes were black plastic, the once-expensive wallpaper had peeled off the walls, and what remained of the carpet had worn through to wood. Jackson and Dixie arrived after midnight and followed the music into the main auditorium. The floor had been ripped out and replaced with clear acrylic that refracted the overhead lasers into rainbows of color. Even though it was late on a weeknight, crowds of stylishly dressed people danced to five thousand watts of music on the dance floor. Heels wide apart, a nearby woman rippled to the rhythm as if she were made of water. The motion started in her knees, worked up through her midsection, and made her head snap.

Far up on one wall, in what had once been a box seat, two DJs sat in an intricate nest of wire and amplifiers, headphones over their ears and fingers flying across control boards. One song merged with the next. The booming beat grew faster and faster.

Avoiding arms and elbows, Jackson cut through the crowd. The weapons under Jackson's vest stuck to his skin.

He led Dixie up the creaking stairs to the top floor, once a lobby for the balcony. Here, the music was slow and subdued, the ambiance thick with shadows. A young woman with long hair sat on a glass cube in the corner. Every few seconds, a light flashed and illuminated her legs. On the floor, couples entwined. *Get a room*, Jackson thought.

He found a corner and pulled Dixie into it. Everything narrowed to the two of them, a tiny bit of quiet in a world of motion. It might have been the music, or it might have been that he was lonely, but whatever it was, he found himself caught in her eyes. When she returned his stare, the smoky depths of her eyes stirred his soul. She moved closer, and he felt the warmth of her body pressing against his side.

The song changed. Another night. Another club. Another face. He was slow dancing with Suzanne at Sly's on Marshal Law Night, the two of them so close that one of the club's "Lawmen," a bright silver star affixed to his shirt and a plastic pistol in his belt, threw them into "Jail" until Jackson paid twenty dollars for charity. He pressed his fingers to his eyes.

"You okay?" Dixie asked.

He tried to focus. "What?"

"We have a few minutes. You want to get somethin' to drink?"

"Sure." He looked around for an empty table, saw one, and borrowed a pair of chairs. A waitress took their order.

Dixie counted the ice cubes in her soda. "This reminds me of when I used to go clubbin' with Bobby Hallett."

This was definitely not what he'd expected. "Your old college boyfriend in Houston?"

"It's the song. I thought it wouldn't bother me, but I guess it does."

She always cut him off when he asked about her past. They both had their secrets, and she was entitled to hers. Stones and glass houses.

She knocked back the last of her drink. "Bobby was a systems programmer for the university. He's why I wrote Genesis and why I'm havin' such fun gettin' shot at. He didn't have the equipment we do, but I've never seen anyone like him. I didn't think anybody could catch him until the NSA tagged him. I don't know if he got careless, or he got into somethin' he didn't understand. I had an exam and was home studyin', or I would have been arrested with him. The government thought he was Chinese or Russian or somebody from Anonymous, so they were paranoid. He's doin' ten years at a Federal pen in Oklahoma. I'd like to go see him, just to give him some support, but if I did, the FBI would lock me up."

Jackson watched a young couple attempt an awkward turn. The girl watched the young man's feet while he peeked inside her blouse. Jackson leaned his head closer, so he could hear over the music.

"Bobby taught me how to crack an encrypted SE Linux kernel—like the one you found earlier today. Infectin' an encrypted kernel with a virus won't work unless the virus is encrypted usin' the same key. If it's not, it can't read the system requests or issue its own, makin' it useless. The campus computer didn't have enough CPU cycles to break itself, let alone anythin' big enough to be of value, so even if I was able to break the crypt key once, I would have to break it again for each different machine. Even with a grid of supercomputers, it would take millions of years to break even one code if the law of averages held up."

"So you went after the I/O?"

She nodded. "The only way the operatin' system could pass requests to the hardware was through the kernel, so I worked on catchin' the crypt keys from the I/O requests and encryptin' the virus with the keys. Once the virus had the keys, it could attach itself to the kernel when the I/O request was serviced."

A waitress walked past, picked up a tray of drinks, and left again. Dixie blinked, thinking, and when she resumed speaking, Jackson could barely hear her.

"Bobby was sentenced on a Monday, and I missed it. I was supposed to be one of his character witnesses. I had spent three days trying to crack the problem with the I/O and hadn't slept. I was passed out on my keyboard when he went to court. I had no idea what day it was. He called after it was over. They'd given him ten years. I felt horrible and wasn't thinkin' straight. I jumped onto the Internet and looked around until I found a low-level mail gateway in D.C. that had the network alias of the machine that had caught Bobby in its HOSTS file. I created a binary message tellin' the government to screw itself, attached the virus, sent it off, and went to bed a happy, vindicated woman."

She shook the ice in her drink.

"Genesis spread through the big commercial networks like the plague. The government told everyone to physically pull their wire until they could figure out what had happened. When I woke up, I realized what I had done and threw up in the bathroom sink. I felt like I had pushed the big red button and blown up the world."

Jackson laughed. She glared at him.

"Bobby cut a deal with the Feds, blamin' everythin' on me. Here I was thinkin' I had done somethin' noble for the man I loved, only he had already let me down. I killed the entire world for nothin'. But that's not the worst part. Gettin' involved with Bobby was like playin' with matches. Gettin' hooked up with you is like playin' with dynamite with a blow torch."

"I never forced you into this."

Her dark eyes flashed. "What was I supposed to do? You showed up the mornin' after they arrested me, paid cash for my bond, and offered me a new life chasing Daemon without tellin' me the terms. I could have been out of prison by now. Maybe even gone back in grad school—if they'd let me. The real issue was that the government was angry they hadn't thought of it first. Genesis is now required readin' at the NSA. Did you know that? I wasn't a criminal then—just an idiot. Now I'm both."

"You can quit. The way things are going, that would probably be a smart idea."

"And do what? I have no future and a terrible past."

"You have a future if you want one. We've made a lot of money chasing Daemon. You know how to hide. The world's a big place. Find somewhere quiet and keep your head down. That's what I'd do."

"I don't see you leavin'. My prospects are the same as yours and we both know it. That's why we've got to get Daemon. One of these days he's goin' to find out you're still chasin' him, and then it's only a question of *when* he finds you—and me."

She checked the time on her phone. "Don't these people work? It's almost one in the mornin'. Let's get this over with before what's left of my good sense catches up."

They went up a dark stairway to a door padlocked shut. Dixie removed a battery-powered electronic locksmith from her purse, inserted the slender metal head into the housing, and pressed the button. The unit clicked twice, and the hasp sprang apart.

Jackson withdrew a radio earpiece, a frequency sniffer, and a stunner from his jacket. He clipped the sniffer to his lapel, plugged it into his radio, and pushed the earpiece into his ear. A burst of static made him wince. After adjusting the volume, he slid the stunner into the belt holster below his left elbow and checked his pistol's clip. Lifting his sleeve, he turned on the small microphone attached to the inside of his shirt cuff.

"You there, Doc?"

"Loud and clear," O'Connell answered from the street out front.

Dixie tapped her microphone. Jackson held up two fingers.

She nodded. Slinging her purse across her body, she clipped it to the back of her belt.

"Ready?" he asked.

She moved to his left and crouched close to the wall. Jackson nudged the door open and slipped through.

15

ALEC JANNÉ STEPPED inside the restaurant and waited for his
eyes to adjust to the gloom. Music played softly, just enough to
be heard, but not loud enough to make it hard to talk. Couples
sipped cocktails and whispered over food. He moved into the
corner where he could watch the crowd. A waitress asked
what he wanted. Janné ordered a cocktail.

Ten minutes later, she arrived. Dressed entirely in form-
fitting gold silk, she moved through the crowd with the self-
confidence of a finely groomed Persian cat. Platinum hair
spilled down the nape of her slender neck and over her pale,
bare shoulders.

"Do you like her?" a low voice purred at his elbow.

Sing wore a short, tight black dress. Where the woman in
gold flashed, Sing shrouded herself in darkness. Most men had
to look twice to see her, and most never got the chance.

Sing touched his hand and disappeared into the crowd.
Even in heels, she moved like a shadow.

Janné turned back toward the woman in gold and found
her speaking with a tall man dressed in a sports jacket and
loafers. A loosely knotted tie hung from the open collar of his

wrinkled shirt. His smile was easygoing. He said something and the woman laughed, her voice drowned out by the music.

A slender man dressed in an expensive European suit stopped beside Janné.

"May I have a moment of your time, my friend?" Jean-Paul Brossard inquired softly in French. "It's important."

Two men Janné hadn't noticed before slid smoothly in front of them; their roving eyes watched the crowd. Brossard turned, back placed strategically so no one could read his lips.

"The *Directeur général* has received an unusual request from the US government," he said in his perfectly cultured voice.

"Unusual?"

"It seems a number of this country's international companies have had," he paused to inspect his manicured fingernails, "difficulty with their intellectual and technological property in France. The State Department has requested our cooperation in solving the problem."

"What do they want?"

As if truly unhappy about delivering bad news, the diplomat frowned. "Recently our intelligence service was caught in an embarrassing situation by this country's FBI. Washington is most upset and is threatening official retribution unless a compromise can be reached."

"What sort of compromise?"

"That should be obvious by my presence," Brossard said.

Janné swore. The bodyguards shifted uneasily.

"What are the terms of the compromise?" Janné asked.

"Unfortunately, I am not at liberty to say."

"Officially or unofficially?"

"Both are the same in this business, I am afraid," Brossard replied. "I am sorry, but such is the way of politics."

He stepped between the two men without another word and disappeared.

When he saw that Brossard had left, Janné went over to Sing.

"*Qu'est-ce qui ne va pas?*" she asked.

"The French are cooperating with the US government. Full disclosure."

Her dark eyes narrowed. "Should we take what we have and leave for the islands?"

"No. By the time both governments understand what has happened, it will not matter. If the US goes down, France will follow."

She handed him two glasses and leaned close to his ear.

"I'll see you in an hour, then," she said, the words spoken so quietly that he wasn't sure if he'd heard them right. Looking at the glasses, he raised an inquiring eyebrow, but she moved off again.

The tall man and the woman in gold were still standing together talking, but almost as if Sing had orchestrated the situation, the man drained the last of his drink and pointed to his glass. The woman nodded, and he excused himself.

Weaving through the tables to the bar, the man ordered another pair of drinks. The man went to pull out his wallet but found it missing. He patted his jacket pocket, and then Sing dangled it like a cat toy. An inviting smile lit her eyes. Fingers three inches short of his wallet, the man paused. After a moment, she put a twenty on the bar and scooped up both drinks. Eyes never leaving his, she took a sip from one of the glasses and handed him the other. He glanced at the woman in gold, looked back at Sing, and allowed himself to be led outside.

Janné cut through the tables. The woman in the gold dress waited alone, dress shimmering in a pool of light thrown from one of the overhead lights. He waited for her to look at her watch, then introduced himself.

Her name was Patricia Myer. She worked for the Mayor's office and handled bookings for the Chicago Jazz Festival. Her family lived in Decatur, Illinois, and, after graduating with a degree in Management Relations from the University of Illinois, she had moved to city. She lived in a one-bedroom apartment with a dog named Butch, a gift from her father to protect her from the crazies he saw on the evening news. When she paused, Janné maneuvered her to a table. More talk, leaning forward, then, almost accidentally, he let his fingers brush against hers and his thigh touch her knee.

~

HE TOOK her across town to a condominium complex and whisked her into one of the corporate suites on the top floor. Taking out his cell phone, he turned it off and uncorked a bottle of champagne. Offering a flute and clinking his glass to hers, he brought her to the window and the endless lights of the Chicago skyline.

"Do you realize what it is like to hold an entire nation in the palm of your hand?" he asked.

She swayed slightly and looked up, bleary-eyed. "What was that?"

"Six years ago, I took one hundred billion rubles from the Russian financial reserve and flooded the currency markets. The ruble plummeted, taking most of the smaller currencies with it. The international traders fled into the bigger, more stable currencies—which only made the ruble fall more. Three months later, it hit bottom. By that time, the Russian economy was worth twenty percent less than it had been. Years of hard work encouraging foreign investment dried up overnight. Millions of people lost their jobs."

"I don't understand what you're saying."

He turned from the window. "Archimedes said that given a place to stand and a big enough lever, he could move the earth. The United States' economy is eighty-seven times the size of the Russian Federation's. Moving something that large requires a monstrous lever. I would need hundreds of billions of dollars just to start, and even that would not be enough.

There simply is not a way to get enough leverage. For years, I tried to find a way to repeat what I had done with the ruble, but I could not come up with enough funds to leverage the dollar adequately. I was very close to giving up. My investments were doing well. I could have let *Directeur* Byrnes triumph. But then my brother gave me the answer. Adrian called it *the psychology of leverage*. Don't target the dollar, he said. Target instead the *psychology* of the dollar, and then leverage the resulting uncertainty. He was quite brilliant, my brother, until the Owl shot him in the head. For that I will never forgive."

He slipped the golden dress over her head. "Can you feel the hum under your feet, pretty one? Bit by bit, kilobyte by kilobyte, the leverage grows."

He carried her to the bed. The bedroom door opened behind them, and Sing slid into the room. She was nude. Snakelike, she moved toward the bed. Her beautiful, bottomless eyes were eager.

"I could hardly stand waiting," she purred, the long silver razor dangling loosely from her fingertips. "She's exquisite, Alec. This is going to be so much fun."

16

JACKSON CREPT onto the landing and peered across the breezeway at the other building's stairs. At this end of the building, there were two doors. One opened onto the emergency exit across the way, the other into the alley forty feet below. He ducked under the railing, leapt across the four-foot gap, and grabbed the other railing. The stairway groaned. For a moment, he thought the fire escape would break free, and then he realized he was the one moving and not the stairs. Grabbing the railing with his other hand, he ducked underneath and flattened himself against the wall. The support bolts' tortured squeal stopped.

Dixie closed the night club's door behind her. She gauged the distance between the fire escapes, tensed, and sprang across. Her foot landed first. He clasped her wrist. She ducked under the rail and crouched to one side of the door. The locksmith glinted dully in her hands. He heard a slight scrape, an electric whir, and then a click. Moving to her left in case the exit was booby-trapped, she tugged on the knob. The door creaked open.

A single security light lit the top of the stairwell. The walls were gouged with holes. The ceiling had been ripped out, exposing the joists, and, above them, the underside of the roof itself. Knob-and-tube wiring hung from the ceiling. Some fool had even burnt a hole in the floor.

Carefully placing each foot in the debris before shifting his weight, Jackson started toward the light below. People, or a work light to deter vandals? No way to tell unless he looked. His electronics chirped in his ear and then, at the top of the stairs, chattered. He waited for the warning warble of multiple frequency ultrasonic, but the tone remained steady.

Dixie opened her purse, withdrew a frequency jammer and a slender spool of sixty-pound fishing line. Snapping open the jammer's display cover, she switched it on. The tiny screen came to life, showing the frequency of the building's ultrasonic and the inverse frequency that would jam it. Jackson tied the fishing line to the handle of the jammer, eased silently forward across the landing, and slowly lowered it over the edge. The steady chatter in his ear immediately changed to an isolated chirp. When the jammer reached the bottom, the chirping stopped.

So far, so good. No one had noticed their presence. He slipped out of the darkness and, with Dixie following close behind, tiptoed down the stairs. When he reached the bottom, he pressed against a wall and looked in both directions. Plaster and lath had been torn from the studs. A sledgehammer lay on the bottom tread. He stepped over it and stood in the entry hall.

"You sure we have the right place?" Dixie whispered.

"Not sure at all," Jackson said.

Yes, the building was only a couple of blocks from the Starbucks where ImTech had been hacked, but other than the building's excessive security, nothing pointed to Daemon's being here. There certainly wasn't enough for the FBI to get a search warrant or even watch the place. Daemon could have flown into Chicago from anywhere, picked a random Starbucks to work on ImTech, and then skipped town. As for the security, maybe the owner was paranoid about break-ins. Or Daemon was waiting here to spring a trap.

A low rattle sounded to their right. Jackson gestured for Dixie to move behind one of the few intact walls. He crouched in the shadow of the stairs. A floorboard popped. A flashlight split the darkness. The light swept the stairs and blinked away.

Another floorboard creaked. A shadow separated from a nearby wall. The man carried a pistol and a flashlight. Jackson waited until he went past, then pushed his stunner against the man's left hip. The man gasped, air exploding from his chest. The pistol fell, and he collapsed to the floor. Jackson dropped his knee on the man's back and quick-clipped his wrists behind him.

"He came from downstairs," Dixie whispered. "C'mon."

Jackson pushed Dixie behind him and, weapon ready, started down the stairs. The air smelled of mold. Bright purple halogens illuminated the room. Networking and computer equipment jammed the basement. A slender cable of optical fiber ran from the computers to a hole jackhammered in the floor.

Jackson ducked behind the equipment and quietly moved to where a tall, thin man sat typing in front of a computer. Dixie crept up behind the man and shoved him away from the table. The man's chair fell. Before he could untangle himself, Dixie slammed her heel into the back of his elbow. The blow sent him sprawling into one of the steel posts. His head hit with a thump that sounded like someone had dropped a watermelon. He collapsed.

Dixie pinned him to the floor and cuffed his wrists. "So much for asking questions." She looked around. "What are all these computers for?"

"Maybe the guy upstairs knows."

Jackson took the stairs two at a time. The man he had stunned lay on his side. Even lying down, he had to be at least twice Jackson's weight. Jackson checked the man's surprisingly small hands. All ten fingertips were covered in calluses, but the rest of his hands were soft. He was still out.

Jackson dragged the man downstairs and cuffed him to the table. Dixie took out her phone and lifted each of his fat fingers to the phone camera's lens.

Jackson pinched the man's oily nose. After a moment, the big man blinked and moaned.

"Man-oh-man," he wheezed, rolling into a ball.

"What's going on down here?" Jackson asked. "What's in the tunnel?"

The man opened his eyes. "Who are you?"

Dixie went over to the computers. Concatenating rapidly down each screen were columns of numbers. The last column had a decimal point.

"Dobrowski might be right," she said. "Look at this."

At Dobrowski's name, the man's head snapped to look at her.

"I take it you know who Hugh Dobrowski is?" Jackson asked.

The man managed a weak smile, the folds of skin tightening around his small eyes. "Who he *was* you mean. The cat's dead."

Dixie righted the fallen chair and started typing on the console. The man watched her fingers and lost the smile.

Jackson followed the cable across the floor and stared down into the hole. An aluminum ladder had been anchored in place by rebar pounded into the floor. Should he go down or not? Making sure he didn't step on the cable, he turned and descended and found himself in a ten-foot-high circular concrete tunnel.

Gray industrial-grade PVC pipes ran along the tunnel's ceiling. He held up a hand to shield his eyes from the spotlights. One of the conduits had been cut open, and an optical cable had been pulled out. Someone had separated the individual strands and connected them to a networking switch.

After climbing back up the ladder, Jackson went over to the big man.

"What's in the tunnel?"

The man grinned. "We got tired of paying for cable. Now we get to watch for free."

Dixie pointed at her display.

"They're moving money. The first column's the bank's routing number. The second is the account where it's going. The last column is the amount."

Jackson's radio earpiece crackled.

"Jackson!" O'Connell snapped. "We have company! Pack it up and get out!"

Jackson turned toward Dixie. "How much can you get?"

She pushed a portable drive into the computer and bent over the keyboard, fingers blurring. The drive's write-indicator light turned red for a few horribly long seconds before turning green. Jumping to her feet, Dixie unplugged the drive. The computer started spitting out error messages. The handcuffed man swore.

With Dixie right behind him, Jackson sprinted up the stairs to the first floor and wove through piles of lath and plaster. Plywood covered the windows on either side of the front door. Dixie kicked the plywood. The wood shook with each blow, but didn't budge. Jackson grabbed the sledgehammer from the stairs and swung at the bottom corner of the plywood. The wood buckled, and the bottom corner sprang free.

Shouts rang out from the rear of the building. Silenced automatic gunfire popped. Bullets hissed past. Jackson swung again. The wood cracked down the middle. He swung a third time. The nails gave way and plywood crashed to the porch. Holding the disk, Dixie jumped through and sprinted for the street. Jackson dropped the sledgehammer and followed.

An engine roared down the block. A sedan accelerated their way. Dixie saw it coming and veered toward the nightclub. The sedan swerved onto the sidewalk and skidded to a stop. The back passenger door flew open.

"Get in!" O'Connell shouted through the window.

Jackson dove into the backseat. Dixie followed, landing on him. O'Connell floored the accelerator, and with a squeal of rubber, the sedan crashed over the curb. The open door caught a light pole and slammed shut with a metal-bending crunch.

Once they were safely away, O'Connell said, "Good thing I took the insurance."

17

AFTER NED DAVIS left the bar, Joe Tresher opened the envelope and went through the private detective's typed report. Sara Branson did, indeed, pay all her bills automatically, even her twice-a-month maid service. He checked the phone bills, but didn't see any long distance or collect calls. As far as he could tell, all she had was local service. Her gas bill was surprisingly small—even during the cold winter months. There was no cable bill.

Flipping a page of the bio Director Byrnes had given him, Tresher examined Sara Branson's photos one more time, admiring the way her smile lit her face. She was a classic model with platinum hair, high cheekbones, and a dancer's legs. There was something in her gray eyes that caught him: a vulnerability that even her professional smile couldn't hide. Alec Janné had met her in New York when she had been working for a fragrance company. They met at a party and hit it off. Long distance relationships were difficult, but even after she'd returned to Chicago, they'd stayed in touch.

After Janné disappeared, Director Byrnes watched Sara, hoping Janné would contact her. As the months passed, Byrnes reduced surveillance, and after a year, he stopped it altogether. The last time anyone had looked at Sara Branson had been three years ago—which meant the trail was hopelessly cold. Tresher had no illusions of succeeding where Byrnes had failed. Tresher could be very persuasive when he wanted to be, but he also knew persuasion could only go so far if Sara didn't know anything. Realistically, the only way he was going to find Janné was if he got lucky.

He gathered up the reports, left money on the table, and went outside. Head down and tongue dripping, a stray dog panted miserably on the sidewalk. Tresher waved down a cab and had the driver drop him off at his hotel. He unpacked, took a cold shower, and watched the last of Navy Pier's evening dinner cruises return from Lake Michigan. One of the boats hosted a crowd of brightly dressed teenagers, and he watched them dance until a building blocked them from sight. He shook his head, unable to imagine voluntarily doing anything but drinking cold fluids in this humidity.

He left his hotel, walked to Lake Point Tower, and waited in the lobby for an elevator. A stylish woman and two men in business suits rode up to the seventh floor, with the woman shivering and looking up at the air conditioning duct in the elevator's ceiling until she exited.

Tresher got off on the fifty-second floor and located Sara Branson's condominium. For such an expensive building, the lock took only seconds to open. The condo was so immaculate he would have sworn the leasing agents used it as a model. And the smell! The condominium had a pervasively pleasant Pine-Sol scent that made his nose run. There was no getting away from it.

Sniffling, he pulled open drawers and looked in closets. All empty. In the bedroom, he looked under the perfectly made bed, searched the nightstand, and even moved the box of tissues on the headboard without finding any of the normal things most single women kept within easy reach. Where was this Sara person's makeup case, toothpaste, and shampoo?

Stepping into the kitchen, he searched the drawers until he found an envelope with the Lake Point Tower's logo on the front. Inside were four copies of the lease — one for each year Sara had lived there. He picked up the most recent lease. Sara's name and address were printed neatly across the top. Her signature looped over the bottom of the last page. The same name and signature were on the second lease and the third. Only the dates were different. He thumbed quickly through the last lease, and then upended the envelope. A dozen or so move-in coupons fell out, followed by a small brown envelope. Inside the envelope were two extra copies of the condominium key. Each shiny key looked as if it had just been freshly cut. He held the keys up to the light.

Had she changed the lock? The keys were similar, but there were several slight variations. He turned over the first key and saw a small 52A stamped into the metal. Setting it on the countertop, he held up the other key, took another look at the number to make sure, and whistled.

The second key was for a different condominium.

18

TYLER JACKSON CALLED Agent Bruce Lambert at home. It was four a.m. on the East Coast, and Lambert was undoubtedly sound asleep. The phone rang for almost a minute before he picked up.

"Hello?" he croaked.

Jackson glanced at O'Connell who, through his binoculars, kept watch on the brownstone through the storefront's blinds. Dixie had dropped them off so she could go to the motel. He wanted her to start working on the stolen transactions before the banks opened on the East Coast.

"It's Jackson. Sorry to call so early. I've already phoned the police, but you'll need to get jurisdiction as quickly as you can. You can't let anyone go in the building."

"What are you talking about?"

"I'm in Chicago. I found Daemon."

"What!"

Jackson checked his pistol as he talked. "A week ago, a network engineer named Todd Ferguson received money from an account Daemon's used in the past. That's what I tried to tell you yesterday in New York before Wilkens's visit. At the time, I had no idea what Daemon wanted with Ferguson.

None of it made sense, but now I understand. Daemon needed a way to crack live optical fiber. It's supposed to be physically impossible since you can't tap or bend light, but Ferguson found a way. Once Daemon had physical access to the network he wanted, he added himself as a node."

"To what network?"

"I don't know yet. My bet is it belongs to a bank or maybe the government. Look, we don't have a lot of time here. I'm watching Daemon's building right now. My guess is that he's wiring it with explosives. If anyone goes through the front door, the building will go sky high. Call Chicago PD. They're already on their way, but when I called it in, I didn't know he was rigging the place."

"Daemon's still there?"

"Yes. Call the police, get jurisdiction, then call me back."

Lambert took a deep breath. "I can't get involved, Ty. Wilkens will go nuts without a good investigative reason. You know that."

"Then call in a favor or make something up like one of your informants sent you the information. I don't care. But if the police go inside, a lot of people will get killed."

O'Connell abruptly ducked below the window. "We have company!" he snapped. "You'd better look at this!"

Jackson lowered his voice. "Bruce, hold on. We have activity. Give me a second."

He put down his phone and came to the window, crouching next to O'Connell. O'Connell handed him the binoculars. It was dark outside. Eight men wearing black body armor and carrying assault rifles jogged up the sidewalk toward the building. Behind them, a black armored truck pulled to a stop. Jackson crawled back to his phone.

"SWAT just arrived!" he told Lambert. "You have to tell them to abort!"

O'Connell made a frantic cutting motion with his hand.

"Hang it up!" he whispered. "If they hear us, we're dead!"

"But they're going to get blown up!" Jackson said.

Two men in heavy boots ran up to the building, stuck something on the door, and darted away.

"Since when does SWAT use suppressors?" O'Connell asked.

"Good point." Jackson raised his head to peer through the blinds again. "Listen to me!" Jackson whispered furiously into the phone. "A bunch of bad guys just showed up, all of them heavily armed! You have to move on this now!"

The darkness exploded in a flash. The force of the explosion rolled across the street and hit their building. The windows burst. Jackson dove to the floor and covered his head. Jackson heard Lambert on the phone demanding to know what had happened. No time to talk. He turned off the phone and risked a look through the broken glass. O'Connell grabbed the camera from the tangled wreckage of blinds and glass, crawled back to his computer, and swept the equipment into a crate.

The first flash-bang exploded inside the brownstone's front door. Three more went off in rapid succession, and then the men darted inside the door, weapons ready. One of them fired, muzzle flashing. A second weapon fired; then they were all shooting.

"We have to leave now!" O'Connell hissed. "This entire area's going to be crawling with police!"

"We're so close!"

"We'll get another chance. C'mon."

"Dixie took the van."

"We'll grab a cab."

Carrying the crate, O'Connell ducked out the back door. Jackson followed, just as a second, much bigger explosion, thundered down the street. That was going to wake the neighbors up.

19

THE SECOND LAKE POINT TOWER condominium was identical
to the first, except it was on the north side of the building and
thirty-nine stories closer to the ground. It had the same deep-
pile carpet and ivory walls. It, too, smelled of pine disinfectant,
but it was obviously lived in. A dirty dish sat in the sink, and
food filled the refrigerator. But most telling was the smell of
mint. Mouthwash? Toothpaste?

Sniffing the air, Joe Tresher followed the elusive scent.
There were no pictures on the walls or photos on the dressers.
He searched for a utility bill or anything else that would tell
him who rented the condominium, but he didn't find anything.
The only things that attracted any attention were the eight
unusual display cases decorating the bedroom walls. They
were all made of stainless steel and had heavy lead-glass doors.
He went to work on one and had a much harder time with its
lock than the condo's front door. Part of the reason was the
light, but mostly it was because the case had been made in
Switzerland, and the tiny steel tumblers had the delicate mech-
anisms of a clock.

After three annoying minutes, the lock finally clicked, and
the door popped open. Inside sat a cross between a garden tool

and something used at an amusement park to snare plastic baubles. The soft rubber grip fit his hand perfectly. At the other end of the steel handle were three sharp, inward-facing claws. When he squeezed the handle, the claws retracted into a fist. Was this a robotic arm?

Intrigued, he went from case to case. What the heck were these objects used for? One was shaped like an eel while another vaguely resembled a misshapen vegetable steamer. About half of the objects had handles, an indication they were designed to be held, but he had no idea why. Some had sharp edges, while others were blunt. One case held an object that appeared to be something Houdini would have used. Like a giant four-armed squid, the device consisted of a large master ring connected by stainless steel chains to four small locking hooks. The workmanship was excellent, but what could they used for?

Looking for clues, he left the bedroom and searched the living room and entertainment center. The television remote was handy, so he pressed the button. Nothing happened. He pressed it again, then got up to manually turn on the television and the stereo. Everything worked fine, but the remote did not. He examined the stereo. The remote had been manufactured by Sony, but all the audio and video components were Samsung. Opening the top drawer, he found the Samsung's remote and hit the power button. The television, stereo, and DVD player all switched off.

So why the Sony remote?

Walking into the bathroom, he closed the door and turned on the light. It only took a second to discover the Sony cam.

Switching off the light, he searched the entertainment unit and eventually located the Sony's instruction manual and warranty. Whoever lived here was highly organized. A place for everything and everything in its place.

Straightening, Tresher returned to the bedroom and tried to jog his memory. The bed would have made a drill sergeant proud. The nightstand was so clean it could have been used as a plate. Every article of clothing was ironed, folded, and properly stored.

What didn't fit?

Bending down, he looked under the bed again, pulled the blinds back from the window, and searched the nightstand and the walk-in closet. Finally, his eyes fell on a ventilation grate half hidden under the neatly hung business suits. He peered up into the shadows and found an open wall duct where the grille should have been.

He grabbed a kitchen chair and climbed up for a look. The interior of the duct was the first dusty thing he had seen in the condominium, but the small Sony video cam bolted into the top was sparkling clean. He stared thoughtfully at the bed for a second then returned to the living room and searched the entertainment center until he found a locked video case in the bottom drawer. One second with his lock-picking tool, and the cheap Korean lock popped open. Inside were DVDs and a neat bundle of women's business cards. Intrigued, he removed the disc labeled *Sara Branson* and slid it inside the DVD player. Using the remote, he turned on the television and hit PLAY.

The video began with Sara Branson lying on the mahogany bed. The recording was so clear Joe Tresher could see the blood vessels beneath her pale skin. It wasn't long until he knew what each of the items was used for. The claw-like thing in the living room crushed joints. The eel-shaped object in the bathroom was a whip. The acceptance in Sara's tear-filled eyes left him feeling fragile and wounded, as though he'd been a silent accomplice.

The last time Tresher had seen eyes like hers had been when he had shot a doe in a thick stand of New Mexico piñon pine. Just as he'd pulled the trigger, the doe had jumped and staggered off into the scrub to bleed to death. He found her twenty minutes later in a cedar thicket. The doe tried to get up but lacked the strength, and they both just watched each other in the hot mountain sunshine until a smoky film passed over the deer's soft eyes.

He heard a chiming sound and followed it to a tablet sitting on the kitchen table. A video call popped up. He stepped aside, out of view of the camera.

"Hey, baby," Sara purred from the small speakers. Her long, blond hair hung fashionably into her brilliant eyes. "Are you still working? I'm going to go for an early run and then try on my new bathing suit." She sighed, her mouth turning into a perfect pout. "I know we won't be going for a few days, but I'll entertain myself somehow. Call me when you get in."

The call ended. Tresher deleted the message, removed Sara's DVD and modeling agency card, and left the condominium. On the way, he phoned Director Byrnes.

"I've found Janné," he said as the elevator dinged downward. "You were watching the wrong condo. He's on a different floor." He heard Byrnes's sharp intake of breath and behind it, the wail of sirens. "What's going on? What's all that noise?"

"We got some intel earlier today on Janné," Byrnes said. There was an angry, hoarse edge to his voice. "Hugh Dobrowski found the network Janné used to move his funds. We got the address about two hours ago and moved on it. Janné had it wired with explosives. I had to leave three good men behind. The police are on their way, and they won't like finding three dead agents in full government-issue tactical gear."

Tresher didn't like cases that spiraled out of control. Too much danger that his own neck would wind up in a noose. Byrnes had been around a long time, and if anyone could spin it the right way, he could. But something told Tresher that a building wasn't going to be the only thing falling if Janné wasn't found. The people Byrnes worked for would make sure of that. Tresher might even be the one sent to kill him.

He rubbed his chin, thinking of the DVDs, the business

cards, and the expensive playthings tucked into their custom-made cabinets.

"He'll run, Director. If it were me, I'd already be gone. You'll need to move now. Bring everyone you have over here as soon as you can."

He gave Byrnes the address, repeating it twice over the sirens, then told Byrnes he was leaving.

Surprise replaced the anger in the Director's voice. "What? Where are you going?"

"New York. I'm going to talk to Wilkens's people about the Owl."

"Who are you going to start with?"

"Bruce Lambert oversees Daemon. I'll start there."

20

NEVER IMAGINING that he'd be crawling out of a manhole and running for his life, Alec Janné parked the BMW in his normal parking space in the Lake Point Tower's underground garage. He took the elevator up. In the late sixties, Lake Point Tower had been the tallest residential building in the world and the only high rise east of Lake Shore Drive. At dawn, the bronze-tinted glass gave the glass and steel spire a golden glow. The building had given him a prestige address where he'd felt completely safe—until today.

With his automatic pressed against his leg, he stepped inside his condo. Nothing moved in the darkness. He slid the automatic into his belt holster and got to work gathering the few things he would not leave behind. How had the Owl and Byrnes located the brownstone? What stray thread had led them to Chicago and, most important, why today of all days?

No time for a shower. But, yes, he should change his tennis shoes. He was tracking mud across the floor. His first stop was the built-in safe in the master bedroom. He withdrew his passports, his emergency cash, and another gun. The money and the pistol went into the bottom of a backpack. He wasn't expecting more trouble. *Directeur* Byrnes had lost some of his men and would need time to regroup. By then, Janné would be gone.

From the entertainment unit in the living room, he removed the case holding the women's DVDs and their business cards. He picked up his laptop and tablet and added his toothbrush and shaving kit from the bathroom. His cell phone beeped.

"Are you done?" Sing asked.

"I'm just finishing up."

"Are you still convinced the man and woman who hit us earlier were not with Byrnes?"

He stopped by his living room window overlooking Navy Pier. The giant Centennial Wheel carried passengers skyward and brought them back to the ground. He had been so sure that he was on the ascent, that the Ferris wheel would stop when he'd reached the top and give him time to survey the damage.

"Knowing he meant to send a strike team, Brynes would have been crazy to send a man and woman in first. It had to be the Owl."

"Byrnes's arrival was just coincidence?"

"I believe so, yes."

"There are too many unknowns with this, Alec. To come this far only to fail —"

"We have not failed!" he said. "*Directeur* Byrnes will fall. I will take him down. That is the most important thing. It is the only thing!" He took a breath. "Have Tarazi and Jester found the accounts the Owl took?"

"They just started. I'm not sure how far they'll get before we have to go."

"I am done packing. I'll see you in twenty minutes."

Her voice changed into a breathy whisper. "*Ciao.*"

On the way to the front door, he opened the coat closet. Should he take his leather coat? In the French Caribbean, the temperature rarely dropped into the sixties. He had purchased the coat in London almost six years ago, and the leather was soft and supple. It was also in London, while touring the Central Bank of the United Kingdom, where he had come up with the idea of breaking into the United States Federal Reserve. After six years of planning, everything had worked far better than he could have possibly hoped. No matter what else happened, he had won, and *Directeur* Byrnes and the secret deadly cabal behind him had lost. Nothing else, not even the Owl, was as important.

So why did he feel so irritated?

In his pocket he found a stick of Wrigley's gum and folded it into his mouth. The classic spearmint taste exploded on his tongue. Chicago, he decided, wasn't about the Sears Tower, the Cubbies, or the Field Museum. Chicago was about Wrigley's gum. That was what he would remember.

He was just reaching for the coat when the front door clicked. Catching his breath, he slipped inside the closet and closed the door, leaving only a narrow crack. The doorknob turned, hinges squeaked, and two men dressed in black windbreakers crept into the condominium. They wore armored vests, black baseball caps, and radio headsets, and they carried silenced carbines. With his backpack flattened against the closet wall, Janné waited and held his breath.

One of the men stopped outside the closet and sniffed. Janné cursed silently. The man moved his head slightly from side to side, nostrils flaring. An eternity passed before he moved into the living room. Janné counted to five, then stepped noiselessly out of the closet. For the briefest moment, he thought about killing them. But even with the element of surprise, there were too many risks, and he did not like to gamble with fate.

He threw open the open front door and flung himself into the hallway.

Byrnes, with his back turned, held a phone to his ear. "Get forensics up here," Byrnes growled. "Whatever we don't need,

I want sanitized. I want nothing left behind for the police when—"

Janné caught the briefest glimpse of Byrnes's sunburned face before they went down in a tangle of elbows and knees. Janné recovered first and slammed his automatic into Byrnes' ear.

"I could kill you now, but the game is only starting, *Monsieur*. I must insist you watch."

He got to his feet and sprinted for the stairs. A strangled, garbled shout crashed through the silence, followed by the whine of a bullet. Janné made the stairwell door and banged through. Three bullets tore through the wall above his shoulder; drywall exploded. Holding onto the railing with his left hand, he leapt down the steps, bouncing back and forth between the railing and the wall. Bullets ricocheted against the treads. He reached the tenth floor. Above him, the stairwell door screeched open. He paused. A man peered over the railing. A silencer popped. The bullet caught the stairs and ricocheted away.

It was not a good idea to run pell-mell down the stairs. Byrnes might have help waiting below, but with the two men chasing him from up above, Janné could only hope that Byrnes hadn't set up a proper perimeter. If there were men at the bottom, he wouldn't stand a chance.

He reached the first floor, brought up his automatic, and cracked open the stairway door. The building's janitorial crew was buffing the lobby floor. Behind them, a pair of joggers headed out the main entrance. None of them looked in his direction.

A suppressor coughed, and a bullet hit the wall above Janné's head. He tore down the final level to the underground parking garage, yanked open the stairwell door, and hustled past the empty valet stand.

Outside at last and washed by the humid air, Janné ran past the swimming pool and through the lightly forested grounds. When he reached the southern edge of the property, he scrambled up a block wall. An armored Navistar truck barreled past on Illinois Street. He waited until it had skidded into the Lake Point Tower's main entrance before he dropped onto the sidewalk. Shouts split the morning stillness, but by the time he had crossed Streeter Drive and made it onto Navy Pier, he had left Byrnes and his goons far behind. Still, maybe they'd come looking. He ran north to Olive Park, reached Lakefront Trail, ran past the Ohio Street Beach, and jumped off the trail onto East Ohio, using it to run under the Drive. A woman walking her dog gave him an up-and-down look, but she didn't say anything. Too bad if his mud-stained, khaki pants and sweat-soaked shirt attracted attention. Janné kept running until he could flag down a passing cab.

"What's on fire?" the cabbie asked, voice only barely interested as Janné yanked the door open and collapsed inside.

"Take me to Montrose Harbor," he gasped, pulling air into his heaving lungs. "I will pay you fifty to make it in ten minutes."

The cab leapt away from the curb. Janné slumped against the scarred seat and wiped the sweat off his face. He turned and watched through the rear window. No one followed. Five quiet minutes passed. His heart slowed. The thump of the tires on cement and the occasional squawk of the cab company's dispatcher were the only sounds. The driver was not in the mood for conversation, and Janné didn't encourage any. He needed to think.

How had Byrnes linked his condominium to the brownstone? Would Byrnes be able to follow him to Corolas Del Mar? Were Byrnes's men even now in St. Louis, waiting at the airport by his jet? Discarding possibilities and searching for mistakes, he went over every decision he had made: the holding corporations and the carefully constructed paper trails. Nowhere could he find an error.

The cab pulled into Montrose Harbor. Janné paid the driver, got out, and called Sing.

"Byrnes is at my condominium," he said. "We must leave Chicago immediately. I'll call Sara and tell her."

"If Byrnes knows about your condo, he'll know about her."

He stopped. Had Byrnes found him through Sara? Was that the loose thread?

"I'm at Montrose Harbor. Come pick me up."

He walked over to the lake and stopped at the top of the storm wall, remembering the night three years before when he'd shot Agent Tyler Jackson. It had been winter then. A quiet snowy evening on Lake Michigan. That had been the last time anyone had gotten close to him until now.

"Another time, *Directeur*," he promised, gazing at the Lake Point Tower, shining like a golden needle in the morning sun. "Another time, *mon ami*."

He spat the gum into the water and left.

21

FROWNING at the wall-mounted security camera and the closed-circuit monitor that showed her worried face, Dr. Leigh Zins, Director of Financial Computing for the Seventh Federal Reserve District, hurried up the ramp and toward the data center. She had been awoken at home after the Federal Building's external WAN link went down, and her morning had only gotten worse from there. She hadn't had time to do more than comb her hair in her car's rearview mirror, and this morning, with her eyebrows pinched together, she looked every one of her fifty-seven years.

The instant she punched in the access code and opened the door, the roar of air conditioning and the relentless drone of spinning power-supply fans struck her. Inside the room were thousands of simulation, backup, database, software development, and network servers from dozens of different vendors ranging from Hitachi storage systems and IBM mainframes to very thin, densely stacked Linux machines—all clustered tightly in hundreds of refrigerator-sized racks. The harsh lighting made her squint.

She hurried through the machines to where Manny Rodriguez and Dr. Kyle McCarthy hunched awkwardly in front of two portable desks pushed against the back of one of the racks. Manny was her lead UNIX administrator in charge of network operations, while Kyle was her most senior systems' programmer. Both men were brilliant professionals, but that was where the similarities ended.

Manny, in a pair of baggy khaki cargo shorts and sandals, was a short, barrel-chested Hispanic with bronze skin and black hair pulled back in a ponytail. He was in his early forties, but already had a gray goatee. His people skills were nonexistent, and he refused to follow protocols, procedures or even dress codes. Today of all days, he wore a black T-shirt with the IP address 127.0.0.1 printed on the front and a subtitle that read THERE'S NO PLACE LIKE HOME.

While Manny appeared to belong at a Black Hat convention, Dr. Kyle McCarthy, seated and balancing a laptop on his knees, looked like a proper Federal Reserve employee. He was six feet tall and weighed a trim two hundred pounds. He wore slacks, a starched blue-collared shirt with a dark blue tie, and Clark Falcon leather shoes. He was clean-shaven with thick reddish-blond hair that hung into his pale, Irish-green eyes, and his clipped Irish accent was hard to understand. When he spoke, Leigh had to listen carefully.

"Gentlemen, have you figured out what's going on?" she asked.

Both men glanced up from their screens. Manny stopped typing—which was about as close as she would ever get to having his full, undivided attention. He was famous for his multitasking. Legend had it he'd once taken a laptop into his supervisor's office so he could send e-mails during a performance review.

"The domain servers are operational," Manny said, giving her the unfocused stare of a man whose eyes looked in opposite directions. "The disk arrays, the computer grid, network gateways, and database servers are all down. The only system still running is the Network Information Service master, and that was because we had physical backups of the boot disks locked up. When everything went down, we swapped out the corrupted boot disks, and NIS came up."

"Do you have physical backups of the other critical servers' boot disks?" Leigh asked.

"Some, but not all. We have extensive disaster recovery procedures, but most of them need the backup servers, and they're down as well."

"How did the intruder take down so many critical systems all at once?"

"We don't know that yet," Kyle replied. His Irish brogue was as thick as a tall glass of stout.

Glancing at her watch, she bit her lip. "We've been down for six hours. That's a record. The Board of Governors will demand answers. I need to know where we are."

The two men glanced at one another. Kyle sighed. "We're working on getting the disk arrays operational. We believe the firmware's been changed, and without the correct revision, they won't boot."

"How did that happen?" she asked.

"We don't know yet," Kyle said.

She took a frustrated breath. "The Chairman scheduled a video conference in fifteen minutes, and our status will be the first thing he asks about. I need whatever progress you've made."

Manny looked annoyed.

Kyle pushed his chair back from the desk. He brushed his bangs aside. "Our status right now, Leigh, is not bloody well good. We tried to bring up the disk arrays, but they immediately crashed. Hitachi will be here in a few minutes to look at the firmware. We think they were backdated to a previous version that is incompatible with the software. The network switches are functional, so the network is available, but we need the disk arrays operational before we can look at the authentication logs to see what happened. That's assuming, of course, that there *are* logs to examine. Off-site replication is up. The master backup server is operational, but the image databases are corrupt. The file system hosting the database filled up sometime last night, and when it got full, the database crashed."

"What? How did it fill up?" she asked.

"A blank six-hundred gigabyte file was created in the backup file system just before it kicked off last night," Manny said. "With nowhere to write, the backup processes crashed and corrupted the catalog. We're running consistency checks, but with the amount of data on that system, it could take days to run."

"Isn't file system usage on all the critical machines proactively monitored so we have enough time to figure out what's going on before space becomes a problem?"

"The monitoring software was turned off," Manny said. "The first we knew there was a problem was when the WAN link went down."

"The software was turned off! How is that possible?"

"I don't know yet."

She glanced at the hundreds of idle racks. All that computing power and each cycle useless. It was absurd.

"There has to be a way out of this. We've done bare metal restores, buried millions of terabytes of data off-site in the vault, replicated trillions of transactions between sites, and spent millions of the taxpayers' money on high availability." She took a breath. "What about the off-site replication between the different regional districts? It worked before everything crashed. If we can get our data to sync back from the other sites, we'll be able to return to where we were before the arrays went down."

"That's assuming syncing the transactions back here doesn't make the problem worse," Manny countered. "We could lose everything needed to understand what happened." He held up a finger. "Anyone smart enough to turn off the monitoring and auditing procedures, flash the disk array firmware back to an incompatible version, fill up the master backup server's database file system, and corrupt the root disks of all the critical machines would not forget about the replication unless they had a reason to leave it running."

"You don't know that, mate," Kyle said. "At least not yet."

"I know it!" Manny snapped his head back and forth; his ponytail swung across his shoulders. "The people who did this knew exactly how to hit us! They knew the other sites are monitored. If replication stops, alarms go off, but if replication doesn't stop, there's no alert, and we think everything is fine until it's too late. They add themselves as a node on the network and capture every packet, every account number and transaction that bursts down the fiber. Simple, elegant, and deadly. Whoever did this is very, very smart."

Leigh walked down the nearest aisle. Power lights on. Fans humming. The room cold as a morgue. The machines were dead. "How many transactions did they get before the WAN went down?"

"No way to tell without knowing when they first got access," Manny said.

"How could this happen?" Leigh asked. "How could it be so targeted and precise?"

"They knew both sides of the bloody equation," Kyle answered. "They knew everything about our systems—how to use them and how to attack them. My bet right now is a foreign government is involved. Probably the Russians or Chinese or North Koreans. Remember how they took out Sony? They're always trying to crack our security."

No one said anything until Leigh's cell phone went off. She looked at the number on the display, then went to a landline and picked up the phone. She dialed the number, listened for a minute, then hung up. When she turned around, her face was grave.

"A statement was just released to the worldwide media.

Someone named Daemon has just claimed responsibility for the intrusion. The CIA and FBI say he's the one who cracked the Russian Ministry of Finance three years ago."

Both men gaped at her.

"The Russians got hacked?" Manny asked. "Why didn't we know? If we could have studied it, we might have been able to keep this from happening."

"They'd never let us in to look at their systems," Kyle said.

Leigh took a breath. "The Federal Reserve has suspended all financial operations until we can get this fixed. Everything from banks to credit unions to ATM machines to wire transfers will be offline until further notice. Any transaction involving anything but cash will not work." Her voice quivered slightly. "In case you don't know your history, that's never happened before. Not even during the Great Depression or after 9/11. I have an emergency video call with the Board of Governors. They're going to brief the President on what's happened so he can make a statement to the press." She took a breath. "Gentlemen, you're the best I have. Please fix this. Do whatever you must to get this place operational again."

She opened her cell phone and dialed.

If they couldn't fix it, there would be hell to pay.

22

HANDS on the back of her chair, Jackson leaned over Dixie's shoulder. She typed Ralf Wilkens' unlisted home phone number into the app on her computer. Four hours had gone by since Daemon had blown up the brownstone. It had been a long night, but Jackson wasn't tired. He needed to keep moving and move fast.

The phone rang three times.

"Hello?" Elaine Wilkens said.

"Is Ralphy there?" Dixie drawled into her headset.

"What?"

Dixie put more syrup into her accent. "Oh, I'm so sorry, honey. I mean, is Ralphy Wilkens there? I tried him at his office at the FBI, but his assistant said he was running late."

A moment went by. Dixie smiled up at Jackson. No doubt Elaine Wilkens was trying to figure out why another woman would be calling "Ralphy" at home.

"Yes, he is. May I ask who is calling?"

"Yes, you may, thanks. This is Dixie Stevens. Ralphy wanted to see me yesterday."

Jackson listened to a heated exchange on the other end. Then Wilkens took the phone.

"What is this about?" he demanded.

Dixie handed the headset across to Jackson and returned to her computer. Columns of numbers scrolled down her screen. In another window, a single yellow line stretched from Chicago to Wilkens' home phone number in New York. Voice-over IP routing messages scrolled across the bottom of the display.

"Did I interrupt breakfast?" Jackson asked. "I debated whether to wait until you were at work, but decided you would want to hear the latest."

"Tyler Jackson!" Wilkens growled. "I should have known. Don't you have enough to do?"

A flurry of automatic number identification requests rolled across the screen.

"He just got the bad news about tracin' the call," Dixie whispered.

"I don't want to hold you up," Jackson said. "Would you prefer we talk sometime later?"

"Just tell me what you want."

Jackson smiled. "I found Satan's Gold last night. It's quite the story. It should be on the news soon. Before I go into details, though, I'll need a letter from your legal department. I don't mean to imply I don't trust you, but to be honest, I trusted you once before. I won't do it again."

Wilkens's voice abruptly became cordial. "We don't need that kind of formality, Jackson. Give me what I want, and your legal issues will quietly go away. Getting lawyers involved only complicates the issue."

Jackson frowned. "Criminal investigations are complicated affairs. After all, I could give you exactly what you want, and you could still continue your vendetta."

"Tell me where you are, and I'll come see you."

"Sorry, I can never find my way around Chicago. Put an *I* between the *D* and the *O* of Illinois Department of Transportation, and it would be aptly named."

"You're a funny guy."

Jackson watched Dixie type. As she identified active accounts from the logs she had gotten from Daemon's basement, she dropped the account information into a program Jackson had written that morning. The program transferred the funds through a series of virtual e-banks headquartered throughout the Caribbean. The banks, if you could call them that, had no branches, no tellers, and no ATMs. Most were loosely affiliated with legitimate banks, but since they were virtual, they were mostly used to move funds—and make money doing so.

"Yesterday after we talked, I had an unexpected visit from your old friend Hugh Dobrowski," Jackson said. "He told me Daemon was in Chicago. He didn't know where, but after putting his information together with what I already knew, I was eventually able to figure out where Daemon was, so I paid him a visit."

Wilkens swore. "That wasn't our agreement! You were only supposed to find him! Dammit, Jackson, this is the reason why you got shot! You don't follow rules and end up in trouble. Now tell me where you are and what's happened so I can contain it."

"I'll need immunity for me and my people. Get it all drawn up, and I'll give you everything I have."

"We don't have time for that right now! Just tell me where you are and what you have!"

"I will—after I get the agreement. Call after it's done."

He terminated the link before Wilkens could argue.

"You certainly have a talent for makin' people angry," Dixie observed, giving him a sideways look. "What do we do now?"

"Finish up with the accounts then get out of here. After that, I don't know. Maybe take a vacation somewhere."

"I love your leadership skills."

❧

HE PAID cash for a private charter to New York, arriving just as the Friday afternoon sun lit Manhattan's glass and steel spires. A storm was on its way but had not yet arrived. Once they were on the ground, Jackson tried calling Suzanne at home. With eyes as sullen as the darkening sky, Dixie wordlessly waited for him finish. After the fourth ring, a computer told him Suzanne's phone had been disconnected.

23

SNOW FELL LIKE CONFETTI. Slow waves undulated across the lake. The silence split with a shriek and the first bullet tore through his chest, driving him back against Montrose Harbor's storm wall. A second bullet bellowed like a freight train, cutting his heart in half.

The dream skittered away, leaving Jackson's shout ringing in the air. He lifted his head off a pile of unpaid bills. Writing checks must have put him to sleep. He pushed the envelopes away and noticed Suzanne's cell phone bill. The total was over a hundred dollars in out-of-network charges from New Jersey to her parents' home in Arizona. Suzanne had never liked Jersey and had threatened more than once to move home.

Footsteps came down the hall, and Dixie stepped into his office. "Another bright and sunshiny day."

"You should be asleep," he said.

She sank down in a chair. "I am. Just ask anybody on the freeway. I'm gonna kill you if you've made me into an insomniac." She stretched until her neck popped. "Did you hear about Daemon? He's taken credit for breakin' into the Fed. He announced it on Twitter if you can believe it."

Jackson frowned. "Why would he do that? He's always stayed quiet. That's why it's so hard to find him."

"I dunno. I can forward you the link if you want." She noticed the envelopes on his desk. "What are you doin'?"

"Paying bills. After I'm done, I'll let you take them over to the post office and mail them."

She gave him a dark look. "The entire world is after us, and you're payin' your cable bill? I must be nuts to hitch my wagon to your star." She closed her eyes. "I finished moving the accounts we got from Chicago. The source and destination accounts were logged, which made it easy. It was more tedious than anythin'."

"How much?"

"Ten zeros."

"How much is that? I can't even count that high."

"Four billion, give or take."

"What! Where were they going?"

"A better question would be where they weren't." She took a breath. "From what I've been able to piece together, Daemon hijacked thousands of legitimate accounts and used them to move funds into the Fed. He must have been on their network for days or weeks without them knowing it. He used source accounts all over the world."

"The transactions went *into* the Fed?"

"Yes."

"But that makes no sense!" Jackson said. "Why would he move money into the Fed?"

"I don't know yet."

Frowning as he tried to think, Jackson rubbed his eyes. He hated not having enough information.

"You've buried the money?"

"Yes."

"Good. I don't want to know where. The less I know, the better. Wilkens found me before. He could do it again. My bet is he's already got the blue suits coming our way. Let's go."

24

AGENT BRUCE LAMBERT was tall and thin, with jet-black hair and the pale complexion of someone who spent most of his time indoors. As a kid, he had always dressed up as a ghost on Halloween. He never needed makeup. Later, in college, he had donned a black suit and had been an instant hit as an undertaker. The running joke at work was that given the right lighting conditions, he could pass for a body in the morgue.

Lambert had been in the FBI for twenty years, the last six at the FBI's elite New York counterterrorism office. International conflict had increasingly become a struggle for economic and commercial success. Competition for global consumer goods, exports, and market share had never been so cutthroat. In his first year in New York, China's foreign intelligence agency's budget had been increased seventy percent, with many of the new agents being sent to the US. The head of the Chinese Ministry of State Security had even gone on record saying China's espionage was essentially economic, scientific, technological, and financial.

In other words, the spooks had traded in their cloaks and daggers for business suits and briefcases. The United States, and especially New York, was a magnet for sophisticated international thieves. Lambert's caseload was always on overload.

He was washing his hands in the restroom at work when his cell phone rang with a number he didn't recognize.

"Hello?"

"I'm looking for some Mets tickets. You wouldn't happen to have a couple of extras?"

Lambert glanced around the restroom. No one else was inside, but he lowered his voice anyway. "I'll call you back."

The connection cut away.

He left work and drove to a nearby mall to use a pay phone. It was never a good idea to talk on a cell phone. It was too easy for anyone to listen. He dialed the number Jackson had called him from.

Jackson's office phone picked up.

"Wilkens is going to issue a material witness warrant for your arrest," Lambert said. "He wants to find out everything you know until he can charge you with something. You know the routine as well as I do."

"How bad is the breach?"

"The financial district's offline. Everything's down."

"Wow."

Lambert turned, back against the wall, and looked for feet in the stalls. "What part of global financial meltdown do you not understand?" he asked, voice low and his hand cupped around the receiver. "This will make the housing bust look like a bunch of neighborhood kids playing banker with change from their mother's purse. Remember back in the 1920s when people hid their savings in the backyard? Investment went to hell and took the economy with it. That was before there were computers and networks linking everything. This will be much worse. Look, Tyler, we're friends, but I'll only go so far with you on this. It's too big. I won't throw myself under the bus because you and Wilkens can't get along."

"It won't get that far," Jackson said. "At least I hope it won't. I can force him to play nice, but I don't want to."

Lambert closed his eyes and sighed. "That's assuming he won't put a bullet in your ear."

"You need my help," Jackson said. "I tried to give it to Wilkens, but he turned on me. But, Bruce, I trust you. I'll give it to you."

"I shouldn't do this," Lambert said, "but all right. I need everything you have on what happened. When you're done, disappear. I don't want you hiding out anywhere the government has jurisdiction or extradition treaties. Understand?"

"Got it," Jackson said.

Lambert hung up, and for the first time noticed that the food court was nearly empty. Handwritten signs said credit and debit card transactions weren't working. A nearby ATM machine had an out-of-order sign taped over its screen.

Staring at the empty stores and returning to his car, he tried to comprehend the enormity of what Daemon had done. Trillions of dollars went through the world's financial systems each day. If anything stopped the flow of money, he didn't want to think about what would happen. The news someone had broken into the most secure financial network on the planet would have an immediate, cataclysmic effect. The financial markets wouldn't just drop. They would collapse unless the Fed could somehow unravel which of the millions of transactions in the past few days were real and which were fraudulent.

The only thing worse than cracking the Fed, he decided, would be if an actual nuclear bomb were to go off on Wall Street—and maybe not even that, since a bomb was easy for the public to understand. Very few people, however, could immediately grasp what would happen if no one could trust the world's financial systems. But everyone from the oldest grandmother to the youngest institutional investor would immediately understand what would happen if savings and pensions disappeared overnight.

What made this worse was that even though he had seen the exact same thing before when Daemon had gone after the Russians, Lambert hadn't been able to do a damn thing about stopping Daemon from doing it again. If history repeated itself, and he was pretty sure it had, Daemon hadn't taken a single penny. What he had done instead was to use the Fed to push billions of automated, trusted transactions. It was much easier than robbing a bank and better than printing money. All it took were a few bits here to debit an account there. All of it at gigabit speeds.

In short, to err is human, but to really screw things up took a computer — or in this case, every single bank on the planet.

Money really did make the world go around — or stop.

But why had Daemon been moving money *into* the Fed? It made no sense.

He stopped in a deli with a CASH ONLY sign taped to the register and scrounged around in his pockets for enough cash to pay for an early lunch. He wasn't hungry, but he doubted he would have time to eat later. Hoping the food would stay down, he bought a sandwich and soup and then returned to the pay phone. He didn't blame Wilkens for going after Jackson. Jackson wasn't in the FBI anymore. He was an easy target. Wilkens could charge Jackson with just about anything he wanted, ranging from obstruction of justice to interfering with an official investigation.

He replayed the conversation with Jackson.

I can force him to play nice.

What had Jackson meant by that? Did he have a bargaining chip he hadn't mentioned, and if so, what was it?

He fed the slot with his dwindling change and redialed Jackson's new number. It rang and did not go to voicemail. Annoyed, he hung up and called Jackson's office. After the third ring, the voicemail system politely asked him to leave a message.

Disturbed, he left the mall and drove to Jackson's office. It was unusually quiet for a workday. Two business executives whispered in the lobby near a decorative tree while an attractive paralegal secretary clicked across the marble tile in her high heels. Lambert had the elevator to himself for the ride up. He saw no one on Jackson's floor. He punched in the office's lock code, pressed his thumb against the door's optical scanner, and, when the lock clicked, pushed inside.

The foyer was professionally decorated with expensive prints, uncomfortable designer furniture, and paintings from artists he'd never heard of. The receptionist's desk was much nicer than his desk in the Federal Building. No one was inside.

He walked down the hall past the reception area, the data center, the break room, and shared workspace where Pavak wrote up his reports, O'Connell dusted the photos of his kids, and Dixie worked her magic. Jackson should be along any time. He went into his office to wait. A half hour later, Jackson still hadn't shown up. Lambert tried Jackson's cell phone once more, and then removed a sheet of paper from a printer and left Jackson a pointed note. Suzanne's phone bill sat in the middle of Jackson's desk, and he tucked the note underneath.

He stood up to leave then stopped and stole a Snickers candy bar from the case Jackson kept hidden in his bottom drawer. He stripped the wrapper and dropped it on the note. Jackson was extremely protective of his Snickers stash. There was no way Jackson would miss his note. No way at all.

He took the elevator down to the lobby. He had seventy-two cents in his pocket. Hopefully, he had enough gasoline in his car to make it back to work.

~

HOPING TO GET LAMBERT ALONE, Tresher had been following the agent since he'd left home. Lambert was the agent in charge of finding Daemon. If the Owl was going to work with anyone, Lambert would be the logical choice.

Tresher had been surprised when Lambert left work and drove to a mall. Lambert was one of those people who could never be accused of having a poker face. Whatever he was thinking sat on his pale, narrow features. He was obviously unhappy about something—something that bothered him enough to make two calls from a public pay phone even though he had a perfectly good cell phone on his hip. After the mall Lambert had gone to an expensive, yet curiously unmarked, office on the top floor of one of New York's corporate skyscrapers.

Two hours later, Tresher stepped out of the same elevator Lambert had used earlier that morning. In one hand, he carried a clipboard, and in the other, an unmarked package. A brown baseball cap sat smashed low across his eyes, and even though it was hot outside, he wore a matching brown jacket. Studiously checking his clipboard against the addresses on the offices, he strode down the hall. He ignored the unmarked door Lambert had exited earlier. An electronic codebreaker or a crowbar would get him inside, but breaking through the door was the least of his concerns. It was the alarms on the other side of the door that worried him. As he checked addresses, he didn't see any outward signs of hidden security devices, but that didn't mean there were none. He was a careful man and always gave his target the benefit of the doubt.

After he had completed his circuit of the floor, Tresher exited into the stairwell and stuffed the package inside his jacket. It was muggy outside, but he kept the jacket zipped until he was out of sight. Choosing a dumpster at random, he got rid of the cap, clipboard, jacket, and empty package. Each item had been purchased with cash, and he had been very careful not to leave fingerprints or receipts.

Leaving the area by a different route, he took a series of cabs across town just to make sure he wasn't being followed. That was where Lambert had made a mistake—not in watching to see if he had been followed but by forgetting to assume that he had been. Of course, being six and a half feet tall and as thin as a chewed bone hadn't helped. Tresher could easily follow him from blocks away.

Twelve hours later, in the middle of the night, Tresher returned to the building and entered by the stairwell. The top floor custodial closet's lock was easy to pick, and he was inside in seconds. The floor shared the same electricity, wiring, and ductwork, so it was a simple matter to climb up into the ceiling, find a shared wall to the office Lambert had visited, push a few tiles neatly out of the way, and drop inside.

He walked up and down the hall. The office did not employ any motion sensors. The front door had an alarm, but Tresher had no intention of using the door, so he had the run of the place until morning. However, as fate would have it, he didn't need more than a couple of minutes until he found exactly what he needed. It was sitting in plain sight next to an empty Snickers wrapper.

Reaching out a gloved hand, he picked up Suzanne Williams' phone bill.

25

JACKSON DROVE BACK to Jersey to talk to Suzanne. She prob-ably wouldn't see him, but he had to try. The weather forecast called for rain, but for now, the sun was bright. The road wove through the forested Jersey countryside. He sped through the curves, enjoying the way his car handled the hairpin turns.

His cell beeped, and he checked the number.

"Did you go home to bed?" he asked.

"No," Dixie grumbled. "I fell asleep on my keyboard. My face looks like someone hit me."

"So it's an improvement, then. Good. A happy employee is a productive employee."

"I hate you." She sighed. "I just got off the phone with Pavak. I filled him in on what happened in Chicago. I e-mailed him the fingerprints we took of the two men in the building. He made some inquiries. You're not gonna believe this. Both men used to work for the government. The overweight gentle-man's name is Carl Jester. He grew up in Southern California and has a doctorate in Computer Science from Stanford. But that isn't the best part. He used to work for the Chicago Federal Reserve. The Fed gave him a Homer Award."

"A Homer what?"

"A Homer Simpson Achievement Award. According to Pavak's sources, it's a joke award given to somebody who really screws somethin' up. They took an old bowlin' trophy, ripped off the plastic bowlin' pin from the top, and stuck a plastic figure of Homer Simpson in its place. On the back of the trophy is a slot where they keep the list of who's gotten the award and why. When somebody fouls up, the department gets together and has a big laugh at his expense. The guy with the award then has to keep it on his desk until someone else screws up, and it gets passed on."

"What did Jester do to get it?"

"He got in a minor traffic altercation in Germany while attending a conference. The next day, during his presentation, the police showed up and arrested him for leaving the scene of an accident. He had to spend the night in jail. His coworkers took the video of him being hauled off in handcuffs, added in *The Simpsons'* music, and presented him the award. A week later, he quit."

"He quit because of a joke?"

"I'm sure it wasn't just the award. It was his credibility. I know I wouldn't put up with something like that."

"Yes, you do. Remember the T-shirt we got you for your birthday?"

Her drawl became deadly. "I prefer to forget it, sir. And no, I won't wear it. Ever."

Jackson laughed. "What about the other man?"

"His name is Hassan Tarazi. Both parents are naturalized citizens from Iraq. He was born in New York. He earned his master's in mathematics at Rutgers. He worked for the NSA as a systems programmer. Rumor has it his software allows the government to play banker pretty much anywhere they want."

"Why did he quit?"

"His nephew got shot by police outside a mosque. The police said the nephew was threatening harm, but no weapons were found."

Jackson whistled. "Do you have an address for either one of these upstanding citizens?"

"No."

"What about Hugh Dobrowski?" he asked.

"Pavak can't find anything on him. Either Dobrowski works in a classified organization, or he didn't tell you his real name, which wouldn't surprise me. The one thing I can't figure out is why he would bring the Chicago FBI office in on Daemon. Why not just go to Wilkens here in New York?"

"I got the impression Dobrowski doesn't like Wilkens any more than I do."

"What about Bruce, then?" she asked. "Daemon is his responsibility."

"We can ask Bruce when we see him."

She didn't respond for a moment. "There are too many unknowns with this, Tyler. All we have are guesses and conjecture, and none of it makes any sense. Why recruit two former government employees to break into the Fed just to move money into it? They could have gotten caught at any time for nothin'. Speakin' of crazy, you haven't had any of your hunches about this, have you?"

"Not yet."

"I've written bios for Jester, Tarazi, and Dobrowski. Would you like to see if I missed anything?"

"Let's do it later. I'm on my way to talk to Suzanne."

"What? You're goin' to see her now? This is not the time for a soap opera, Tyler! Somethin' is gonna break. What happens if Daemon or the FBI comes after us?"

Jackson gripped his car's steering wheel. "So I shouldn't tell Suzanne about Wilkens until he arrests her? 'Hey, honey, I heard the FBI came and threw you in jail. Sorry to hear that. I'll call later this week to see how you're doing, okay?'" He slowed for a U-Haul. "She needs to be told."

"Then say hello to Wilkens, Captain Obvious! Suzanne's will be the first place he'll look!"

She hung up.

A white cinder-block building appeared on the right. Jackson parked under the building's sign, cut across the empty parking lot, and went inside. Jerry Newman, the pub's owner was just finishing a solitary game of eight ball. Jackson bumped the end of his stick just enough to make the cue ball clip the eight and scratch into the side pocket.

Jerry scowled. "Don't you ever just say hello?"

"You feel like a beer?"

"You'll have to pay cash. I can't take credit cards. The banks are closed."

"No problem."

They walked to the solid oak bar Jerry claimed was the longest in all of New Jersey. It probably wasn't, but since no one cared to dispute it, the claim had stood by default. Jackson slid onto a stool. Jerry pulled two bottles from the fridge, popped the caps, and pushed one across the bar. He was an overweight man with a bald, bullet-shaped head, arms the size of sledgehammers, fleshy, heavy face, and small, intelligent gray eyes.

"Where have you been the last couple of months?" he asked. "The guy you decked has been here three times looking for you. Last time he had a Sheriff's deputy with him. They said you are one hard guy to find."

Jackson flushed. "Sorry about that. I can't remember the last time I did something so stupid."

Jerry waved the apology aside, but his eyes were sharp. "Are you and Suzanne still separated?"

"Yeah. But I'm going out to see her and patch things up."

Jerry reached under the bar and retrieved a rag to run over the varnished wood. "Suzanne's parents want her to go home. Her father has lined up a job for her at one of the commercial agencies back in Arizona. She seemed set on going."

"When was that?"

"Yesterday. I'm telling you this because I like you both.

She's one of the nicest people around, and you're the toughest runt I've ever known."

Jackson put a ten on the counter.

"Thanks for the drink. I owe you."

"Don't tell her I told you."

"I won't."

He slid off the stool and headed out. Jerry let him open the door before he cleared his throat. "One more thing, Tyler. If it doesn't work out, then drive on by, understand? If she says no, I don't want you coming in here trying to kill somebody. I cut you a favor the last time, but I won't do it again."

Jackson nodded and limped outside. It was sunny now, but dark clouds were moving in from the east.

26

CARRYING FLOWERS, Jackson parked two blocks away and cut through the trees. His backyard looked exactly as it had the last time he had visited, except the grass needed to be mowed. If it rained tonight, the landscapers would need a riding mower.

After five quiet minutes, he slid out of the trees, walked across the grass to the back door, and set the flowers on his patio table. He peered through the kitchen window. Counters clean. Dishtowels hanging on the oven door. Nothing amiss.

He unlocked the door and carried the flowers inside. There were packing boxes scattered around the living room. On the counter by the microwave, he found a list of moving companies. Best to ignore that. If he gave up now, he was lost.

It was still early for Suzanne to come home from work. While he waited, he looked at the news on his phone. It wasn't good. Closing the banks had paralyzed the country. The news outlets were already saying the shutdown could tip the country into a recession.

He heard the garage door open and grabbed the flowers. She was halfway into the garage before she hit the brakes. For a second, he thought she might back out and drive off, but she finally let off the brake and finished pulling inside. Her door opened, and she got out. She wore her blond hair swept back, showing the diamond-stud earrings he'd given her. His engagement ring wasn't on her finger.

He forced a smile and held out the flowers. "There was a sign in the window of the florist shop that asked: 'How Mad Is She?' and underneath were these three vases arranged in size from 'Sort of Mad' to 'Better Get A Lawyer'. I went inside and told the salesclerk you would probably rather kill me than give me a chance to say I'm sorry, so she recommended roses."

Suzanne looked at the bouquet, but didn't take it.

Surely, when she saw him making a sincere effort, she'd soften up. She just needed time. He put the flowers on one of the shelves that held their camping equipment and took an envelope from his pocket. "I also got you this."

Mouth set in the unhappy line, she didn't move. "What is it?"

"One-way tickets home. As soon as I finish what I'm working on, we'll leave."

Anger tightened her eyes. "It's too late for this, Ty! If you wanted *us* to work, you should have quit chasing Daemon months ago. I can't keep holding out hope."

"I couldn't quit then. I wanted to but couldn't."

"And now you can? What exactly has changed in the last three days?" She threw up her hands. "Just look at you. You're a wreck. I can see every bone in your face, and you're so skinny a strong wind could blow you over. I don't think your mother would recognize you. You talk about trying to stay alive, but you're killing yourself. You have two bullet holes in your chest, and there isn't enough left of your stomach to tie a knot." She reached under his jacket and jerked the Colt free of its holster.

"Whoa! Hold on." He threw up his arms in surrender.

She turned the gun around and held it out by the barrel. He took it.

"You know where your heart is," she said. "If you're going to kill yourself, then you might as well do it now."

"I love you," he said. "I want us to be together. Every time I see you, I can't look away."

"That's not enough. Not after everything that's happened."

"Love is always enough," he said, "or it should be."

He put the Colt away, picked up the flowers, and returned to the kitchen, laying the roses on the dinette and hoping she'd come around. He heard the utility room door creak and then her footsteps on the stairs. Five minutes later, she came down wearing blue jeans and a cotton blouse. She picked up one of the roses and sat down at the dinette.

"I heard this song on the radio today," she said, looking at the flower. "Something about a man having five minutes to tell his wife what she wanted to hear, or else she was out the door. That's the problem with country music. Most every tune hits close enough to sting. I gave you five minutes years ago. I can't give you any more. I'm tired of you killing yourself—and us— over a wild goose chase that never ends."

"It will be over in the next few days. I have to get Daemon by the end of the week, or Ralf Wilkens will throw me in jail."

"Why would he do that?"

"I don't have enough time to tell you everything, but I found Daemon in Chicago yesterday. I knew Daemon was moving money, but it turned out to be a lot more than I had anticipated. He broke into the Chicago Federal Reserve. He drilled a hole into a communication tunnel and spliced into a cable used by the Fed. That's why all the banks are closed. Wilkens is furious I didn't call for help, and he's holding me responsible." He dropped his chin against his chest. "That's why we couldn't get together for dinner the other night. I wanted to, but couldn't."

Her lower lip quivered. "Oh, Tyler, life isn't about absolutes. Call Wilkens and work something out. He has to listen to reason."

"We have too much history. He needs someone to blame, and I'm an easy target."

Reaching into his pocket, he took her plane ticket and set it on the table. "Please come home with me. We may not get another chance."

She stood suddenly and wrapped her arms around his waist. He held her tight, and, closing his eyes, felt her body press against his. She was still his woman. His life. It was not too late. The magic was still there.

"I've missed this," she whispered.

He started to reply, but his phone went off. She let go and stepped back. Anger pooled into Suzanne's eyes, something Jackson had seen far too often.

"Take the call outside if you must."

"I'm sorry."

"Just think about me, you, and us, and then decide what's important. My heart wants this, Tyler. Don't give my head a reason to talk me out of it."

Jackson stopped and sighed. "You're right."

He was about to return his phone to his pocket but saw Dixie's SUV squeal to a stop in front of the house. She jumped out and stalked across the grass. Jackson went outside. The wind had picked up, and she gave him a shove.

"What the hell do you think you're doin'?" she asked. "The FBI is lookin' for us! Do you have any idea what they'll do if they catch us with all those numbers?"

Her voice faltered as she noticed Suzanne standing in the doorway holding the rose. Dixie stiffened in sudden understanding and started to back away.

"...no, no, no, no..."

"Dixie, hold on a second."

"Tyler, don't do this!" she whispered fiercely. "Not now. Oh. My. God. Don't do this!"

She stumbled backwards to the truck, got inside, and roared away.

Jackson watched her taillights disappear. For a moment he thought about going after her, but Suzanne needed him, too.

Inside, she sat very straight on one of the dining room chairs.

"I thought about locking you out," she said. "Then I remembered the last time you left."

"The night you ground up my key in the garbage disposal?"

"It cost me three hundred dollars to have it fixed, but it was worth it." She sighed and lifted her gaze. "I have something to tell you. I've thought it through a hundred times, but for some reason the words just refuse to work the way I want them to." Love, hate, and pity crossed her face before she continued. "I know I've said this before, but the only thing worse than being apart is being together for the wrong reasons." Her voice softened. "Have you talked to Bruce Lambert about what's going on?"

"Multiple times. Wilkens won't let him do anything."

"Is there anyone else you can talk to?"

"No." Nothing he'd said sounded at all persuasive, even to him. He curled his fingers and waited.

She shook her head and sighed. "Do you know what it feels like, having to constantly risk everything for nothing? All I want is to go home to Arizona with the person I love. How long has it been since we've eaten Sunday dinner with family? Is that too much to ask?"

"No. Of course not," he said.

"Family is what life is about. Nothing else is as important. Call Bruce again. If he won't take your call, I'll call Leesa and talk to her. Give Wilkens whatever he wants. You don't have to be the one risking your life all the time."

"Our world will end if I don't."

"What did you say?"

"I said our world—"

She pushed back her chair and stood, and then he felt her fingers on his cheeks.

"You just said *our*." A smile lit her face. "Do you know how long I have waited for that? For you to come back to me. For you to come back to *us*."

She put her arms around his neck. For a second, as their lips met, he couldn't think or even breathe. This was what he wanted, what he had dreamed of, what he desired more than anything.

"I have never stopped loving you," he said. "Even when I hated you for breaking it off, I never stopped. Not for a second. You deserve everything I have to give, and I've kept you waiting."

"I never stopped loving you either."

Eyes closed, he stood unmoving for a few long moments before he let go. It would be easy to stay with her, but if he did, Wilkens would make their lives a living hell. One of his college philosophy professors had once said fate was nothing more than a bowling alley where people either bowled or were bowled over. Those who determined their fate were the ones who threw the balls. Those who didn't were the pins.

"I have to go," he said. "The FBI's on my tail."

She clutched his arm. "Just come back to me. When it's over, come back to me. Come back to us."

"I will. I promise."

"Tonight?"

"I hope so. I'll try."

He let her go and went outside, wondering if she understood that trying didn't necessarily mean he could. There were a thousand things that could happen between the moment he drove away and the time he could return, and most of what could happen did not depend on him.

27

HE WAS tired of playing defense. Wilkins and Daemon had him backed in a corner. Wilkens could sic the whole apparatus of the FBI on him if he had a mind to, and Daemon, with his billions, could hire the worst kind of help. Jackson had done his best to keep his office in Manhattan secret, but by now Wilkens or Daemon would be looking for it. For the time being, he needed to hide out and come up with a plan.

Jackson met Dixie, O'Connell, and Pavak at his storage unit in the basement of an old building on the East Side. The building had a lobby with three cracked leather couches and a toilet in the custodian's closet; however, what was most desirable, from Jackson's point of view, was the building's high speed WiFi network and the fact that neither Wilkens nor Daemon would think to look for him here.

Jackson caught Dixie's angry frown, but there was nothing he could do. This storage unit was going to have to be their temporary base of operations. Pavak had brought bags of Chinese take-out, and O'Connell made a makeshift table of cardboard boxes and used desk chairs. Dixie unpacked the white containers and paper plates.

O'Connell unwrapped his chopsticks. "So what's the plan?"

"That's the thing," Jackson said, opening a box of chow mein. "We need to put our heads together."

For the moment, at least, operating capital wasn't their problem. Using the log she'd found in Daemon's basement, Dixie had transferred funds to virtual banks in the Caribbean. The accounts should cover their expenses—even high-ticket items. As they ate, they talked about how to keep the money safe.

"What about your buddy, Lambert?" Pavak said.

"Yeah, Bruce. We've been playing phone tag."

Lambert had left messages on Jackson's voicemail, saying it was urgent he call back. Jackson had left a message telling Lambert he'd gone out to see Suzanne but was back in the city. No return call so far, and he couldn't just sit around, hoping Lambert would come up with the break they needed.

Once they'd finished eating, he opened a cardboard box and removed the files inside.

Dixie saw what he was doing and made a face. "None of that's gonna help. We've been through those files so many times I can recite everythin' word for word."

"We're missing something," Jackson said. "We have to be."

"The only thing we're missin' is a deal. Call Wilkens."

"I've tried. He's angry."

"I wonder why."

Pavak patted his stomach and belched. "I'm going upstairs."

"What's upstairs?" O'Connell said.

"A long leather couch with my name on it."

Jackson dropped the files on the floor and opened the first folder. Dixie muttered something about wasting her life. She cleared the paper plates. "You all are gonna have to handle this on your own."

"Where are you going?" Jackson said.

"Goin' upstairs to the nap room."

Jackson sighed and looked over at O'Connell.

"I told my wife I'd be home to read the kids a bedtime story," O'Connell said, "but I can stay for a while. Why don't you talk it through?"

"Okay, sure. This is past history, but I can't believe we missed the significance of Todd Ferguson. Daemon didn't just wake up one morning and decide he was going to break into the Fed. They have the most secure network in the world. Finding out where the cables were, leasing the building, and getting the right software and equipment had to take years. I would bet this all started before I got shot. The big question is how he broke the Fed's encryption. Without the crypt keys, hacking the line wouldn't have made a difference. How did he get the keys?"

"Maybe Carl Jester got them. He used to work at the Fed before he got the Homer Award and quit."

"Access to the Fed's network is time encrypted. Even if Jester had a way in, without the time key, it wouldn't work. Where did he get the key?"

"Good question."

"Too bad I'm missing all the good answers."

He handed Ferguson's folder to O'Connell. "Maybe you can see something I've missed."

O'Connell, leaned back, read through the documents, and handed back the folder. Yawning, he stood. "I'm not coming up with anything, and given that there's nothing urgent at the moment, I'd like to go home and sleep in my own bed."

"Sure, Doc. Say hi to the wife." Jackson put Ferguson's folder back in the box and chose another folder. An hour became two until his phone rang once. He swiped the screen, noted the number, and called Suzanne. She should have been asleep by now. Her phone rang six times before switching to voicemail. He thought about leaving a message, but didn't. She would see his call and ring him back.

Dixie walked in and slouched into a chair.

"You should go to bed," she said.

"I'm too tired to sleep."

"Pavak went home. Did you know he sleeps with his eyes open?"

Jackson picked up another report and started flipping pages. "Uh-huh."

Dixie gave him a sideways glance. "You want to find a hotel somewhere and get naked? I could cover you in honey and bird seed, hide your clothes, and pull the fire alarm."

"Sure."

"You're not listenin' to a word I'm sayin', are you?"

"Uh-huh."

Her voice lowered. "Uh-huh as in you want to get naked or uh-huh as in you want me to cover you in bird seed?"

He noticed the change in her tone and looked up in annoyance. "What are you saying?"

"I'm tired. I want to go."

"Then go. Nobody's keeping you here."

Her eyes narrowed into barbed, brown points. "We've been over those files a million times! Once more isn't going to matter. It can wait."

He scowled at her. "What if we left something behind in Chicago? What if Daemon traces the money? All he needs is one loose end and everything will unravel. We have to find him before he finds us."

"You have to sleep sometime. Walkin' around like a zombie will only get you a broken neck."

He sighed, trying to remember the last time he felt rested. He pushed his chair back and stood. "Fine. I'll look at it tomorrow."

He returned the files to the box and followed Dixie upstairs to the building's dingy lobby. The East Manhattan skyline angled sharply outside a rain-streaked window. Lightning flicked and jumped through the clouds. He paused to watch, wondering if he was going to miss the city. Contrary to popular belief, New York wasn't found at the top of the Empire State

Building or in one of the shops proclaiming unbelievable discounts on everything from cameras to weapons. It wasn't a postcard or a T-shirt. The real New York was roaming Times Square with his wallet in his front pocket and a knife in his sleeve while a half million of his closest friends tried to sell him a shirt or take it off his back. The black stretch limos on Broadway and the billion-dollar business plazas were only the city's crisp, juicy red skin. Beneath that—the place Daemon would be doing his dirty work—was the soft underbelly of New York.

He called Suzanne again, but she didn't answer.

"Why do you keep crawling back to her?" Dixie demanded, taking her car keys from her purse.

"I'm not sure that's your concern."

She stiffened. "Not my concern! This isn't just about you! You risk all our lives every time you see her. What do you think will happen if Wilkens takes her downtown for a chat? She'll fall apart. I'm not being mean, and I'm certainly not tellin' you somethin' you don't already know, but this life you've selfishly dragged her into is not what she wants! The only person who can't understand that is you!"

Her SUV was parked at the curb. He called to her to stop, but she ignored him, got in, and squealed away.

28

WITH A BLANKET WRAPPED TIGHTLY around her shoulders, Suzanne waited for the teakettle to whistle. The house felt cold, or maybe it was the icy lump inside. Hatred, was it? Fear? Something heavy and frigid that nothing seemed to thaw.

The chills had started after Tyler had left and had gotten steadily worse throughout the evening until she thought she was coming down with the flu. Even calling her folks in Arizona hadn't brought warmth and connectedness back to her life.

Huddling under her blanket, she waited for the kettle to boil. She couldn't ever remember being so cold. Even the time she had almost drowned ice-skating as a teenager hadn't been this bad. At least then, she'd been able to warm up afterwards. Nothing helped tonight.

The teakettle whistled. She poured hot water into a coffee mug and dropped in a bag of Autumn Cinnamon herbal tea. Wrapping her hands around the cup, she sniffed the aromatic steam, her nose almost in the dark liquid. She took a cautious sip. The tea burned her lips but felt wonderful as it went down. The sensation reminded her of late October nights sipping hot chocolate with Tyler outside a neighborhood spook house as they waited their turn to go inside. It was always cold standing in line, but it was fun because she could put her chilly hands inside Tyler's shirt and make him jump. He retaliated by trying to get his hands inside her shirt, but that was part of the game, part of the fun. If only he were home, he would baby her or, better yet, get into bed next to her, and wrap her in a warm embrace. The cold couldn't reach her there. It couldn't sneak under the covers and make her shiver.

He'd promised to return that night, and when he did, she was sure he would stay. She searched through her dresser for something to celebrate their reconciliation and found a silk nightgown he'd given her just after they were engaged. Maybe if she called, he'd come home.

He didn't pick up.

Well, it wouldn't be too long, and when he showed up, she'd greet him with a kiss. She turned the water on in the bathtub as hot as she could stand and waited until it was full before getting in. The water nearly scalded her skin, but the heat chased away the cold.

Even with this reclining Kohler tub, New Jersey would never be home. She missed the hot high-country Arizona summers, the groves of ponderosa pine, and the narrow dirt roads.

She had spent most of her teenage years rambling along those back roads in jacked-up pickups, her arm linked around whatever boy she was going out with that week and listening to country songs. They never had a destination in mind. They just drove and talked the miles away. One night when she was nineteen, she and one of her boyfriends had driven all the way to Vegas just to see the lights. She couldn't remember the boy's name, but she could easily recall the growl of tires on the interstate.

Here in Jersey, all she had to do was drive half an hour in any direction to see all the lights she wanted, but she could never get far enough away to see the stars in a clear night sky. The only reason she had stayed this long was for Tyler.

The water in the tub had cooled. Time to towel off.

Stepping out of the tub, she saw that the mirror had fogged. Tyler's finger had left a message. "See you soon." She slipped the nightgown over her head and wrapped a towel-turban around her head. With the house so cold, it wouldn't be good to climb in bed with a wet head. She unwound the towel and picked up a comb. The mirror had cleared.

Just as she ran the comb down her part, she looked in the mirror and then looked again. Sitting in the middle of the bed was a white Stetson hat. The chills came roaring back.

29

JACKSON HAD JUST GOTTEN into his car when he received a text from Suzanne. He called her phone again, but it rang straight to voicemail. Why had she texted him if she was going to turn off her phone? Disturbed, he left his building and headed south. Something didn't feel right.

A half hour later he crossed the Raritan River Bridge, leaving North Jersey's industrial blight behind. Trees and bushes replaced the chemical storage complexes. Forty minutes later, he slowed to take the Brookdale exit. Once off the Interstate, he pushed his car through the twisting curves. As he drove past Jerry's Tavern and turned onto Monroe Avenue, it started to rain. A rodent darted in front of the headlights, and he braked. It might be smart not to come roaring up the driveway.

Switching off the headlights, he coasted down the empty cul-de-sac and stopped a hundred yards short of his house. He examined the dark windows. Maybe he had overreacted. The texts could have been from earlier in the day, been delayed getting to his phone. It had happened before.

He got out into the rain, made sure he had his knife and pistol, and walked slowly up the block. A dog barked. Raindrops plopped in puddles. Nothing out of the ordinary. He cut across his front yard and headed for the kitchen door. No sign of a break-in. He was probably just being paranoid. He took care to insert the key quietly, but the tumblers still clicked like marbles. He stepped inside, locked the door behind him, and stood listening to the familiar creaks. He shivered. The house felt like a meat locker. Was the thermostat on the fritz?

He tiptoed across the tile floor and stopped at the foot of the stairs. Darkness pooled at the top. He took out his pistol and, hearing a scraping sound, froze, breath caught in his chest. Only the elm tree, scratching the glass.

He took the safety off his pistol and crept upstairs. At the top he started forward, eyes searching the darkness. Lightning flashed through the open master bedroom door, and for an instant light spilled into the hall. The dark returned.

He took hold of the door jamb with his left hand, waved his gun hand inside, pulled back, and waited. Except for the tree scratching the window and the rain gurgling through the gutters, the house was silent

Switching to the other side of the opening, he placed his back against the wall and nudged the door open with his foot. He took a quick look inside and straightened. Hair fanned around her head on the pillow, Suzanne slept on her side of the bed. The heavy down comforter was pulled tight around her shoulders the way she liked it, even in the middle of the summer when the humidity turned the covers into a smothering cocoon. No wonder she'd turned up the air conditioning. He couldn't wait to climb in bed and cuddle.

He returned downstairs to take off his jacket and vest. He switched on the small lamp by the coat closet and never saw the man step out of the shadows behind him. Pain exploded from the back of his neck. The table and the Colt went flying. A blackjack whistled past and hit the wall. He lashed out blindly with his right foot. His boot connected, but his balance was wrong — he nearly fell. The blackjack circled in a small, deadly arc, slamming into his vest. He was leaning into the blow, but the force still sent him crashing backward into the front door.

The man was on him in an instant, his left fist coming in straight while the blackjack looped in from his right. Jackson ducked inside the weapon and snapped his right hand sideways. His knife clicked. The skin on the man's arm split smoothly. Blood followed the arcing steel and splattered the wall. The man's knee slammed into Jackson's thigh, and the intruder followed with a hard left that caught Jackson on the jaw.

The edges of his vision turned fuzzy. His legs belonged to someone else. Stumbling backward, he snapped his right hand up toward the man's face. The man jerked his chin back and hit him again. Roaring filled Jackson's ears. He slowly toppled onto his side. The floor felt wet. His blood, not the man's.

The man kicked the knife away. "Put your hands out where I can see them," he commanded, a small automatic held in his fist. He was tall, thin as boiled rawhide, and heavily tanned. "You've already made this much harder than it had to be."

Jackson did as he was told. The man dragged him across the kitchen floor.

IN THE BASEMENT, Bruce Lambert sat slumped in one of the workshop's wooden chairs. Lambert's narrow chin hung against his bony chest. His matted hair dripped blood. His hands, arms, and long legs were duct-taped to the chair. On the floor next to a pair of pliers and a scattered set of screwdrivers lay a bloody hammer.

"A million and one uses, that's what the package advertises," the man said, dumping Jackson into a second chair and picking up a roll of duct tape. He ripped a long piece free, wrapped one end around the back of the chair, and the other across Jackson's collarbone. "Your former partner and I have been having a long talk about you chasing Daemon. He doesn't know nearly as much as he should. I'm surprised Wilkens hasn't thrown you both in jail."

He stepped behind Jackson and grabbed the roll of duct tape, winching it tight around Jackson's elbows and taping his forearms to the armrests.

"Now listen carefully, Jackson. Your pretty fiancée is upstairs tied to your bed. If you are anything less than cooperative, I'll cut her with the knife you used on me. How do you think she'll look missing her nose?"

Jackson tried to focus. "What do you want?"

"You've been tracking Daemon's money for years. I want everything you have. In exchange, your lovely fiancée will be allowed to live. Understand?"

Jackson let his head drop. There was nothing else he could do. Drawing air into his bruised chest, he fixed his good eye on his basement workbench. One shot. That's all he wanted—but he had to make it count.

The floor creaked overhead. The man looked up, then stuffed a rag in Jackson's mouth and taped it shut.

"You move, and I'll hurt her a lot more than I have to!" he hissed.

The man reached above his head, caught the pull chain, and manually turned off the light. As he climbed the stairs, the basement steps creaked. Then the basement door clicked open. Silence returned.

Eyes fixed on the workbench in front of him, Jackson drew in a painful breath. Using all his strength, he forced himself to stand.

The pain hit him, but the gag kept the scream from ripping free. Pushing his left foot a few inches forward, he shifted his weight. The chair dug into the backs of his knees. The tape bit into his elbows and neck. He forced his right foot forward and then the left. He had to hurry. If he didn't, Suzanne was dead.

Six inches at a time, he shuffled through a sticky puddle of Lambert's blood and finally bumped into the workbench. He stood gasping, the darkness spinning around him, then turned until his right arm was parallel to the edge of the bench. He reached underneath. His fingers found the rough stock, and he pulled the hidden pistol free of its holster.

Now that he had the gun, what should he do? The ringing in his ears scared him. His left eye wouldn't focus. With his forearms immobilized, he wasn't even sure he could lift the gun, let alone aim it, and it wasn't like the guy would stand still and let Jackson get off a clear shot.

He moved toward the stairs, but the basement spun, toppling him sideways, against the workbench. Somehow, all four legs of the chair landed at the same time and caught his weight. Gasping, he told himself to stand and find something to cut the tape, but his feet wouldn't obey.

Above Jackson's head, footsteps returned to the stairs. The bastard was coming back. He had to do something. An idea flitted across the back of his mind, but before he could catch the thought, it danced away. Lambert shifted and mumbled. Jackson listened to his friend's ragged breathing and found the strength to move once more. Something light touched his face. He flinched, then realized it was the end of the pull chain. It reminded him of something, something important. The man had manually turned off the basement light. The only way he could turn it back on was to pull the chain. The switch at the top of the stairs wouldn't work. He would come into the basement blind.

Backing up, Jackson marshaled the last of his strength. All he had to do was keep from passing out.

Come on, he thought. *You got me before. Let's see you do it again, now I know you're here.*

Upstairs, glass shattered. Running footsteps pounded across the floor. A feminine shout rang out, the cry edged in surprise. Three gunshots exploded. Jackson opened his mouth to scream at Suzanne to run, but the gag reduced his shout to a croak. A warm, frustrated tear squeezed free.

Five long, quiet minutes went by before the basement door opened. The stairs creaked. A dim silhouette appeared. Jackson put the Colt alongside his leg and kept his good eye on where the pull chain hung from the ceiling. Cautious footsteps sounded, followed by the pull chain's mechanical click. Light flooded the room. Jackson brought up the Colt, aimed at Dixie's chest, and tried again and again to pull the trigger until she took the gun away.

"Tyler, what's goin' on? Are you all right? Who was that man upstairs?"

He mumbled at her until she took the tape off his mouth. He spat out the gag.

"Suzanne. She's upstairs. I . . . I tried to help her, but I couldn't."

Dixie checked the Colt's safety. "It's a good thing you're not thinkin' straight, or I'd be dead."

She cut his arms free and helped him to his feet. The basement spun.

"Hurry," he said. "He might come back."

"Let him. I've been lookin' for a stand-up fight all night, and you're in no shape to make it interestin'."

Lambert stirred at the sound of their voices and opened his eyes. Dixie pulled the tape off his mouth, withdrew the gag, and cut him free.

"Bruce," she said, "we're gonna make sure he's gone then call for help. One of us will be back in a minute."

Jackson took his Colt from Dixie and lurched toward the stairs. Each tread was a bronco, trying to buck him off. He finally made it into the kitchen and staggered across the tile. Stumbling upstairs, hands grasping the railing while his feet tried to keep up, he tripped and started to fall. Dixie caught him from behind, her fingers steel vices on his ribs.

Blood hammered his ears. He put his shoulder against the

wall and half slid, half staggered, down the hall. He grabbed hold of the bedroom door and pulled himself inside.

The lights were off, but the blinds were up. Facing away from him, Suzanne lay on the far side of the bed. He dropped the pistol on the comforter and fell to his knees. He didn't want to look, couldn't bear to look, but did anyway, and the pain was so fierce he thought his heart would stop.

30

BRUCE LAMBERT POSITIONED himself stiffly in front of the urinal and unzipped his fly with his right hand. The fingernails on his left hand were gone, and his left arm was so swollen he could barely move it. There was blood in his urine and more of the same when he spat in the sink. The doctors at the emergency room had told him internal bleeding was normal for injuries such as his, but they weren't the ones staring at the red stain on the porcelain.

Lambert's left eye had swollen shut, and his face was a patchwork of bruises. Spidery rows of stitches tracked across his cheekbone, the corner of his mouth, and the back of his ear. His elbow had ballooned to twice its normal size and sent shock waves through him whenever he moved it. He still couldn't believe it wasn't broken. The man who'd worked him over had been right-handed and knew exactly where and how to swing the hammer.

Leaving the restroom, he shuffled slowly to the corner office. Ralph Wilkens's new assistant, Laura Patterson, typed on her computer but stopped when he halted in front of her desk. She was the latest in the steady stream of young, well-built women that Wilkens obviously preferred. He was due to retire in two years and numerous bets had been placed as to whether his weakened heart could stand the strain of looking at her every day.

"Hello," Lambert croaked, carefully working the stitches inside his mouth around each syllable. "You look like you got some sun."

A shocked look crossed the young woman's sunburnt face. She didn't ask what had happened, which meant that Wilkens had already told her. "You should have seen me earlier in the week." She gave him a forced smile. "Next time I go to the beach, I'm not going to forget my sunscreen."

He didn't necessarily feel like making small talk, but he didn't want to see Wilkens either.

He leaned on her desk. "Where did you go?"

"Oyster Point on the Shore. It's a really nice place. They have a great beach."

Lambert pictured her in a swimsuit and made sure he kept his gaze firmly fixed above her neck.

"Who did you go with?"

"A friend," she answered, her voice changing just enough so he would know not to ask.

Lucky guy, Lambert thought. "Is Wilkens in?"

"He's been expecting you for the last twenty minutes."

Lambert shuffled to the door behind her desk, knocked softly with his right hand, and let himself in. In the middle of the office sat a round table with four chairs. Lambert slid into one of the chairs and winced as his elbow bumped the table. Wilkens ignored him for a full minute until he finished what he was doing. Then he swiveled his chair around, his small, dark eyes flicking over Lambert's injuries.

"Thanks for coming in, Bruce," he said. "How are you feeling?"

"I've been better."

Wilkens nodded. "I know you should be in the hospital, but I needed to talk to you about what happened yesterday." He picked up a folder off his desk. "According to your report, Suzanne Williams called and asked you over to her house."

"That's right."

"What was the reason?"

"She didn't give me the chance to ask why. She was frantic."

"So you raced over and conveniently arrived just in time to get assaulted."

Lambert glanced up sharply. "Suzanne and Tyler are friends of mine. If Tyler hadn't come home, I would be dead right now."

Wilkens flipped a page, then closed the folder and tossed it on his desk. "You should think carefully about who you call friends. It would be in your best interest to distance yourself from Jackson."

"You're telling me to ignore what happened?"

"No, I'm telling you to be careful. Jackson isn't in the FBI. You shouldn't be involved with him."

"Jackson's working with the Russian government recovering the money Daemon took from them. It's natural our paths should cross."

"I know what he does. What concerns me is what you're doing with him and how it will affect your career."

"Why would being friends with Tyler and his wife affect my career?"

Wilkens leaned back so that his chair creaked; his eyelids closed into slits. "You're in no condition for this kind of discussion, so I'll keep it brief. I retire in two years, and you are the logical choice to take over. According to the numbers, you are well past due. You're on a first-name basis with the New York Attorney General, and if he could get you to work for him, he would. He's asked me confidentially more than once. You're rated in the top ten percent of your experience cohort, and you get along with everybody here."

The old, lidded eyes didn't blink as Wilkens picked up his coffee cup. "You would be surprised at how many people are snapping at my heels for this job. The only place with more criminals than New York is Washington, and most of those are politicians. Why do you think Laura left her cushy job on Capitol Hill to work for me? Before she transferred here, all she had to do was wear clingy sweaters, make her department head happy once or twice a week, and she could do whatever she wanted. She'll never admit it, and neither will her former boss, whom I know very well. A pretty young thing like that bouncing around, and everybody thought I would have another heart attack."

He laughed lightly and took another sip. When he finished, his face was grave.

"Here's how it's going to be going forward. Get everything Jackson has on Daemon. Names, dates, places, accounts, etc. Forward everything to me. I'll review what you have."

"You're giving Daemon to someone else?"

"An outside opinion can't hurt."

Lambert took a ragged breath. "Jackson found the intrusion into the Federal Reserve. He tried to involve me multiple times, but I said I couldn't help him because you told me not to. I would rather have his voluntary cooperation than force him to cooperate."

Wilkens's eyes narrowed into dangerous points. "Tyler Jackson is an ex-agent who illegally employs the services of hackers and worse. Dixie Stevens is wanted for dozens of computer crimes. Quinten Pavak is a former New York detective suspected in the disappearance of two government witnesses. Tracy O'Connell used to work for the CIA in military black ops. He's a very dangerous man. I don't even want to think what he's doing with Jackson. You have a choice,

Bruce. You can find out what Jackson knows and sever your relationship with him before it affects your future, or you can stand in my way. If you're anywhere nearby when I go after Jackson, I'll hang you both. It's just as easy to throw two ropes over the limb as one."

31

The first time CIA Deputy Director Marcus Byrnes had heard of Joe Tresher was after he killed the ambitious nephew of a powerful Colombian general. Without the general's knowledge or blessing, the nephew, Luis, had been blackmailing the cartels. If the cartels paid him, he guaranteed the military would look the other way.

Luis made a lot of money playing one side against the other. Then, a few high-ranking members of the Colombian government got uneasy. The United States pumped a lot of money south, fighting drugs, and the last thing they wanted was a scandal to stop the inflow of cash. The general's powerful friends made quiet inquiries about a quid pro quo. Eventually, Washington got an extradition treaty and continued to pour money into the army. In exchange, the CIA promised to get rid of the nephew.

Tresher took the contract and went south. The cartels had been trying to kill Luis for a long time, so he was very hard to find, but Tresher did it. That should have been the end of it, except the kid was secretly engaged to the premier's daughter. As the young man and his fiancée were announcing their engagement at a private party held in their honor on the premier's patio, Tresher made the hit. One moment, Romeo was dancing with Juliet under the steamy Colombian summer sky; the next he lay in a puddle of expensive French champagne.

The premier asked some pointed questions, and it wasn't long before he found the right people in his own government who were more than happy to tell him what had happened—in exchange for being allowed to keep their heads. A phone call later, and he had the undivided attention of the US ambassador, who wasn't happy to find the premier thinking about terminating the extradition treaty.

The Justice Department promised they would investigate the allegations, and a month later, they quietly figured out enough of what had happened to shake some trees at the CIA. But a few slapped wrists didn't even the score, and a month later, some Harvard-educated Colombian lawyers and two highly paid cartel killers went north.

The lawyers reviewed the Justice Department's investigation records and sent the assassins after a career CIA case manager named Paul Schuster. They wired his wife to a kitchen chair, put her in a bathtub filled with water, and made their six-year-old son watch while they cooked her with a cut extension cord. Schuster told them everything they wanted to know, but they didn't stop; and, after they were through with her, they did the same to his son, and then, eventually, to him. Two days later, the assassins went after Tresher, and that's when their journey ended. Even though the FBI tore the country apart looking for the hit men and lawyers, the Colombians were never seen again.

Byrnes got out of his car and squinted up at the ozone-white Jersey sky. Last night's rain had moved into the Atlantic, leaving the afternoon hot and muggy. Loosening his tie, he walked across the wet pavement and entered the pipe assembly plant. The building was as hot inside as out, and the air stunk of machine oil. If anybody could find the Owl, Tresher could, but time was running out. No news was not necessarily good news, especially after what had happened Thursday night in Chicago. Janné had blown up his building. Where was he now and, more important, where was the money?

Trying not to get his shoes dirty, Byrnes dodged metal lathes and silvery piles of pipe shavings. No telling how long it would take Tresher to get here. Whatever, Byrnes was sure it would be worth the wait. Between two steel columns, a furry spider repaired its web, its black hairy body jerking as it negotiated its sticky snare.

"Director." Wearing his white Stetson, hands buried in an old-fashioned yellow slicker that made him look like he had just gotten back from herding cattle on the Wyoming frontier, Joe Tresher stepped out of the gloom. He handed a thumb drive to Byrnes. "I have some information you'll find interesting. It's a recording of Agent Bruce Lambert explaining his relationship with his former partner Tyler Jackson."

"Isn't Jackson the agent Janné shot in Chicago?"

Tresher nodded. "Tyler Jackson is the Owl. Lambert didn't exactly say it, but I think Jackson also has some or all of the money Janné took from the Fed. Jackson got to Janné just before you did. That's why Janné wired the building to explode."

His mind turning with the new information, Byrnes put the thumb drive in his pocket. "Do you know where Jackson is?"

Tresher adjusted the brim of his Stetson. "Not yet. I was working on it when you called."

"This might be an opportunity. If we can acquire the money, then Jackson can be blamed for the theft."

"Lambert won't go for it."

"Lambert will if he doesn't have a choice. If word leaks that a disgruntled ex-FBI agent broke into the Federal Reserve and stole billions of dollars, Lambert won't matter. The account transfers are the key. No numbers, no sacrificial goat."

"If we don't locate the accounts in the next day or so, Ralph

Wilkens will grab Jackson on an arrest warrant, and you'll never get close to him or the money again. Hugh Dobrowski will strike a deal with the FBI about your involvement with Janné, and that will be the end of it."

Byrnes glanced at his watch. "Not if we find Jackson first. Where will he run to?"

"I don't know that yet." Tresher handed over an envelope. "Here's Jackson's information. Tell your people to be careful. The FBI's watching him. I'm going to try and have another conversation with Lambert. He's the key."

32

BRUCE LAMBERT LIMPED SLOWLY across an alfalfa field toward the giant oak tree standing on the top of the hill. The field had been irrigated recently, and after getting deeper and deeper in the mud, he wondered if it had been such a good idea to come the back way instead of driving to Jackson's house on the road. After struggling up an incline, he stopped under a tree's umbrella of spreading limbs and caught his breath. In the shade was a wooden bench.

Tyler Jackson sat holding a small red-velvet box. Lambert sat next to him.

"Suzanne loved it up here," Jackson said, turning the box. "Said it was the best view in town. That's why I put the bench here. Sort of a king's chair. Lord of all he could survey. This was back when I thought the future was a piece of red carpet leading from here to forever. Now, I guess there's no such thing. Suzanne's gone, Bruce, and I wrecked everything as much as Daemon did. I had to go after him. I couldn't just hang it up and walk away. The hardest part though is understanding why. Suzanne wasn't a part of this. She didn't know anything. She just got in the way. Have you identified who it was yet?"

"We dusted the house, but the guy didn't leave any prints. He was obviously a pro. Be glad you came home when you did."

"I thought Suzanne was going to be mad about me getting home so late. You remember when she turned the hose on me for inviting you and Leesa over for dinner and not telling her beforehand?"

Lambert smiled. "She could move like lightning when she got mad."

"And call it from the sky if the mood suited her." Jackson stared out at the valley, following the irrigation canals with a farmer's instinctive eye.

Far below, a dun-colored colt ran circles in the long grass. Lambert watched the colt run, and then he leaned down to shake mud from the cuffs of his pants.

"I had this dream last night," Jackson said, "where I came home and found him killing her. He did it nice and slow, really enjoying it. I told him to leave her alone and try his luck with me, but he wouldn't stop. He wanted me to see it happen. I grabbed his hair, putting my knee in between his shoulder blades for leverage, and pulled his head back. I'm ready to cut his throat but stop because I realize it's too easy. I want him to pay. Give him exactly what he gives her. We play this game. He cuts her, I cut him. I cut him, he cuts her. Over and over all night long, until I realize I'm so damned caught up in killing him, he's already killed her. I just couldn't quit and walk away."

"The story of your life lately," Lambert said.

Down below, the colt rolled on its back in the grass and kicked up its white-stockinged legs.

"I'll get him," Lambert said quietly. "I promise I'll get him."

"You said that three years ago."

"I know."

He sighed. "I spoke with Wilkens this morning. He's going to issue a warrant for your arrest. He's made it clear if he gets hold of you, there won't be a single thing I can do except watch."

Jackson scowled and turned his head to meet Lambert's eyes. "Maybe he hasn't been keeping up with current events. Going after me is a waste of time he doesn't have. Daemon's stolen billions and made it abundantly clear he can and will do so again. The world is offline. The SEC has suspended trading on Wall Street. The banks are closed. Economists are already wondering if this will throw us into the mother of all depressions."

"Wilkens doesn't care."

"So what do we do?"

"For the first time, we have the advantage," Lambert said. "Daemon wants the money you took from him. He'll try to get it back."

"And who will get hurt then, Bruce? Your kids? My family? How would you feel if Leesa packed her stuff and told you she never wanted to see you again?"

"You and Suzanne have worked it out in the past. Give her a couple of days, then call her. She'll come around. It could be worse. You could be putting her in the ground."

Jackson handed the velvet box to Lambert and slumped against the bench. "There won't be another reconciliation. All my second chances are gone."

Lambert opened the box. Inside was Suzanne's diamond engagement ring.

"I never realized until now just how simple severing the most important part of my life could be," Jackson said. "She says goodbye, and suddenly all our plans for the future are no more. Even getting shot didn't hurt as much as watching her leave."

"I'm sorry. She's a wonderful woman."

"She got tired of waiting. Last night was the last straw."

"Have you found out anything more about Hugh Dobrowski? He seems to be the key to all of this."

Jackson shook his head. "No. The first and last time I saw Dobrowski was in New York at the paint warehouse. He had information on Daemon, so I flew to Chicago to see if the intel was solid."

"You should have called for help."

"I tried to, but it's not like I can just dial 911. Look, Bruce, I know I don't have any credibility with the Bureau, but there has to be a way we can pool our resources."

"That may not be possible. You're an easy target, and there are people involved who want to make an example of us both."

"What should we do?"

Lambert sighed, air hissing through his swollen lips. "What we always do. Follow the money. I'll get access to the Fed before Wilkens cuts me off. We'll go through how Daemon got in, and more importantly, how he moved the money out. I'll need the accounts you got from him—where they came from, how they were moved, and where they were going. Maybe we can find a pattern."

"Hugh Dobrowski knew enough to send me after Daemon," Jackson said. "We find Dobrowski, we find Daemon. I'll track him while you chase the money."

Lambert stood up. "Get out of town. There are more sharks than you know of on this case, and every one of them is smelling blood."

33

JACKSON LIMPED DOWNHILL and went in the back door. He kicked off his muddy shoes and walked down the hall in his stockinged feet. Dixie waited in his office. She was looking at framed photographs on the walls. The first was of an old fence, stretching into a lake at sunset. The second showed a waterfall in the desert. A third photograph captured a mountain stream in winter. The ice covering the water was spider-web thin. The last photo showed a lonely tree out in the middle of rolling sagebrush hills. On the tree hung a NO TRESPASSING sign that had been shot to pieces. The picture had been taken at sundown, and the branches were silhouetted against the fiery sky.

"Where is this?" she asked, pointing at the last picture.

"Northwestern Utah, up by the Idaho border," he replied. "It's some of the most desolate country I've ever seen."

"What were you doin' up there?"

"A buddy of mine invited me to go bow hunting in the Hogbacks. Our trailer blew a tire about fifty miles from the Idaho border. I stayed to keep an eye on it while he went over to Snowville to get it fixed. I can't ever remember being that alone. There were hundreds of miles of sagebrush to the north, the Great Salt Lake to the south, and nothing in between. An old set of railroad tracks cut around the top of the lake, and I passed the time catching rattlesnakes. They were trying to soak up the heat from the railroad ties. I pinned a couple before they could slide down their holes. If you keep them off the ground, they get cold and stiffen up. After a while they're just like sticks. I saw the tree and wondered what idiot would put up a No Trespassing sign out in the middle of nowhere. If you look closely, you can see some white things in the distance behind it."

She squinted at the picture. "What are they?"

"Antelope. What you can see are their tails. At the time, I had no idea they were even there." His voice caught. "I guess that's how life is. You never appreciate what you have until it's too late."

He slumped against the wall. "Have you ever felt like the ground's so soft under your feet that you're afraid of breaking through? I feel like I'm walking on cracked ice. Everything touches some memory."

Dixie checked the time. "What did Bruce want?"

"Wilkens has issued a warrant for my arrest. We need to disappear."

"You shouldn't have made him angry."

"He would have gone after us either way, unless you trust him to be anything other than what he is."

"I do not."

Sun streamed through the windows. "I'm going to change clothes. I'll be down in a few minutes, and we can go."

"Where to? Another hole in Jersey?"

"I was thinking something a bit further away. Have you been to Vancouver in the summer?"

Dixie blinked. "I have not. I've heard it's nice."

"It's better than nice if you're up to it. There's worse places to disappear for a few months."

"Sounds good," she said.

He went upstairs and, trying not to look at the clothes Suzanne had left behind, rummaged through his closet until he located an old pair of boots. The heels were worn down, but at least the boots still fit. He rolled his dress shirt into a ball and tossed it across the room into the wastebasket.

Two points.

"Tyler?" Dixie yelled up the stairs. "Can you come down here for a second?"

He went downstairs.

Dixie knelt on the entryway floor. She appeared to be examining the splotches of dried blood. "Look at this."

Jackson crouched next to her. Using a pair of tweezers, Dixie picked up a business card and held it out.

"Who is Sara Branson, and why is her modelin' business card on your floor?"

———

34

THE BEAUTIFUL NAPERVILLE RIVERWALK sat in the heart of the town's small but picturesque town center. The brochure in Dobrowski's hotel room said the Riverwalk had won the Illinois Governor's Award for Best City Park. It was easy to see why. Expensive brick pathways wound along both sides of the scenic DuPage River. *The city must have floated one hell of a large bond issue*, he thought. Lawns, flowerbeds, shrubs. The annual maintenance budget had to run at least a million a year.

Shutting off the engine and the all-important air conditioning, he climbed out into the humidity. The first thing he noticed was the noise. Screaming kids of all ages, shapes, and sizes raced down the paths and across the bridges.

The surly mood he'd been dragging around since Alec Janné had broken into the Fed deepened. He tried to remember where the week had gone, but the hours ran together. For the last two weeks he had spent most of his time running from one place to another, usually at night, and he hadn't gotten much sleep. He remembered meeting with Tyler Jackson in New York on Monday and then running when CIA Deputy Director Marcus Byrnes—Dobrowski's former boss— had shown up. After that he'd lost track of time.

Hunching his shoulders against the sun, Dobrowski left the parking lot. His wool suit made him sweat, and he needed somewhere shady and quiet to think. No one else smoked, and the cheerful crowds gave him a wide berth. How times had changed. Back in the sixties, when he had been young, smoking had been fashionable. Everybody did it. Actors and actresses exhaled blue clouds and then kissed passionately without stopping for a breath mint. The American Cancer Society didn't exist, and no one worried about emphysema. Smoking was as American as apple pie, cheap gasoline, and driving Chevys with grilles as wide as tanks.

Now, everything had changed. Smokers puffed in designated areas or were banished outside, even in the winter. People wore nicotine patches and went to seminars on kicking the habit. Smokers' families sued tobacco companies for billions, while the tobacco industry fought back like a befuddled giant throwing haymakers at clouds of flies.

Heading down to the water, Dobrowski thumped moodily across a wooden bridge. A path off to one side led to a secluded spot beneath the bridge's supports. And a bench. Just what he was looking for. He wasn't far from the car, but the short walk had left him wheezing, and he hoped he could make it back up the hill.

This was a pleasant spot. Out of the sun and away from the chaos. TheDuPage River gurgled past, and children begged for bread to feed the ducks. "Please! Please! Please!" echoed across the river. A pair of mothers handed out bags of stale bread, and their children galloped down a stairway to the water's edge. Ducks sniped at the food and each other.

Dobrowski watched the children and thought about CIA Deputy Director Marcus Byrnes and the quiet, vicious people above him. Dobrowski had no idea who they were—very few did—but what he did know was enough to make him extremely cautious. They were well-funded, silent, and deadly serious. Frankly, he felt fortunate to be alive.

He thought about his ex-wife and daughter in Ohio. He didn't know if it was the young children or the realization of his deteriorating health, but for once the anger left him, and he remembered his ex the way she had been when they both were young, just after their daughter Marjorie had been born. He hadn't had a kind thought for Joyce in a very long time, and the sudden welling of emotion surprised him. Why had he traded his family for this dangerous, hollow life?

His cigarette smoldered and went out. He flipped it in the water where it caught the current and floated away. One of the ducks pecked it expectantly and gave him a disappointed look. Dobrowski's fingers twitched. He wanted another cigarette, but knew he should stop. Gripping his knees, he forced himself to consider his choices.

He had been Catholic all his life, but like many, he hadn't attended church in years. But that didn't mean he didn't believe. The older he got, the more firmly convinced he became that there were other forces at work. Considering the amount of bad in the world, there had to be. Either God was asleep at the wheel, or the devil was doing the driving. Either way, Dobrowski had happily done his part in making sure the bad guys stayed ahead on the scoreboard. That's how Director Byrnes had set the hook and reeled him in.

What if the Bible stories about God and Jesus weren't just fairy tales? Would he be saved by grace, or would he go to hell because he had been an unrepentant son-of-a-bitch? There was no way to know for sure. That had been where Judas had screwed up. Judas believed Jesus had been the Messiah sent from God to destroy the Romans. For forty pieces of silver Judas had sold his self-respect. In a classic case of buyer's remorse, he'd thrown away his ill-gotten gains, but that hadn't saved him. It was all a matter of scope and understanding the big picture. Judas hadn't, but God did. Jesus's death had given everyone had another spin of the wheel.

Dobrowski started to get up, then froze. Across the river, a figure moved under one of the trees, and one of Byrnes's hired guns stepped into sight. The man, with blunt features and powerful shoulders, stood over six feet tall. He wore jeans, Adidas running shoes, and a loose, oversized sweatshirt that hid the pistol on his hip. He slowly swept both banks of the river, looked right at the bush Dobrowski hid behind, and then continued. His eyes lit on something above Dobrowski and to his right.

Half-standing, Dobrowski dared not move. He listened and caught the faint sound of careful footsteps. The second killer wore black jeans, a dark shirt, running shoes, and mirrored sunglasses. He stood so close, Dobrowski could hear him chewing gum.

Dobrowski's lungs couldn't hold much air. He felt the pressure to breathe first in his left temple and then at the back of his neck. His heart hammered. His chest tightened. Sparks flashed before his eyes. *Hold on*, he told himself. A horribly long moment passed before the killer turned and retraced his steps. A second later, he had gone.

Chest heaving, Dobrowski sagged against the bridge pylon. He tried to breathe without making noise, but couldn't, and for the first time that day, he was grateful for the pounding of little energetic feet on the wooden bridge above his head.

By the time he recovered his breath, both assassins were nowhere in sight. He had been planning on striking a deal with the FBI. The office was less than an hour's drive downtown from Naperville to the Federal Building in Chicago, but earlier that morning, he had changed his mind. The FBI would love to know everything, but even if Dobrowski wrote an autobiography, there were no guarantees those responsible would be brought down. He wasn't about to pay the bus fare all the way to hell by himself.

He threw his cell phone into the river and, staying off the main sidewalks, walked to the other end of the park. At the softball diamond, he found a pay phone and called a cab.

Byrnes's men would be watching his car, which meant they knew about his room at the Marriott. Good thing he traveled light. It didn't matter how they'd found him. Like weeds, the killers were just the bushy part.

It was the root he had to pull.

35

JACKSON AND DIXIE met O'Connell and Pavak at Teeterboro, the airport for private planes. Jackson had paid cash to book a charter flight to Chicago. During the afternoon, a weather front, bringing powerful thunderstorms and high winds, had boiled out of the southwest. Waiting in a private terminal where the food kiosk offered pre-wrapped sandwiches and pizza slices, business travelers thumbed through the *Wall Street Journal* and *New York Times*. Headlines read "Banks Still Closed" and "Fed Sees China Threat."

Needing time to think, Jackson walked over to a window and watched dark clouds rush across the sky.

Dixie found him. "You okay?"

He shrugged. "The more I push everything away, the harder it blindsides me."

"That's one of the reasons I'm glad I'm not a man. You can't just break down and get it out. You can cry when nobody's lookin', but you can't always choose the time when the hurt comes to call. You have to take it like a man and be a big boy right up until you fall flat on your face."

The plane took off two hours later in a booming thunderstorm. Normally he didn't have a problem flying, but the weather, combined with the greasy pizza he had eaten at the airport, made him wish he had taken a Dramamine. A gust of wind nearly turned the small plane onto its side before the pilot regained control. Dixie, pale and leaning on the seat in front of her, sat with her hands clamped on her armrests. He unwrapped a Snickers bar and took a bite.

"Wow, the last time I saw you look this bad was last year on that United Airlines flight when you threw up all over the sales rep for Pepto-Bismol," he said as he chewed. "Amazing when you think about the odds involved. Fate must really have a sense of humor. Too bad he was married."

She glared. "I will get you for that. Even if the plane crashes and we're both killed, I will make you pay."

He laughed but put the candy away. The plane eventually broke through the clouds. The charter's copilot started handing out sandwiches.

"You're welcome to mine," Dixie said. She closed her eyes and folded her arms over her chest. In the seat behind them, Pavak and O'Connell snored.

Jackson pulled down his tray and dealt a hand of solitaire.

The plane landed in Chicago a few minutes after two in the morning. Jackson paid cash for the after-hours pickup fee and the passenger van. O'Connell, Pavak, and Dixie threw their belongings inside and climbed in. Jackson started the engine and followed the maze of exit signs leading out to the I-190. Contrary to common sense, some IDOT idiot had decided there only needed to be one way in and out of O'Hare, and at rush hour, the funnel turned into a bottleneck of taxi cabs and limousines. The only time traffic moved effectively was in the middle of the night, so Jackson figured that, at least in one respect, he'd caught a break. A few short minutes later, he found himself on the Kennedy Expressway heading east.

The City of Chicago had numbered addresses, but only the post office understood what those numbers meant. Jackson needed an address on Buchanan Street—the address on Sara

Branson's business card. Even Google Maps couldn't help. Buchanan was on the map, but every time Jackson started to get close, the road either changed names or dead-ended at the Chicago River. He finally took a wrong turn and ended up near Loyola University. Three fraternity brothers returning from a night on the town pointed out a small side street.

Sara lived in an upscale area of stately brownstones. In the dark, her building looked like a single long structure. Fifty-year-old maples dwarfed the occasional streetlight and hid the house numbers.

Dixie rolled down her window and aimed a pencil light at the porches. "That's it!" she said.

Jackson made a quick U-turn and parked between a Honda with a Loyola parking decal in the back window and an orange Volkswagen Beetle with an old bumper sticker that read, "God is not spelled G.O.P."

He switched off the lights and squeezed between the seats. "Pavak, trade places with me and keep the engine warm."

"Yes, boss." Pavak moved forward.

Looking out the side window with a pair of low light binoculars, O'Connell inspected the brownstone.

"There's a lamp on, but no movement." O'Connell handed the binoculars across to Jackson. "You take a look."

The old house had aged well, Jackson thought. The wood trim had been painted recently and the decorative fence surrounding the small yard stood straight and clean.

Jackson returned the binoculars to O'Connell and opened his suitcase. He'd packed his Browning automatic shotgun in foam. He assembled it and hefted it for balance, slipped the strap over his right shoulder, and tested the release to make sure it wouldn't get tangled up with his coat.

"Yell if you hear or see anything," he told Dixie. "Once things are stable, you can switch with O'Connell."

He and O'Connell got out of the van, moved up the walk through the darkness, and stepped onto the brownstone's porch. O'Connell knelt in front of the doorknob and withdrew a credit card from his wallet. With the card's edge angled for maximum leverage, he slipped it against the bolt. The door clicked. He caught the knob before the door could swing open.

O'Connell went in first. With a scratch of claws on the floor, a black Persian cat scrambled away. O'Connell followed the cat into a bedroom. Jackson peeked in the kitchen and then switched on the light. O'Connell met him in the hall and silently shook his head. No one home.

Jackson tried to get a feel for what sort of person this Sara was. The light in the window came from a lamp in the corner next to a glass and steel entertainment unit holding an expensive television. The opposite wall held a bookcase filled with stuffed animals. Her favorites seemed to be cats and mice. Why would a grown woman decorate her house with children's toys? A stuffed kitten suddenly came to life and sprang down on an oversized Little Princess doll propped against a couch cushion. Jackson nearly shot a hole in the wall before he got hold of himself.

On the corner of the coffee table sat Sara Branson's modeling portfolio. He paged slowly through the glossy photographs. She modeled designer clothing, perfume, makeup, lingerie, and nothing at all. He ignored the miniskirts, bustiers, teddies, and corsets, and studied her beautiful face, noticing the way her gray eyes sparkled.

On a small end table sat an amateur snapshot of Sara's family. Three women. Lace tablecloth. Turkey waiting to be carved. Like Sara, her mother and sister had thick blond hair, freckled noses, and fair complexions, but her mother's face had wrinkled and her smile looked forced. In contrast, Sara, in a sweater that showed off her figure, leaned in toward the camera and smiled with an urgency that said *like me, like me, like me.*

A cat bed covered with black fur lay on the end of the couch. Next to it, Jackson saw a crumpled ball of aluminum foil and a catnip mouse. He picked up the ball and threw it toward the door. The kitten leapt out from behind the doll, pounced on the toy, and rolled on its side so its back claws could come into play.

O'Connell walked into the living room. "Nobody's home."

"Are her clothes gone?"

"No. Just the opposite. I think she has at least five hundred pairs of shoes. You want me to send Dixie up?"

"Sure, but keep an ear on the police scanner, and yell if there's a problem."

A minute later, Dixie came into the house. "Where do you want me?"

"Take the master bedroom. You'll know what to look for better than I do."

"Thanks a lot," she grumbled.

Jackson started with the entertainment center, moved to the bookcase, then got down on his hands and knees to search under the furniture. Something caught the light by the wall, and he fished a dusty photograph out from behind the couch.

It was another picture of Sara's family, but this one wasn't nearly as formal as the one on the end table. It had been taken in a pizzeria with a strong flash that highlighted every wrinkle and freckle. Sara's mother, another worn smile on her lined face, sat at the center of the table. A sheet cake with yellow frosting read "HAPPY BIRTHDAY MOM!" Sara's sister was younger, but just as striking as her older sibling. Sara had a different hairstyle than she'd had in the modeling photographs, but he would have recognized her anywhere.

Jackson went up the stairs into the master bedroom. Perfume bottles covered Sara's dressing table. Dixie must have opened one. The smell of violets and made his nose run. Sitting on the bed, Dixie thumbed through a pile of glossy black-and-white photos. She peeled one off and held it out—a nude photo of Sara.

"I absolutely shudder to think what Pavak will do when he sees these," she said.

Jackson lifted it up to the marginal light, glanced sideways at Dixie, and made a show of putting it in his pocket. "I'll need to keep this as evidence."

"You're worse than Pavak."

Jackson laughed, returned the photo, and went down to the kitchen. The postcards covering the side of the refrigerator caught his eye, and he sorted through them. Most were from the United States, but a few were from Canada, Europe, the Caribbean, and Mexico. The majority had been sent to Sara by herself. She had signed them "Me" as if she were doing an autobiographical trip report.

He went to put them back, and then stopped to look more closely at a card that had been custom-made from a 35mm color print. It showed a sign listing beach restrictions—or the lack thereof. The only thing the place seemed to prohibit was glass bottles. The sign was written in both French and English.

He turned the card over and found a man's neatly lettered script telling Sara his vacation wasn't the same without her, and he wished she was there. Jackson read the signature, blinked, and read it again. The kitten made a funny noise in the living room and bolted past the kitchen door and into the bathroom at the end of the hall. Something had spooked the cat. He cocked his head to listen. A floorboard in the living room creaked.

Sliding the postcard into his pocket, he lifted the shotgun and stole across the linoleum floor to the doorway. The hall was empty, as was the part of the living room he could see from inside the kitchen. He shivered. Why was it so damn cold in the house? Had the air conditioning switched on? Putting each foot down as if walking barefoot through glass, he started down the hall.

He had almost reached the end when the feeling went away. He stopped and waited. From where he stood, he could see the entertainment unit, the front door, the kitten's aluminum ball, and the arm of the couch. There were no unexplained shadows or sounds. Nothing seemed to have changed, but every fiber of his being told him that something had. His thumb found the safety of the shotgun, and he slipped it off. Taking a deep breath, he stepped to the far wall, crouched, and took a quick look around the corner.

The room was empty.

Only he would have sworn it shouldn't have been.

He let the trapped breath out of his chest and straightened. The strain was starting to get to him. It had been months since he'd gotten enough sleep, and he was jumpy. Pretty soon, he would start making mistakes. He took a quick look at the timer on his phone. Fifteen minutes had gone by since O'Connell had left for the van. No telling when Sara would come home.

He went up to the bedroom. Dixie sat on Sara's bed and paged through a daytimer.

"What's that?" he asked.

"Her life since January," Dixie said. "The woman schedules everything. She even made appointments with herself to go swimsuit shopping yesterday." She glanced up. "Did something happen?"

He shivered, recalling the feeling he'd had in the kitchen. "Bring what you have and let's go. We've been here too long."

"Gladly."

He locked the front door and left the house to the cats. Pavak had started the van. O'Connell, in the passenger seat, turned. "Okay if I ride shotgun, boss?"

"Be my guest," Jackson jumped in back and gave Dixie a hand up. She shut the door and fastened her seatbelt.

"Did you see anything in Sara's daytimer about someone named Alec?" Jackson asked, keeping his voice even.

Dixie thumbed the book open. "There's an address for an Alec Janné and three phone numbers. She writes his name with two hearts if you can believe it. Please tell me I wasn't ever this bad as a teenager."

She stopped at his expression.

"What is it?"

"Alec Janné is a financial analyst for the French General Directorate for External Security." Jackson took the daytimer. "His field of expertise is computer banking networks. He's one of the guys Bruce and I were looking at him before I got shot."

"What are you saying? Is . . . is he Daemon?"

"I believe so."

She stared, eyes widening, before she unexpectedly leaned over and gave him a hug. "You did it, Tyler! You found him! After all this time, after losing so much, you did it! I'm so happy for you!" She let go and smiled, eyes bright.

"Thanks," he said, "but we don't, in fact, have *him*."

"We have his address, though," Dixie said.

"We do," Jackson said. He tapped Pavak on the shoulder. "Come on, Q. Let's pay the man a call."

Pavak drove to Lake Point Tower and parked on the street. O'Connell broke into a service door. The elevator shot skyward while a cheerful chime announced each floor. When they got off, a pleasant synthetic voice thanked them. The apartment's lock was harder to pick than lock on Sara's house, but that wasn't saying much, and seconds later O'Connell had them inside.

Only they were too late. The condominium was empty. The carpet had been cleaned, the appliances scrubbed, and the walls shone from a wet layer of fresh paint. The refrigerator had been unplugged and hung open.

The elevator down seemed to last forever.

36

SAYING HE NEEDED A CATNAP, O'Connell curled up in the back of the van. Jackson took the keys from Pavak and climbed in. A moment after the engine roared to life, he felt the light touch of Dixie's hand on his shoulder. "Where to now?"

"Sara's brownstone," he said.

Pavak, leaning against the passenger door, harrumphed. "Why?"

"I don't know."

He heard Dixie settle back in her seat. "No doubt Pavak has a better idea. What is it, Pavak? Where do you think we should go?"

"I don't know." Pavak turned to the window. "But looks to me like we're going around in circles."

True, it was probably stupid to go back to Sara's place, but he couldn't think what else to do, and at least the traffic wasn't bad. Because of the banks being closed and not being able to use credit cards to buy gas or pay for parking, most people used public transportation to get to work. By 8:30, the downtown sidewalks were crowded with professionals walking to their offices, but the Mercantile Exchange had a CLOSED sign on the door. Cabs drove the empty streets with CASH ONLY signs in their windows.

At stoplights, Jackson searched the crowds. Janné may have run, but that didn't mean that he had gone to ground. If Sara was one of his minions, he might have an army of helpers. The well-dressed man standing on the corner and talking on his cell phone might have a gun under his suit. The woman running for a taxi could easily be Janné's associate.

Hunger was making him see bogeymen on every corner. The others must be hungry, too. He needed to find some breakfast. Jackson headed north, and a few blocks from Sara Branson's brownstone, he stopped at a convenience store. Inside, the cinnamon rolls smelled good, and he paid cash for a dozen.

He returned to the van, propped the daytimer on the steering wheel, and ate one-handed as his finger ran down the page. If Janné wasn't at his apartment and his basement operation was buried under rubble, where would he go?

"We should have a party after all of this is over," Pavak said. "Take a break with señoritas, margaritas, and sunshine."

"Do you have somewhere in mind?" Jackson asked. "It would have to be somewhere nice enough for Doc to bring his family."

"Cozumel, Mexico is nice. There's always Cancun if we don't mind crowds. Just be careful about who's invited. Last time you told Dixie she could bring her significant other, she showed up with her vibrator and a case of batteries."

Dixie sputtered and socked Pavak's shoulder.

"Children, children," Jackson said, the acid in his stomach boiling up to the back of his throat.

He handed the daytimer back to Dixie and returned to the store for some Rolaids. As he stood by the door, unwrapping the roll, a moving truck pulled into the fifteen-minute loading zone. Three muscular men wearing overalls and caps passed him. The biggest looked like he could carry a piano single-handed.

Jackson turned to watch them microwave burritos. He ran to the van and yanked open the door. "Wake up, O'Connell."

"I'm awake." O'Connell climbed over the backseat. "What's going on?"

Jackson pulled away from the curb and sped toward Buchanan. He parked down the block from Sara's place. A white Lexus ES sedan had parked in front of her house.

"Want me to run the plate?" O'Connell said.

"Don't bother," Jackson said. "There's a moving van at the 7-Eleven down the street. Ten bucks says she's inside packing."

"Do you think they're the same people who cleaned out the other address?" Dixie asked.

"That shouldn't be too hard to find out," Jackson said.

The front door of the house opened, and out came a beautiful woman wearing heels, a short black skirt, and a brilliant red blouse Sara Branson was taller than Jackson had expected, and her hair was darker, but he easily recognized her. She swung up the walk in her heels.

"That woman's got to be a speeding ticket because she's got 'fine' written all over her," Pavak observed.

"What do you do, wake up in the mornin' and put 'annoy Dixie with sexist comments' at the top of your to-do list?" Dixie asked.

Pavak thought about it. "No, but that's not a bad idea."

Sara put the suitcase in the Lexus then swung back up the walk and disappeared inside the house. Jackson pulled his automatic from its holster, but O'Connell shook his head. "Let's see where she takes us. She might be going to Janné."

Five minutes later, carrying a leather briefcase, she emerged from the house. Then, she folded her legs into the sedan and pulled smoothly away from the curb.

Jackson waited for Sara to reach the stop sign and then followed. She made the most of the light traffic by switching lanes and speeding through intersections. For a few minutes, Jackson was convinced Sara knew they were following her, but she didn't run any red lights or make sudden turns. He eventually decided she was either late for something or had a lead foot. He did his best to stay with her without being obvious, but quickly gave up and just tried to keep her in sight.

"She must know a good mechanic," O'Connell said. "I didn't know a luxury sedan could corner like that. Every one of her hundred and twenty pounds must be in her right foot."

Almost as if she had heard him, Sara took a hard right, and disappeared into a forest preserve. Jackson flattened the van's accelerator. Fifteen long seconds went by before he reached the entrance and skidded inside using both lanes. Trees closed around the road. The Lexus was nowhere in sight.

"I don't like it," Dixie said, searching the undergrowth.

Jackson didn't either but accelerated anyway. The road split. A small sign reading PICNIC AREA pointed to the right. The left fork had no sign. He turned right towards the picnic area. Straight ahead stood the main pavilion; the Lexus had parked in front of it. He slowed and pulled behind some trees. O'Connell jumped out the back door and disappeared. A minute later he climbed back inside.

"She's sitting in her car looking at her phone. It's five of ten. We'd better find someplace else to wait."

Jackson flipped a quick U-turn, drove back to the fork, and took the other road. It made a scenic loop through the other end of the preserve and eventually turned back the way he'd come. He sped through the narrow roads, eyes jumping from the pavement to the clock on the dash and back again. He finally caught sight of the pavilion through the trees and stopped where he could see Sara sitting in her car. Dixie handed him a pair of binoculars and he settled down to watch.

A squirrel ran across the road, grabbed an acorn from under a bush, and bolted for the safety of a nearby tree. Jackson watched Sara take another look at her phone and wondered why Daemon would leave such an obvious link behind if he had plans to disappear.

An old gray Chevy Celebrity drove up. The tires were mismatched, paint on the hood had oxidized, and the sedan needed a new trunk lid. The passenger wore a tight-fitting black stocking cap, while the driver had an unmarked baseball cap pulled low over his eyes. Both wore sunglasses. The Celebrity turned into the picnic area and accelerated toward the Lexus.

Jackson swore and dropped the van into gear. The tires spat mud and grabbed hold of the pavement. The road looped to the left—away from where he wanted to go. Undergrowth came in to flank the road, and he lost sight of both vehicles. The picnic area was only a few hundred feet away on the other side of the trees, but it might as well have been on the moon. O'Connell pulled the side door open, locked it into place, and removed his pistol. Dixie retreated into the van's back corner and braced her feet against the rear door. Pavak checked his revolver.

The road emerged through the last of the trees just as the Celebrity stopped behind the Lexus. Jackson floored the accelerator and hit the horn, hoping Sara would notice, but fearing she wouldn't react in time.

The Celebrity's passenger door opened and one of the men jumped out; he was holding a gun. Sara gaped at the weapon but didn't move. They had her pinned. The man brought up the pistol, but it fell from his fingers and clattered to the pavement. A look of surprise crossed his face. He turned partway toward the Celebrity and slowly toppled over. The other man shouted, but before he could move, a neat round hole appeared in the Chevy's windshield.

Sara threw the Lexus in reverse and slammed backwards into the Chevy. The two cars bucked with the impact before the Lexus wrenched free, ripping both bumpers and the Chevy's rear side-panel away. She dropped the transmission into drive, but before the car moved, her left front tire exploded, and then both her rears.

"Shooter in the trees!" O'Connell yelled.

Holding a rifle, the tall, thin man from Jackson's basement stepped into the road in front of the van. The weapon bucked against his shoulder.

The windshield exploded in Jackson's face. He spun the wheel and hit the brakes. With a wail of rubber, the back end whipped around. He wrenched the wheel in the other direction. The van's rear end hit the gravel and took the rest of the van with it. He caught a split-second glimpse of a tree. Brilliant, multicolored lights detonated behind his eyes. A high-pitched shriek filled his ears.

37

WHEN JACKSON WOKE UP, he lay in the back of the van. O'Connell was poking his jaw, and even the lightest touch shot pain to Jackson's temple. The van's engine made a bad grinding noise that sounded like a chainsaw.

"What happened?" he whispered.

"You swerved the van into the tree. You hit your head and dislocated your shoulder. I had to pop it back into place." He shone a light in Jackson's eyes. "You'll have one hell of a headache."

"My jaw hurts. It's hard to talk."

"Yeah, you'll have a nice bruise to show the ladies."

"I can't afford this right now. Can you give me something?"

O'Connell hesitated then turned to his med kit. "I'm going to give you a shot. It's not for you, but to get Dixie off my back. Every time you groan, she goes crazy."

"Why is she driving?"

"It was better than her hovering around back here." O'Connell loaded a needle from a glass vial and squirted the air. "The FDA outlawed this about twenty years ago. It fries the nerves, but it'll kill the pain for a couple of hours."

Jackson stared at the wall. The crash had torn a hole in the roof. Sun shone through and buildings moved past.

He felt a pinch below his jaw, then, like wildfire through dry patch timber, a horrible burning sensation flashed across his face. He opened his mouth to scream. O'Connell put the shoulder strap of his backpack between Jackson's teeth. For a moment, Jackson thought his eyes were going to pop out of their sockets, and then abruptly the burning went away and took the pain with it.

Panting and sweating, he spit out the strap. "What was that?" The words sounded garbled, but at least he could move his jaw.

"I got sent to Latin America a long time ago to teach our friends and neighbors how to kill one another. Only they already knew a lot more than I did, so I patched the poor bastards up after they practiced on each other. Sometimes this was all I had. It hurts, but you'll be glad you have it. Give the stuff five minutes, and you wouldn't notice if I pried your head open with my fingernails. Now hold on while I give you another in your shoulder."

Jackson waited for the pain to hit him, but this time all he felt was a warm sensation deep in the socket. O'Connell put the needle away and gave Jackson some water.

"What happened to Sara?" Jackson's face still felt hot, but at least he could talk. "The last thing I remember is sliding off the road."

"We don't know. By the time we got the van off the tree, she was gone. The two guys she left behind weren't so lucky. The driver got it through the head, the shooter in the throat. Very clean, very professional." The van hit a bump and tried to shake itself apart.

Dixie stopped at a red light. A man in a pickup pulled alongside and asked if Dixie had tangled with a bulldozer; he offered to buy her a beer. The light changed, and she rattled away without answering. From his prone position in back,

Jackson figured the accident had smashed the fender into the wheel-well, and as far as the shot-out windshield, he was still picking glass off his shirt.

O'Connell removed a crumpled five-dollar bill from his pocket. "I've tried to figure out how many times you could have been killed in the last week, but I've lost count. Lotto's at thirty million. You pick the numbers. All I want is one ticket. That kind of money will go a long way on an island down south."

Something clicked in Jackson's mind, and he tried to sit up. A wave of nausea swept over him, and he slumped back to the carpet.

"I wouldn't do that again," O'Connell warned.

"Get Dixie. I need to ask her something."

O'Connell went up front and told Dixie to pull over. She found an alley and stopped. O'Connell opened the side door. Using his right arm, Jackson slid out. He could see his feet but couldn't feel them. He told the right one to move anyway. The other followed. His stomach convulsed, and he threw up. Dixie handed him some tissue.

"You okay?" she asked.

He wiped his mouth. "Ask me again after I'm dead. I'll feel better then."

Dixie put her arm around his waist and helped him back into the van. A loud ringing sounded in his ears, but at least he didn't feel like throwing up again. He eased himself onto the seat, keeping hold of the van's sliding door so his head would stop spinning.

She touched his chin and gently turned his head.

"You need to go to the hospital," she said.

"I don't have time." He removed the postcard he'd found in Sara's house and gave it to her.

She read the postcard. "Beach Restrictions. No glass bottles." She flipped the postcard over and read the back. "Where did you get this?"

"It was on Sara's refrigerator. Can you get online and check the FBI's file on Adrian Laroque? I want to see where this photograph was taken. As I recall, Laroque had the same sign on his wall at the mental hospital. At least, that what his FBI file said."

"You remember that? I'm impressed."

"It's hard to forget Laroque trying to kill me."

Jackson checked the St. Vincent postmark and gave it to O'Connell. "Doc, have you ever been to the Grenadines?"

O'Connell nodded. "There's a maze of small islands down there. Most of them are so small, they don't have names. This picture could have been taken on any of them." He handed the card back.

Jackson looked sideways at Dixie. "I have a hunch Laroque will know where it is. You need to go talk to him."

"Me? Why am I always on the receivin' end of your crazy ideas?" She glared. "This is just my luck!"

"Speaking of luck," O'Connell said, "there's a gas station up the road that sells lotto tickets."

38

JOE TRESHER WIPED the final coin free of fingerprints before dropping it into the pay phone. He could have used the cell phone in his pocket, but he always used pay phones when he was working. It was getting harder and harder to find them, but the inconvenience was preferable to the police being able to listen without a warrant.

Turning to face the parking lot, he watched more FBI agents drive by. Sara Branson had become a very popular woman. The phone clicked and beeped. He hung up, worked a stick of gum free, and returned to his car.

Ten minutes later, the phone rang. Tresher spat the gum into its wrapper. Lifting the handset, he turned and leaned against the building so he could watch the street.

"Something better be on fire," Director Byrnes growled. "I was in a meeting with the senior staff."

"Janné's left town, and the FBI wants to know exactly where. They're sitting down the road right now waiting for his girlfriend to come home."

Byrnes let out an angry rumble. "Do they have him?"

"No. He saw them coming and bailed. Oh, and one more

thing. Jackson's here. I winged him, but couldn't get a clear shot."

"This is starting to sound familiar, Joe."

"I'll get him. I brought it up because you'd better start thinking of damage control. I don't have to tell you what will happen if the FBI gets hold of Janné or Dobrowski."

"What's your next move?"

"Janné has a bolt hole he's jumped into. Locating it will be difficult. I'll find him though. Everybody has a few loose threads. I just need to find the right one to pull. Are you leaving?"

"No. If I can't hide in D.C., then I should have retired long ago."

A government car with more FBI agents pulled into the parking lot and stopped in front of Tresher.

"I'll call you when I know more."

He hung up and drove to his motel. Sara Branson lay trussed up on the bed. Her eyes were open and clear, which meant the drug had worn off. He watched her in the half-light thrown by the room's blinds and remembered the afternoon he had found the doe lying on its side in a stand of wind-gnarled pinion, head in a patch of late summer New Mexico sunshine and misty brown eyes as soft as velvet.

Taking out his knife, he sliced through the duct tape binding her ankles and knees, but left the tape on her wrists, elbows, and mouth. She flinched at his touch but didn't move. She learned quickly.

"So where were you and all that luggage going?" he asked.

39

AT MIDNIGHT, Bruce Lambert let himself into Jackson's office. Nearby buildings cast a kaleidoscope of color across the reception room's carpet, but other rooms had no exterior walls. Good thing he'd been here before. The hall was so dark he could have been the last person on earth. Leaving the lights off and playing Blind Man's Buff, he felt his way past the supply room, the data room, the break room, the room Dixie, Pavak, and O'Connell shared when they were all in the office together, and the suite Jackson kept for himself.

At the end of the hall, he arrived at the conference room where he intended to set up for the night. Lambert unlocked his briefcase, removing his laptop, twelve feet of shielded CAT 5 wire, and a small flexible clip light. He plugged the laptop into a nearby network jack, clipped the light to the underside of the conference table, and pointed the beam towards the carpet. With the table in the way, no light showed from outside the room. The last thing he wanted was for building security to call the police.

Feeling his way back to the break room, he removed two cans of Coke from the refrigerator and bumped the door shut with his good knee. It was going to be a long night, and he

210 | MICHAEL RAY EWING

needed the caffeine. Then, seated at the table and popping open a can, he logged into one of Jackson's database servers and started running queries against the SQL data warehouse. The servers were linked with a Wall Street research firm's compute-cloud through a high-speed link, and the amount of information he could access was staggering. There were database feeds from the government, the Internet, most of the commercial online services, and even data from overseas that hadn't yet been translated. His first query on anything with the words "Daemon" in it netted almost eighty-thousand responses. Narrowing the scope of the queries reduced the number somewhat, but there were still too many to wade through in one night. He finally just went through the entries for the last month.

Two hours later, he went to get another soda and stopped. The refrigerator was empty. The sign on the door said the last person to empty the refrigerator was supposed to put more inside. Lambert thought back to his previous visit, trying to recall how many sodas he had removed, but decided he didn't care. With one working arm he certainly wasn't going to carry a heavy case of soda from the supply room. He would just go without.

He closed the refrigerator and started back toward the conference room. But wait. He could see — and not because his eyes had magically adjusted to the dark. How could that be? He turned back toward the entrance. Under the data center's door glowed a bright band of light. Had it been there the whole time?

The carpet muffled his steps. Quietly, he opened the door and slipped inside. The data center was the only room with a raised tile floor. Immediately in front of him were two uninterruptible power supply units. Two rows of racked computers stretched from one end of the room to the other. Dozens of database servers hummed inside the racks. At the end of the racks stood an expensive NetApp disk filer. Thick gray wires disappeared into cut-outs in the floor tiles.

At the other end of the room, two men sat in front of a console monitor. Their backs were turned, and they were arguing quietly back and forth. The one typing had a heavy pockmarked face and long blond hair. A box of cookies, a bag of potato chips, and a can of Dr. Pepper sat by his feet. The second man had a gaunt, intelligent face under a shock of greasy black hair. He talked in short sentences and listened politely whenever the other man interrupted him. A bruise darkened his forehead.

Lambert had a good memory for faces. These were the men in the pictures Jackson had forwarded to him from Chicago.

"Look at those packets hitting the network," Carl Jester said, pointing at one of the console's windows. "Someone's spawning search processes on the VPN. An outside connection just hit the subnet. They're looking for information on Adrian Laroque. This is the third file they've accessed."

"Can you open the document?" Hassan Tarazi asked.

"No. The transcripts are in Microsoft SharePoint. This server is running Linux."

"There's a computer down the hall in Jackson's office. I'll be right back."

Jester grabbed Tarazi's arm. "You do that, and you might as well go introduce yourself."

Lambert watched the two men for a moment, then made a decision. There was a time to be quiet, a time to make noise, and a time to not give a damn anymore.

Jester was reaching for his bag of potato chips when Lambert stepped behind him.

"Eat those things before bedtime, and all that saturated fat will go right to your heart," he said.

Tarazi spun around, hand reaching for his weapon, but froze when he saw Lambert's pistol. Lambert motioned for them to raise their hands, and they did. Reaching into his jacket, he took out two sets of handcuffs and tossed them on Jester's ample lap.

"Have your friend hook his hands through the arms of the chair, and then cuff him nice and tight," Lambert said.

Jester licked his greasy lips then wordlessly did as he was told.

"Now, put the other set on the chair and turn to your left so you're facing him."

Jester turned ninety degrees until he faced Tarazi. Lambert put the pistol's sight on Jester's head and picked up the handcuffs. Snapping the bracelet around the man's right wrist, he threaded the chain through the chair's arm, and closed the other around Jester's left wrist. Stepping back, he let Jester sit sideways. The chair creaked beneath his weight.

Lambert centered the pistol on Tarazi and circled behind him. Placing the muzzle against the man's neck, he reached down, withdrew Tarazi's pistol, and then checked the cuffs. They were snug, but he tightened them anyway until the metal bit into the man's skin. Stepping out of reach, he located another chair, and pushed it toward the two men.

"Do you know who I am?" he asked.

"You're Agent Bruce Lambert," Jester said. "You want vital statistics, or is that enough?"

Lambert nodded and sat down. "I'll get right to the point, then. I'm looking for two men, and I think you can help me. The first is somebody who goes by the name of Daemon. The second is the guy who did the work on my face. I want their names and where I can find them."

"Assuming we know anything, why should we tell you?" Tarazi asked.

"Talk to me now, and I'll help you out later."

"And we were both born yesterday," Jester snorted.

"Then let me put it another way. You can either talk to me voluntarily, or I'll get a needle and set you up with Alice down at the corner of Fifth and Wonderland. Either way, I'll get what I want."

"That's against the law," Tarazi pointed out. "Anything you get will not be admissible in court."

Lambert put his left index finger into his mouth and let them see the rows of black stitching crisscrossing the inside of his cheek. "I don't care."

Jester grinned, showing food fragments. "If you're going to shoot me up, then how about mixing in some of whatever you've been smoking. After we're nice and rosy, we'll all go up on the roof, and you can show us your buzzard imitation."

"Don't blow it, Carl," Lambert said. "I'm offering you a lot better deal than you'll get from anybody else."

"And why's that?"

"I don't know why you quit the Fed to work for Daemon, but I don't think you like where you've ended up. With the terrorism bills passed by Congress after 9/11, you're going to end up in an 8 ×12 for a long, long time."

Jester lunged to his feet, dragging the chair behind him. As Jester's three hundred pounds landed on top of Lambert, his swollen elbow hit the tile, and blazing pain detonated in his arm. Pure blubber, Jester was the size of a sumo wrestler. Pinned down and smothered, Lambert watched the ceiling lights dim. His ears rang, and he heard a splat; the sound of a dropped ripe peach. The weight left him, and Jester's body rolled off. Sweet air rushed into his lungs.

Tarazi watched impassively. The Iraqi held a small caliber pistol with a silencer screwed to the end of its barrel.

"What are you, Houdini?" Lambert said.

"When he went for you, he broke off the arm of my chair, and the keys fell out of your pocket." Tarazi rolled Jester onto his back and dropped Lambert's keys on the work table. "I think you were about to tell me about a possible deal."

Lambert cradled his throbbing left arm and sat up. He'd

felt horrible before Jester crashed into him. Now, he felt worse.

"All I want is Daemon, the guy who tried to kill me, and the money Daemon stole," he said. "Give them to me and you walk."

"A lot of influential people won't like that," Tarazi said.

"I can guarantee your safety."

Tarazi laughed. "You really don't understand who you're dealing with. Your father works for Princeton University. Your wife Leesa works for the phone company in their customer service department. Your youngest daughter is almost ready to start kindergarten. Both of your grandparents on your mother's side live in Florida. Your older sister is married to an insurance broker and lives in upstate New York. We do our homework. But, okay. Let's say we both live long enough for you to give me a new identity."

Tarazi reached into his chest pocket, withdrew a thumb drive, and tossed it across. Lambert caught it.

"That's what you want," Tarazi said. "Just ask yourself if you really want to read it."

Lambert glanced at the stick. "Who's Daemon?"

"His name is Alec Janné."

"The French Agent?"

"He used to work for the French before the CIA recruited him. Now he works for himself."

"And the other guy?"

"My guess is he's CIA, but I don't know." Tarazi gave Lambert a hand up. "You might want to think before you do anything rash." He headed for the door but stopped. "One last thing, if you're looking for somewhere to start, I wouldn't bother with Janné. I doubt he's going to be alive much longer. If the Russians or your government don't kill him, your former partner probably will."

"And the money?"

"Janné moves it constantly through bitcoin. It's all time-encrypted—impossible to hack."

Tarazi turned toward the door.

"But wait," Lambert said. "Where will I find you?"

"For both our sakes," Tarazi said, "it's better if I contact you." The door closed behind him.

Lambert looked down at Jester and the blood pooling beneath his head. The first person at work in the morning would find the corpse. No point wiping the room for prints. He had more important things to deal with.

Lambert made a copy of the thumb drive and put it in a mailing envelope. He'd send the original to Jackson's family in Arizona, along with instructions to put it in a Mason jar and bury the jar on their ranch. In the event of his death, they should let Tyler know that Lambert had left him the drive. Then he made careful edits to the files on the copy and called Ralf Wilkens's secretary, Laura Patterson, to meet him at the office and transcribe the files.

The morning sun had just risen when she finished. Lambert had her print two copies of the files and lock the second flash drive in the FBI's vault.

A lot of bad things could happen in the next few days, and, best of all, he was damn sure most of them would.

40

THE FIRST THING Dixie Stevens noticed as she pulled into the Elgin Mental Health Campus early Tuesday morning was the Old Center building. Sheets of faded plywood boarded up the first-story windows, but the second- and third-story windows stood open to the elements. Weeds flourished around the foundation, choking the few shrubs that had survived after the State had let the building go to hell. *At one time it must have been beautiful*, she thought.

After circling the campus, she stopped at a small building to ask directions. Two security guards grudgingly told her where to go. The building she wanted sat in the far northern corner of the grounds. When she remarked that a sign or two would have made finding the building that held the criminally insane a lot easier, the two men simply shrugged and told her to write the governor. The irony of deliberately making a mental hospital grounds confusing was not lost on her as she left.

If she could pull this off, it would be a miracle. Sure, she wore dress flats, but her eyes looked like they needed a shot of Visine, and her slacks were wrinkled and stained.

Two more security guards sat inside the lobby. The taller

one had iron gray hair, three chins, and a gut that made it hard for him to fit inside his uniform. The shorter, younger guard still had patches of brown in his thinning hair, but he was well into his second chin. Along with their badges, both men wore identical scowls.

Dixie told them she was looking for a missing person and handed them a manila envelope containing a copy of the Cook County police report, a fake private investigator's license, a rough description of who she was looking for, and a facsimile of a color photograph of a man O'Connell had once found years before he'd started working for Jackson. The quality of the fax was not great, and the blurred face could have belonged to half the population, but it was all she could lay her hands on. Dixie just hoped that with the supporting documentation, it would be enough to get her inside.

The two guards slowly went through the material, held the fax up to the light, and then handed everything back and pointed to a plastic seat against the wall. She thanked them for their assistance and sat down. The older guard popped the tab on a diet cola and took a gulp. It was so quiet in the lobby she heard him belch under his breath.

Eventually, the locked door leading into the rest of the building opened, and a large Black man stepped through. He was dressed in white cotton slacks and a matching shirt that showed every muscle in his chest.

"Ms. Stevens?" he asked, his soft voice unexpectedly polite.

"Yes?" she said, standing.

"My name is Elden Campbell. Dr. Rice asked me to escort you to his office."

Elden turned to the guard station and told them to get her a badge. The guard with the soda gave her a log to sign in and a clip-on badge with a large "V" on the front. The other guard pushed a button, and the door clicked open with an electronic hum.

Carrying her briefcase, Elden led the way down the hall,

his long legs forcing her to hurry to keep up. He had an easy way of walking that reminded her of Tracy O'Connell.

"You've come to have a look at Adrian Laroque?" he asked.

She increased her speed to draw even with him. "Excuse me?"

"The John Doe you're looking for with the head injury. His name is Adrian Laroque."

"Has positive identification been made?"

"The CIA seems to think so. That's what they call him. Who are you looking for?"

"A Kansas business executive."

"Why do you think Adrian is the person you're looking for?"

"The time of the disappearance is about the same, and the descriptions on the police reports matched," she lied. "I had a few hours this afternoon, so I decided to check it out."

"I don't know who Adrian was before he came here, but I doubt he was a business executive."

"I doubt it also, but it was worth the gas money."

They stopped in front of an office. Elden knocked softly and opened the door. A tall stooped man looked up from reading a medical chart. His thinning black hair was brushed back from his high forehead, making his widow's peak more pronounced. A small bandage had been taped across the bridge of his nose. He had a mole near his left nostril. She forced herself not to stare.

"Ms. Stevens?" he asked, offering her his hand. "I'm Dr. Glen Rice. I understand you're looking for some information on one of my patients?"

Dixie shook the pale hand, getting a good look at Rice's bloodshot eyes before he straightened his chair and sat down. She wasn't the only one who was tired, it seemed. She lowered herself into the chair by the door. Elden set her briefcase by her foot and closed the door.

"Thanks for seein' me on such short notice," she said. "I'm

lookin' for an executive of a large petroleum company in Wichita, Kansas. His name is William Kotch. You might have read about him in the newspaper. He disappeared last spring just before a business meetin' in Chicago and hasn't been heard from since. His description matched that of one of your patients, so my client asked me to come out and see if it was him."

"That sounds highly improbable."

Dixie smiled. "So is bringin' in psychics or rattlin' a bag of chicken bones, sir, but at this point, I'm just about ready to try anythin'. Just before Mr. Kotch disappeared, he emptied the company's pension accounts. Neither he nor the money has been seen since."

"And you think he's here?"

"I get paid to investigate possibilities, even those that are remote."

"Did you happen to bring a photo?"

Dixie took the envelope from her briefcase and handed it across his desk. "Inside is a fax sent to me this morning from my client after I found the police report on your patient. I wasn't expectin' to find anythin' so I didn't bring his profile with me, and I didn't want to wait until they could e-mail me the original before speakin' with you. The rest I got from the police downtown."

Rice smoothed the contents of the envelope on his blotter and hunched forward, examining the documents. For a moment, Dixie thought he had fallen asleep; then he stirred and returned everything to the envelope.

"I'm sorry to disappoint you, Ms. Stevens, but my patient is not this man."

"Are you positive? I could bring out a better photograph tomorrow."

"My patient is at least ten years younger than the man you are looking for. Certainly, you must have looked at the age of the man on the report?"

"Your patient was admitted to the hospital with a gunshot wound to the head. I took a chance on the approximation of the age. Do you mind if I ask you a few questions anyway? It will only take a minute or two, and then I'll be on my way."

Rice glanced at the clock on the wall and nodded.

Dixie removed her phone, opened the recorder app, and quietly stated where she was, the date, and who she was interviewing.

"Dr. Rice, how would you describe the condition of your patient?"

"He suffers from characteristic delusions, hallucinations, and severe schizoaffective disorder."

"Which means?"

"In layman's terms, he sees and interacts violently with those around him."

"What is the approximate age of your patient?" Dixie asked.

"Early to mid thirties."

"What is his prognosis?"

Rice shrugged. "I can't say at this point. He's still in the early stages of treatment. Cases like this can last for years."

"When was your patient admitted to this hospital?"

"March."

"During his treatment, has he shown any indications of improvement?"

"No."

"To your knowledge, has your patient mentioned anythin' about Kotch Industries or any of its affiliates?"

"No."

"Has your patient ever mentioned the names Charles, Brian or Donna Kotch?"

"No."

"When was the last time your patient had a visitor?"

"Two days ago. The CIA has been visiting my patient monthly since he was admitted here."

She paused, surprised. "Why so often?"

A bit of frustration entered Rice's voice. "They want to know who shot him. Adrian always turns violent afterwards."

"Your assistant, Mr. Campbell, mentioned that the CIA refers to your patient as Adrian Laroque."

Rice nodded. "That's part of the reason why I'm certain he's not the man you're looking for."

"Have they been successful at questionin' him?"

"As I stated before, my patient suffers from characteristic delusions, hallucinations, and schizoaffective disorder. Individuals with those kinds of illnesses have a difficult time communicating coherently, if at all." Rice glanced at the clock again and sat up. "Where is all this leading, Ms. Stevens? We've ascertained that my patient is not the man you're looking for, yet you continue to ask questions."

Dixie smiled disarmingly. "I work closely with federal authorities from all over the country on my cases. They're usually my best sources of information. I'm just surprised to find they would continue to keep questioning a patient sufferin' from severe characteristic disorders—"

"Characteristic delusions," Rice corrected. "Schizoaffective disorder is something else altogether."

"If your patient is as ill as you claim, then what good is it for the government to keep questionin' him?"

Rice scowled. "I've asked the agent that a number of times. From the day I took over this case, I've tried to find out exactly who my patient is and why he was shot. It doesn't sound very complicated, but getting any kind of answer is close to impossible. I don't care if my patient is an undercover agent or a drug dealer or even the man who shot JFK. None of that matters. What's important is having somewhere to start and something to work toward."

"Do you have a case number, or, failing that, a phone number where I can reach this agent?"

Rice found the number in his Rolodex and wrote it on a

piece of scrap paper. Dixie slid it into her pocket.

"I have one final request, and then I'll be on my way. I know the fax of the picture is of extremely poor quality. Is there any way I can visually confirm your patient is not Mr. Kotch before I leave? There's a great deal of money involved, and I would hate to bother you again by havin' to return at a future date."

Rice sighed.

"I'll let you see him if you agree to call Agent Janné and ask him to return my call."

Dixie stiffened at the name but forced her voice to remain even. "Agent Janné? Is he the one leadin' the investigation?"

"Yes."

"I'll be glad to call him. We may have even worked together in the past. May I know what you want to talk to him about?"

"It's confidential." Feeling his bandaged nose, Rice stood abruptly. He had a limp, so the walk down the hallway was much slower than when it had just been Elden and herself. The elevator discharged them onto the fifth floor. In a corner near the ceiling, Dixie saw a rotating security camera. Rice hobbled over to the security station and motioned for her to sign in. Dixie, eyes sweeping the other entries, bent over the book. An Alec Janné had signed in at the top of the page. The metal doors clicked open, and she followed the two men inside the wing.

This side of the building faced east, and the morning sun had heated the air into the eighties. In the hall, Rice hobbled through the puddles of hot sun. Dixie took up the rear. The tile was a seventies-era mucus green. A handful of patients shuffled aimlessly about. Two of the more vocal patients let everyone within earshot know how angry they were at being confined.

"How long have you worked here?" she asked Elden, trying to keep the nervousness out of her voice.

He smiled. "What time is it?"

They arrived at Adrian Laroque's room and stopped. The door had a blacked-out window. Bits of sunshine shone through. Rice touched the glass.

"You are not allowed to ask questions or provoke him in any way," Rice said. "If he threatens you, move into the hallway. Do you understand?"

"Yes, sir."

The lock clicked, and he pushed the door open. Dixie peered tentatively inside, and then squinted to make sure she wasn't seeing things. The entire room had been turned into a tropical beach. Sand and palm trees stretched toward a distant, powder blue sky. The light fixture had been transformed into a sun. White, fluffy clouds rolled across the ceiling. A narrow band of surf cut the room in half. Her side of the room—including the walls, the ceiling, and the inside of the door itself—was black.

At first, she thought the scenery had been painted on, and then she saw that everything, including Adrian Laroque, was covered in chalk. Rocking slowly back and forth, he hunkered down and didn't look up. A white scar from where Jackson had shot him puckered the right side of his forehead. He mumbled softly under his breath.

Big hands balled into fists, Elden moved to one side of the door. Rice limped inside. Dixie took a deep breath and carefully put her dress shoe down on the chalky floor. She had a rough description of Laroque from the FBI's investigative report, but they hadn't gotten him right. Laroque looked more like an adolescent boy than the killer his resume said he was. His dirty face lifted toward Rice. For a moment, the two men simply looked at each other. Then Laroque turned his head towards her. He stopped rocking. His gaze narrowed, and she saw his thighs tense. A low growl, like that of an angry dog, bubbled from his chest. His eyes met hers and sharpened into a sudden, brilliant blue. Laroque wanted to kill her right now where she stood. He wanted her dead.

Heart hammering in her chest, she faltered backwards. Her eyes locked on the far wall. The lettering was cramped, but the sign easy to read.

COROLAS Del Mar BEACH RESTRICTIONS
NO GLASS BOTTLES

"Miss Stevens?" Rice said.

"What?" Dixie said.

"Have you seen enough?"

She swallowed and nodded. "Yes. That's not him."

A hand on her chest, she backed into the hallway. The steel door clanged shut. Rice started back toward his office.

"That was a scary man," she said, stumbling to catch up.

Elden fell in beside her. "Visiting for the first time is always a shock. Don't let him get to you."

"I'll try not to," she said.

They took the elevator down to Rice's office. Her fingers were clumsy as she groped for the handle of her briefcase. Laroque had recognized her. There was no doubt about it. Characteristic delusions and the rest of the psychological bull-shit aside, he had known exactly who she was.

Elden walked her to the lobby. She gave him one of her business cards and circled the number of her answering service.

"If you hear anythin' about another John Doe, let me know," she said. She turned to leave then stopped. "One last thing. Can you confirm Agent Janné's first name? I don't think Dr. Rice wrote it down."

"His name's Alec. Alec Janné."

She smiled. "Thank you, sir. You've been very helpful."

Pushing open the glass door, she stumbled out into the hot sun. Removing her phone from her purse, she dialed Jackson.

"The island's name is Corolas Del Mar."

41

THE PINEY WOODS of east Texas grew so close together that, from a distance, the pecan and evergreens looked black. The sunlight had a fuzzy haze that made it hard to focus. Hugh Dobrowski wondered if it was because of the humidity, his sunglasses, the rental sedan's tinted windshield, or the combination of all three.

He took the Mount Pleasant exit off Interstate 30 and headed south on US 271. Towns dating back to the late seventeen hundreds rolled past, along with fast food stands and junk shops shimmering in the heat. It wasn't much past ten in the morning, yet the temperature was over 100 humid degrees. How did the local citizenry stand it?

Squinting through the glare, he adjusted his sunglasses. He felt listless and tired. It had been almost thirty hours since he had gotten any rest. Lack of sleep hadn't been from personal choice. He just hadn't been able to fall asleep.

The night before, in Dallas, he had picked up a young, glassy-eyed prostitute who had snorted a line of coke off the motel's tiny bathroom vanity before she took off her clothes and sprawled face down onto the bed. For a few moments, he thought she had passed out.

Then she turned her head and glared at him. "Hey, old man, you going to get it up or not?"

Afterward, he blew smoke at the room's dingy ceiling while she dressed in the bathroom. He listened to her heels click on the tile floor, wondering if he should shell out the additional hundred that would keep her with him until morning. She emerged from the bathroom wearing a miniskirt, heels, and a tight cotton top that showed her small breasts. She couldn't have been much over eighteen, if that. For a moment she just looked at him, and he thought he saw real emotion drain from her eyes before she simply left. No *thank you*. No *see you later*. No *goodbye*. Just a click of the door. Well, what had he expected? It was work for her. And for him? A kind of last hurrah.

In the city of Kilgore, he stopped at a barbecue restaurant and activated the prepaid cell phone he had purchased that morning. The overpowering smell of spicy meat filled the air, and his mouth watered. A local country Christian rock station droned from speakers in the ceiling. He tapped in the number for his lawyer in Virginia. The circuits clicked a few times and rang.

"Alts and Young Legal Services," John Alts's daughter Betsy purred in her young, sugary voice.

"Betsy, this is Hugh Dobrowski. Is John available?"

"He's on the phone with a client. Would you like to wait?"

"Do I have a choice?" he muttered under his breath then told her that he would. She clicked away. He watched a man smoke a cigarette at the bar. Raw need ripped through him, and it took every ounce of what remained of his willpower not to go outside, pop the sedan's trunk, and retrieve the little golden key hidden under the tire well. The golden key fit the lock on the briefcase that sat on the floor behind the passenger seat. Inside the briefcase was a .22 caliber automatic, silencer, and three clips of custom hand-loaded, mercury-tipped SS-90 hollow points. The ammunition was as illegal as it was deadly, but that wasn't the real reason why he had put the key in the trunk. The real reason was the lovely pack of red and white tobacco heaven sitting, along with his lighter, inside the briefcase.

His reward.

The phone clicked. "John Alts speaking."

"John, this is Hugh Dobrowski. Did you get the package?"

A cautious undercurrent entered the shark's voice. "It arrived last night. I looked it over this morning."

"Any problems?"

Alts paused. "No. Everything's in order."

"Then we're all set?"

"Yes."

Dobrowski released his breath. "Thank you, John."

"You're still going to go through with it?"

"Yes."

"I wish you luck, then. I hope you get what you want."

"Thanks, John."

The connection dropped. He switched the phone to his other ear and tried to ignore the restaurant's blaring music. Every song seemed to be about God, Jesus, pickup trucks, and failed marriages.

The second, and hardest call, was to Dayton, Ohio. Joyce's phone rang five times, and he almost hung up before the call connected.

"Hello?"

"Marjorie!" He exclaimed at the sound of his daughter's voice. "I was hoping you would be home. How's my little girl?"

"I'm fine, Daddy. Where are you calling from? I can hardly hear you."

He brought the phone closer to his mouth.

"I'm in Texas."

"Where?"

"I'm in Texas!"

"What are you doing there?"

"Sweating mostly," he replied. "It's unbelievably hot down here. I had a few minutes so I thought I would call and tell you I love you."

There was a short pause. "What?"

He tried again with more volume, but she interrupted him and demanded to know what was wrong. He insisted there wasn't anything wrong, but he knew she didn't believe him.

"Can't a guy just call his daughter and tell her how he feels about her?"

"You have bad news, don't you? That's why you never called me about visiting the Fourth of July."

"Marjorie, there's nothing wrong. Everything's great, or it would be if you'd just shut up and let me talk. I was thinking about your birthday and wondered what you wanted."

"My birthday? That's not until November."

"I know, but I could get you something while I'm down here." He tried to think of something mundane. "What's your shoe size?"

"My shoe size? What for?"

"If I told you why, it would ruin the surprise, wouldn't it?"

"You're going to get me some Tony Lamas!" she squealed. "I've been after mom to get me some for school, but she only bought me jeans and shirts."

His insides sank. "Tony Lamas. You want boots?"

She laughed. "Don't try and act surprised. Everyone's wearing them now. I bet you and mom have been planning this for months. I wondered why your support check got here so fast. Mom about had a stroke when she opened it. She tried calling you at least a dozen times to see what's wrong."

"I already told you. Nothing's wrong!" he snapped before he could bite off the words.

When she finally responded, her voice had lost its laughter. "You didn't call about my birthday, did you?"

He needed a cigarette so badly he could taste it.

"Do you have a pen handy? I need you to write down something for me. It's important."

"Hold on and I'll get one."

The phone bumped on the counter, and Dobrowski swore at himself. Why in the hell had he asked her about her birthday? The phone picked up, and she told him to go ahead. He gave her John Alts's name and phone number and told her to put it someplace where she wouldn't lose it. She asked him why, and he told her it was another surprise, but this time she wasn't nearly as willing to take the bait.

"Daddy?"

"Yes?"

"Why didn't you send me an airline ticket to come see you for the Fourth?"

He couldn't breathe.

"I wanted to," he managed, "God knows I did, honey, but I couldn't. You'll understand in a few days. I promise."

"You never called to tell us the results of your tests. Mom and I sat by the phone for a week, but you never called. You're sick, aren't you?" Her little girl's voice was velvety soft, but cut him deeper than a knife.

"The only thing I'm sick about is not being able to see you as often as I want to, and that's the truth," he said.

A door slammed and Dobrowski heard Joyce shout at Marjorie to help her unload the groceries from the car. Marjorie yelled she was on the phone. The utility room door banged, and the two women in his life whispered furiously until Joyce snatched up the phone.

"Hugh! What's going on?" his ex-wife demanded. She had quit smoking in the late seventies, and her clear, angry voice whipped over the phone.

He gritted his teeth. "Nothing."

"Nothing?"

"That's right."

"You send me a box full of money, and you tell me that nothing's going on! What do you think I am, an idiot?"

"You're always complaining I'm late with my support check."

A note of exasperation entered her voice. "This isn't about the money. It's about the reason why. Getting money out of you is like trying to get you to quit smoking."

"What's Marjorie's shoe size?"

"Her shoe size?"

"Size five!" Marjorie crowed from the other extension. "And I want the kind that has soft uppers!"

Joyce snapped at her to hang up. The other extension clicked.

"Where did you get the money, Hugh?"

"I don't want to talk about it."

"All right, then. Let's talk about where you've been the last few months. Marjorie cried for a week when you never called about the Fourth. You kept after me for weeks about that vacation, and then you disappeared. What were you thinking, getting her hopes up like that?"

He didn't answer.

"Well?" she demanded.

"Lay off, Joyce. I have my reasons, and I'm not going to fight with you."

"You don't want to fight? That will be the day." She spat each word like she was firing a gun. "Fighting's the only thing we've ever had in common."

He took a deep breath. "I'll admit that as exes go, you could have done a lot better. I'm sorry."

"You made my life horrible for twenty years, and now you're sorry?"

"You have my money and you have my kid! What else do you want?"

"Some honesty would be nice."

He resisted the impulse to hit the wall. "You want honesty?

All right then, here it is. We may have hated each other, but even at its worst, the good we once had has never gone away. No matter what happens, just remember I honestly love you. I always have and always will."

Stunned silence greeted his words.

"The Devil's Dialing 911" played on the radio as he drove away.

42

WITH PEOPLE TRYING to get out of the country before the weather closed the island down, the tiny Dominican airport was a beehive of activity. A hurricane was barreling their way, and no one wanted to be stuck on the island. Jackson, Dixie, Pavak, and O'Connell were the only arrivals, but every departing flight was fully booked.

The four of them got off the plane and hurried toward the small terminal. The wailing wind nearly sent them sprawling.

A pair of sweating loaders took their luggage to a red minivan and threw the duffel bags in the back. Jackson started to protest, but screaming over the wind hurt his jaw. Dixie gave the loaders a twenty and they left. O'Connell drove while Pavak rode shotgun.

Jackson took the rear seat and leaned against the window. Wind shredded the trees. He saw Dixie sneaking glances at him out of the corner of her eye. He smiled and went back to watching the natives nail everything down. The storm wasn't a category three yet, but the locals weren't taking any chances. The minivan's tires thumped over cracks in the asphalt. The steady, rhythmic noise made him sleepy. After doing nothing but sitting for almost two days, he wasn't tired, but the air conditioner felt good and he closed his eyes.

When he woke, he saw that O'Connell had pulled into a brightly lit resort—the nicest on the island.

"What's this?" Jackson asked.

"It's a hotel, Mr. Jackson," Dixie said. "We tried to find somethin' for fifty bucks a night like you wanted, but the travel agent only laughed."

"Travel agent? Are you trying to get us killed?"

"No, but we'll get a good night's sleep."

He frowned. "Look, my jaw hurts too much to argue. Just get us—"

She unbuckled her seat belt. "It's already settled. Tracy, will you help the invalid while Q and I check us in?"

Dixie and Pavak trooped inside as if they were the best of friends. O'Connell glanced at Jackson, then noticed a smudge on the window and carefully buffed it with his shirtsleeve. Jackson staggered out into the wind.

"At least find somewhere out back to park the van. Somewhere where the van won't attract—"

He was interrupted by a pair of cheerful porters who quickly started emptying the luggage. They were very fast and had half the bags out before he could protest. He gave up and went into lobby. The hotel's atrium had decorative streams stocked with colorful imported Japanese koi. Two kids threw alfalfa pellets into the water. The fish went crazy.

Dixie took his arm and steered him toward a glass elevator. "Isn't this nice, Ty?" she asked, sandals clicking on the marble floor as she pulled him along. "I got us rooms with Jacuzzis and a view of the ocean. You should see the waves. Actually, Tracy, Q, and I all got rooms with Jacuzzis," she amended. "I got you a room in the basement with the janitorial staff. If you clean up after everybody else, you stay free. You even get a commemorative dustpan to keep as a souvenir."

"Very funny," he said. "Ha. Ha."

O'Connell loped across the lobby. "Hold the door."

Jackson put his finger on the button.

Pavak and O'Connell crowded in. The elevator zoomed to the top floor. Jackson didn't know how, but the porters had somehow gotten there first and were unloading luggage into their rooms. Dixie gave them each a twenty and both men bowed.

"You don't buy anonymity by overtipping," Jackson grumbled.

"Don't be such a cheapskate." Dixie took off her shoes and walked barefoot to the bed. She plopped down. "You can always tell a nice place by the mattress. You know what this reminds me of?"

"Nothing in recent memory?" Pavak said.

"Right!"

Dixie and Pavak cackled.

Jackson watched them laugh like old friends. Had the world gone insane?

He located the room with his luggage and limped inside. The suite had two televisions, a microwave, refrigerator, mini-bar, and a king-sized bed. He turned on the light and examined himself in the mirror. The knot on his jaw had turned purple. He looked like somebody had used his face for batting practice.

He retrieved a folder from his overnight bag and withdrew a stack of high resolution black-and-white aerial photographs. Spreading them on the bed, he took another look at Corolas Del Mar. The island was a desolate rock in the South Caribbean Sea. The French government had erected four small bungalows, a clubhouse, swimming pool, and a set of tennis courts.

He took a can of guava juice from the minibar, sat down on the bed, and flipped to the last photograph. For this one, the photographer had used a wide-angle lens. On the eastern side of the island where the buildings were located, he saw a small natural lagoon. Moored in the lagoon was a commercial seaplane, the only way in or out.

He switched to a different photograph. At the far end of the island was another lagoon, somewhat larger and bordered by a reef. He ran a finger along the reef and calculated the distance. At its widest point the lagoon was fifty feet. That wasn't much room to set down a plane, especially at night. One unexpected gust, and the plane would cartwheel into the coral.

His door opened and Dixie walked in. "Sorry about the hotel."

"No, you're not."

"You're right." She looked out the window at the ocean. "Even if it's only for a few hours, we're goin' to enjoy ourselves. We may not get the chance again."

"This isn't an all or nothing thing," he said. "If we don't like what we see, we'll just turn around."

"What happens if Daemon has his DGSE buddies waitin' down there?" She picked up his juice, drank some, and made a face. "The truth is, we know next to nothin' about his little paradise."

"We could still hand this all to Wilkens and get out."

"And let him dictate terms that would ruin our lives?" she said. "No. We found Daemon and know where he's gone. We've broken almost every law there is getting' that information. I am not gonna let Wilkens throw us in prison as a thank you."

He nodded and stood up. "I'm going down to the beach to look at the waves and think. You want to take a walk?"

"Let me change first. Before I forget, Doc wants to go over your medical kit in his room."

Jackson swore and went next door.

O'Connell handed him a small red backpack: the Med-Tek Kit.

Jackson hefted it. "What's inside this thing? It weighs a ton."

"A complete pharmacy." O'Connell unzipped the case and pointed out the different vials of painkillers, antibiotics, needles, bandages, surgical staples, tourniquets, saline, and a small field manual on military first aid.

"Memorize where everything is. Make sure you can pick out what you need in the dark."

Jackson pulled out a vial and squinted at the label. "Hydrocodone. The print is microscopic. How am I supposed to memorize it if I can't read it?"

"That's why you do it before we leave."

Jackson grumbled and lugged the Med-Tek kit downstairs. Dominica was a small, mountainous island. The grainy volcanic rock on its beaches could skin the hide off an alligator. The island authority had closed the beaches, but two happy windsurfers were out sailing. He watched one of the windsurfers fall while jumping a wave. The sail whipped around in the wind and smacked the water with a loud crack.

He dragged a pool chair to the shelter of a changing room and went through the contents of the kit. The rains hadn't arrived yet, and it felt pleasant just sitting outside. His jaw and shoulder hurt, but a cortisone shot had dulled the pain enough that he could move.

Dressed in a pair of shorts and a red bikini top, Dixie arrived at the pool. He found himself staring. He had seen her in less, but he had never really looked at her before.

"I like the bikini much better than the computer T-shirts you usually wear," he said. "I'm never going to allow you to go to Vegas for E3 again. All of the vendors can't wait to give you free junk."

"The shirt that picks up Wi-Fi is cool!"

"It's also a men's large. Whenever you wear it, you look like you're wearing a tent. A stiff wind would lift you off the ground."

"Are you complainin' about how I look, Mr. Jackson?"

He laughed and shook his head. "No man alive would do that. It's a resort. Wear whatever you want."

"I'm glad I have your permission." She laughed, sat down on an adjoining chaise lounge, and stretched out, crossing her ankles.

"It's good for you to have a little fun at my expense."

"Is that what I'm having?" she said.

Jackson opened the medical kit and tilted it in her direction. "Have you memorized all of this?"

"I went through mine on the plane down while you were sleepin'."

He held up the vial of epinephrine. "Why do we have this? Isn't it used for allergic reactions?"

"That and getting your heart started again if you go into cardiac arrest."

"Oh." He put it back.

Dixie looked at the windsurfers. "This is a nice place. I wish we didn't have to go. Let someone else have the fun of landing a plane on a reef in a hurricane."

O'Connell walked out of the hotel and stopped beside them. "Duane's inside."

With his good arm, Jackson helped Dixie to her feet.

"Hey, you look like a babe," O'Connell said.

"I am a babe," Dixie said. "Just none of you seem to realize."

Frowning and holding his injured arm, Jackson walked across the pool deck. Was she a babe? The thought had never crossed his mind. Just as the first fat raindrops landed, he entered the lobby.

43

Hugh Dobrowski stopped at the Sam Rayburn Reservoir where CIA Assistant Deputy Director Marcus Byrnes owned a lake house. The setting sun turned the clouds red and orange. Night birds called from the trees, and in a county park near the water, teenagers barbecued blue crabs on steel grills. He heard laughter as he drove by and, shaking his head, rolled up the window. His youth was a long time ago.

Dobrowski had a map of the lake and followed the gravel roads through the trees. The street dead-ended a few hundred yards from the water. Turning off the engine, he withdrew the briefcase from the backseat and stepped into the twilight. Insects droned in the bushes. A breeze fluttered the leaves.

He removed the key from its hiding place under the spare tire and unlocked the briefcase. Hands shaking, he shook a cigarette free and lit it. The paper caught fire and the tobacco started to burn. He drew the smoke into his lungs and removed his pistol from the briefcase. The weapon smelled of oil and shone in the dim light. He ran his fingers along the barrel, screwed the silencer into place, and put two extra clips in his shirt pocket. He wouldn't need them, but old habits died hard.

He lit another cigarette, removed a brown envelope from

the briefcase, closed the trunk, and got back into the car. Using a felt tip pen, he wrote AGENT BRUCE LAMBERT, FBI, NEW YORK and put the envelope on the seat next to the box of size five Tony Lamas.

Once the sun had completely set, he drove back to the blacktop. A mile down the road, he passed a pair of parked cars with four men sitting inside. They watched him drive by before one of them lifted his radio.

"Too late," Dobrowski sneered as the trees behind him cut off their view. Taking the next gravel road, he negotiated the twists and turns until he saw lights through the trees. Pulling the sedan to the side, he rolled up the window and locked it. The keys he put in the envelope with Lambert's name on it, and the envelope went into his suit pocket.

He stepped into the trees. His dark suit made him nearly invisible. Marcus Byrnes's brightly lit house glowed in the dark. A parked sedan appeared in the gloom. The car's headlights were off, and the interior dark. Two men sat inside. Dobrowski stepped behind a tree.

Bruce Lambert's tall figure was silhouetted behind the wheel. He pulled to the side of the road. The passenger door opened, the dome light switched on, and Ralph Wilkens got out. With a wisp of hair, he looked like an ancient baby. The door clicked shut, the light went out, and the sedan moved slowly up the road toward Byrnes's driveway.

It had been years since Dobrowski had done any covert work, but moving quietly through the woods was a skill more easily learned than forgotten. Wilkens stood where he'd gotten out and watched the house through a pair of binoculars. Dobrowski waited for him to stop whispering into his radio, then stepped out from behind a tree and put his pistol's silencer against the old man's wrinkled neck.

"Hello, Ralph. I heard you were moonlighting at Weight Watchers after your heart attack, but I didn't believe it until now."

Wilkens stiffened. "Hugh! What are you doing here?"

"I'm going to ask you a question, and you're going to answer it. Otherwise, your triple bypass will have been a waste of time. How much help do you have in the woods?"

"Woods? What are you talking about?"

Dobrowski pulled the trigger. There was a small flash and a quiet pop. Wilkens collapsed to the ground.

"You always were a piece of work," Dobrowski said.

He felt very good.

44

JACKSON DIDN'T QUITE KNOW what to expect from O'Connell's friend, but he hoped the guy was a good enough pilot to fly through choppy weather and get them safely to the lagoon. Duane "Cardinal" Morris was a small-time Caribbean-based pilot who owned two military-surplus seaplanes and every '65 327 Nova Super Sport Coupe he could get his hands on. He was tall and long-faced; his shaggy red hair and a sunburned complexion matched his red St. Louis Cardinals T-shirt. Rumor had it he was wanted in five countries on charges ranging from weapons smuggling to tax evasion, but very little of it was true. The truth was he had retired from the Air Force after twenty years and moved south. With his red hair and St. Louis origins, the nickname "Cardinal" had stuck.

He was sitting in the hotel bar drinking Red Stripes and making passes at the two waitresses when Jackson, Dixie, O'Connell, and Pavak walked in. Jackson watched Duane's eyes run up and down Dixie's body. If his jaw hadn't hurt and he hadn't needed the pilot's services, he would have clocked the guy.

"I saved you a seat," the pilot said, patting his lap.

Dixie pointedly looked away.

Good for her, Jackson thought. She had her ways of dealing.

Morris smoothly shifted gears and proposed an extended engagement of a decade or so.

How tiresome this must get for her, Jackson thought. Moving next to Morris, Jackson called for the bartender to bring another beer. He needed to pin down Morris's fee before the storm got worse or the pilot changed his mind.

"How much'll this cost me?" Jackson said.

"Ten grand," Morris said. "All up front."

"Fair enough," Jackson said, offering his hand.

Morris shook it, made one final attempt at Dixie, and left his bar tab on the table. O'Connell walked him out and returned a few minutes later.

"Anything I need to know?" Jackson asked.

"He just wanted to make sure we knew what we're getting into. He's flown by that island. They don't like visitors. They take their privacy seriously."

"In what way?"

"Guards with weapons. He hasn't seen anything firsthand, but he hasn't gone looking."

"How many guards?"

"He doesn't know. Never had a reason to count."

Not for the first time, Jackson debated about what they were getting into. They weren't soldiers. They didn't have a governmental mandate. They were out of their league, depth, and minds.

"Should we still go?" he asked, glancing around. "We could call for help. The military could clear this up."

"And tell them what?" Pavak asked. "That we broke into every bank between Canada and Panama looking for Daemon and tracked him down here? They'll throw us behind bars and lose the key. It's one thing to stay out of Wilkens's way, but if the entire government starts chasing us, we won't stand a chance."

"And we don't even know if Janné's there," Jackson

added. He gave Dixie a sideways look. "I have a *hunch* he is, but we won't know for sure unless we go."

She groaned. "Chimes of doom."

He put a twenty on the bar and stood up. "You all know why we shouldn't go and why we should. If there's anything anyone else wants to say, then do it now."

Dixie fiddled with her cocktail napkin. O'Connell didn't move. Pavak stared at the floor. Jackson nodded. "Then let's go."

Jackson drove the minivan to the airport and parked in commercial parking. He tried calling Lambert, but the call went to voicemail. He didn't leave a message. Working in a vacuum annoyed him. In a perfect world he and his old partner would be coordinating their efforts. But with Wilkens chasing them, they couldn't.

The pilot helped load their gear into the plane and told them to buckle in. "It's likely to be a rough ride," he said.

THE STORM FLUNG the small plane around, but Morris knew what he was doing and kept them airborne.

When the plane leveled off, Jackson pulled the photographs of the island from his attaché case. Looking at them gave him a headache. Too much turbulence. He gave up and closed his eyes, trying to think. The best way to stay alive was to keep moving. So why had Janné gone to ground? Did he think he was safe on his island, or had he gone there to wait for them?

The plane's cramped cabin was dark, but even with the storm, there was enough light to see Dixie next to him. She looked asleep, but he didn't think she was. Pavak sprawled across two seats in the back, snoring as if he hadn't a care in the world. Watching the storm, O'Connell sat in the copilot's seat. The plane had been specially modified for stealth, and the engine had a quiet purr, mostly felt instead of heard.

"You okay?" Dixie asked without opening her eyes.

"I guess," Jackson said.

She sighed. "You don't make it easy, you know? With one hand you're keepin' everythin' tucked in close, while with the other you're stiff-arming anythin' that comes within reach. We're a team, boss. If somethin' is bothering you, speak up."

"I just can't shake the feeling we're setting ourselves up. Without backup and no easy way out, this could get ugly. We should leave it for Bruce and get out."

"Don't lose the glow, Tyler. You start doubtin' yourself, and we may as well turn tail and run for home right now."

"You always know exactly how to make me feel better."

She opened her eyes, the irises so dark they looked like still-pooled water. "A lot has happened, Ty, and we may have a few more bruises now than when we started, but don't forget we're the ones still walkin'. The only person who ever doubts *you* is yourself. Call them hunches or intuition or blind luck, but O'Connell and Q talk all the time about how you're able to see connections and relationships no one else can. That's why Wilkens wanted you to work for him again. You're a twenty-first century information alchemist. You may work with bits and bytes and routers instead of lead, but you still spin gold. If it was any other way, none of us would be here. O'Connell and Pavak would have moved on. Lambert would have cut you loose long ago."

"What about you?"

She searched his face for a moment before dropping her gaze to her lap. "I would have died in the bus terminal in South Holland."

"Except you wouldn't have been there to get shot."

"If it wasn't there, it would have been somewhere else. I have no choice in the matter."

"There are always choices. You lecture me about them all the time."

Her chin lifted. "Not when you love somebody, Tyler Jackson. After that, you can't let go no matter what."

He gaped at her, then mumbled something about going up to check on the weather. Up front, his knees braced against the turbulence, Jackson said, "How's it looking?"

"Good," O'Connell said. Then he looked past him at Dixie in the rear.

"Whoa, boss, she doesn't look happy! What did you say?"

"I said I was going to check on the weather. I'll give you a hundred bucks if you tell her I'm sorry."

"A hundred in cash, and I'll tell her anything you want," Duane said.

Jackson scowled at the pilot. Morris ducked his head to fiddle with the plane's controls.

"Could you at least keep my seat warm until I think of something to say so I won't sound like a fool?" Jackson asked O'Connell.

"I'll give you five minutes," O'Connell said, releasing his seatbelt. "Not that it will make any difference. When women get mad, they're mad for a long time."

Jackson slid into the copilot's seat and put on the headset. The plane's windshield had been coated with a polymer that repelled the rain, but he still couldn't see anything beyond the clouds at the plane's nose.

"How's the storm?" he asked the pilot.

"It was downgraded to a category two about an hour ago," Morris said. "They're calling it Mitch. The last report has it well to our northeast, but it's still packing enough wind and rain to close everything down between here and the mainland. It's a good thing we have long range tanks, or we'd have to sit it out."

"Are you going to be able to land?"

"If we stay on the leeward side of the reef, we'll be okay.

With the headwind we've got, we'll barely be moving when we touch down. There isn't a lot of room inside the lagoon, and the currents will be bad, but I've done drops in worse conditions."

"Worse than this? When?"

"Try doing it with people shooting at you. Besides, this is just a category two blow. If the weather service projections hold true, Mitch will swing northwest into the Gulf. We may even get some sun in the morning."

"What's our ETA?"

"About an hour. We've got one hell of a tailwind behind us."

Jackson glanced back at Dixie. She was beautiful and intelligent and the best friend he had. The last thing he wanted was to risk her life. Telling her how he felt could get them both killed.

He took off his headset and walked back to switch places with O'Connell. Dixie crossed her arms and stared out the window.

"Aren't you going to let me have it?" he said, buckling in.

"I would only be mad if I expected better, sir, which I don't."

He leaned over the armrest. "Look, after all this is over, I promise we'll find somewhere quiet to talk. There's a lot buried inside me that will take some time to work through. The only reason I'm here is because of you. Unfortunately, I wrecked your life by dragging you into this, and I don't want to wreck it again. Too many people have died because of me." He met her brown eyes. "But I just want you to know I have no choice in how I feel either."

Her eyes widened. "What's that supposed to mean?"

"That's a conversation for later." He stood and woke Pavak. "It's time."

Pavak mumbled something about making a career out of working overtime and sat up.

Jackson checked his carbine, blackened his face with military-issue waterproof paint, and pulled on his camouflage desert suit. After he finished, he opened his pack and made sure his radio equipment, night vision goggles, extra paint, water desalination tablets, snorkeling equipment, and the Med-Tek kit were inside where they were supposed to be.

When he was satisfied that he had everything, he screwed a suppressor over the end of his rifle and checked the weapon's action. The AR-15's oiled steel felt good under his fingertips.

Dixie handed him her vest. In the cramped aisle, she unzipped her camouflage suit and braced against the seat back. With the vest's straps tight and her suit zipped, she slid a butterfly knife up her sleeve.

"I'm still waiting for the day when you cut off your hand with that," he said.

"Boy Scout motto," she said. "Be prepared."

"Turn up the air con," he called to O'Connell. "We're hot back here."

O'Connell reached for a dial.

"Get ready," the pilot called.

Jackson cinched his seatbelt and grabbed hold of the armrests. Outside the window, the sea boiled with whitecaps. Morris muscled the plane's nose into the wind and cut speed. A gust caught them and nearly flipped the plane backwards onto its tail. The pilot wrenched it down.

"Good thing flying is the safest way to travel, or I would be getting worried about now!" Pavak yelled over the howling wind.

The island's breakers thundered white under the wings. Jackson had never seen waves so high.

"Hold on!" Morris shouted.

Jackson braced, keeping hold of his seatbelt buckle with one hand. If something happened, he wanted to be able to get out of the restraint in a hurry. The nose of the plane dipped, throwing him forward. The plane bellied into the water. Morris throttled back the engines and turned away from the rocks.

Jackson gazed out the window. The waves beyond the reef were four times the height of the plane. Just off their starboard wing, a wave exploded, its impact shaking the plane.

"My God," Dixie whispered.

Morris cut the engine. The plane grated to a stop on a narrow beach. Jackson unlocked the cabin door and pushed it open. The rain hit him, driving him backwards, before he jumped into the sea. Within seconds his clothing was soaked. The water wasn't deep, but the current tried to cut his feet out from under him. The wind made a wailing, keening cry.

Pavak jumped next, followed by Dixie. O'Donnell handed down the equipment, and they made a fire line. When all the duffel bags had been transferred to the beach, Jackson waded ashore and looked through his night vision goggles at the dunes. Not a sign of life. That was good. With luck the guards would be on the other side of the island, holed up with a beer and waiting for the storm to pass. He waved Pavak and Dixie over.

Trying not to move his jaw, he shouted. "Q, get your sniper rifle up on a dune, and make sure we don't get surprised. Stay out of sight. Don't shoot anyone unless you have too. Dixie, you're with me."

Surprise crossed Pavak's face. "You sure about that, Ty? Dixie's better with a keyboard than anyone I've ever seen, and she's fast with a knife, but I don't think she's ever handled an automatic weapon, and this is going to get hot. You never know how someone is going to respond to getting shot at until it happens."

"I know, but if we get into trouble, I'll need you to bail us out. She won't be able to do that on her own."

Pavak didn't look convinced. "All right. I'll sit this out, but are you sure?"

"You need to guard our escape route."

Dixie dropped her gaze to the sand. Jackson noticed her hands shaking. He went to Morris and shouted over the wind.

"If anyone shows up, you had engine trouble and landed to wait out the storm. Pavak will be up in the dunes watching. Listen in on the radio. We'll call you when we know more. If you don't hear from us, get out."

The pilot pulled out a pistol, checked the clip, and nodded. "I'll be here."

45

THE BYRNES' two-story lake house blazed with lights. Insects did mad circles in front of the windows, while bats swooped and dipped. Bruce Lambert watched the acrobatic hunters and limped up the flagstone walk to a porch full of potted gardenias. The flowers were in bloom, and their fragrance filled the humid air.

Lambert rang the doorbell. A distant clang sounded. The laughter and voices from behind the house paused for a moment before they resumed. He straightened his tie and tried not to scratch the tape holding the wire to his chest.

Deputy Director Marcus Byrnes had over thirty years of service and was considered one of the most knowledgeable men in the CIA. A lot of his early work had even become government policy. Why hadn't he raised the alarm about Alec Janné going after the Federal Reserve? Byrnes's actions made no sense.

Footsteps approached from inside. A young woman dressed in shorts and a T-shirt opened the door. Flipping on the porch light, she inspected his bruised face before motioning him inside.

"Y'all must be Agent Bruce Lambert," she said in her Texas

drawl. "Daddy told me ya would be comin'. I'm Ashley, his youngest. He said for me to take ya out back."

"Sounds like you're having a party."

"Uh-huh. Ya want a beer or somethin'?"

"No, thanks."

She turned and, flip-flops slapping the floor, led the way through the kitchen.

"He's over there," she said, rolling aside the patio door. "Yell if ya want anythin', okay?"

"Thanks."

Lambert saw a brick patio where two dozen party guests in shorts and sundresses nursed glasses of wine. Behind the patio sat an in-ground swimming pool half the length of the house. Roman columns strung with lanterns lit the water. To his immediate right sat a barbecue drum. The sweet smell of barbecue sauce and steamed corn filled the air. Steaks, chicken, hamburger, and hot dogs covered the grate, and an overweight man armed with a fork and a pair of tongs stood watch over the meat.

Off in a corner of the patio and behind a potted cypress, Byrnes sat with an older, white-haired man. Marcus Byrnes was bigger than he looked on his bio, Lambert thought. Byrnes wore a pair of faded khaki shorts, a polo shirt, and leather sandals that had seen a lot of miles. His face and arms were sunburnt, and a maze of wrinkles surrounded his eyes.

The man sitting with him was more formally attired. He wore slacks, stiff Cesare Paciotti leather shoes, a starched white shirt stained with barbecue sauce, a Rolex watch, and a Bugatti silk tie. He had an odd way of sitting that reminded Lambert of a vulture perched on a phone pole. As the men saw him approach, their eyes met. When they looked back at him, their faces were carefully devoid of expression.

"Agent Bruce Lambert?" Byrnes waved him toward an empty chair, but didn't bother standing. "I'm Marcus Byrnes.

Glad you dropped by. This is my buddy Ira Clarke. You want something to eat?"

"Not hungry," Lambert said.

"Too bad," Brynes said. "We have plenty."

Lambert stared at Byrnes for a moment. For somebody in a lot of trouble, Byrnes seemed defiantly jovial.

"What's the occasion?" Lambert asked, taking a seat.

"My niece just got engaged. She's the one sitting with her feet in the swimming pool. My wife's giving the gent the third-degree. You sure I can't get you something to eat or drink? There's a cooler with beer."

"Can I ask you a couple of questions first?"

Byrnes grinned, showing sharp white teeth. "Ask away, but before you do, Clarke here would like to look at your identification. He has a funny way of playing by the rules, but what lawyer doesn't? Hey, do you know the difference between a lawyer and a rat?" He paused expectantly. "The rat has hair on its chest!"

Lambert leaned forward, handing over his identification. Clarke inspected it and handed it back. His intelligent old eyes missed nothing.

"You sure you don't want a steak?" Byrnes asked. "You guys up north don't take the time to eat right, and Cecil over there is a fine grill cook. Put some weight on you."

The stitches in Lambert's mouth made it hard to chew, but he wouldn't have accepted even a drink of water from this guy. "No thanks, Director. I'm fine."

A conspiratorial look crossed the Texan's jowled and sunburnt face. "Spoken like a true married man. You ever notice women hate that word? They ask you how they look, and you tell them 'fine' and they get all bent out of shape." His voice rose to a falsetto. "I just spent a hundred bucks getting my hair all cut and permed, and all I look like is 'fine'? I bet your wife Leesa uses the word as much as my wife does."

Lambert's heart missed a beat. He forced himself to smile,

even though what he wanted more than anything was to tell the whole damn party to eat some brick. He had expected the spook to do his homework, but it wasn't only his own life he was risking. If things went south, Byrnes would be paying Lambert's family a visit.

"Director, would you mind answering a couple of questions?" Lambert asked.

"Be glad to, but you have to call me Mark. Only stuffed shirts like Clarke here call me Director after five o'clock. Isn't that right, Clarke?"

"Yes, Director," Clarke said.

"Have you ever heard of two men named Hassan Tarazi and Carl Jester?" Lambert asked.

"Tarazi and Jester? I can't say I have. They sound like circus people."

"Why do you want to know, Mr. Lambert?" Clarke inquired, voice deceptively soft.

"They're suspected of breaking into the Chicago Federal Reserve. I wondered if Mr. Byrnes knew anything about them."

"My client wouldn't know a computer thief from a car thief," Clarke said smoothly.

Lambert glanced at Byrnes. "Is your parrot going to be the one answering?"

Byrnes plucked an olive from his cocktail, ate it, and used the toothpick as a pointer. "Who's driving depends on where you're headed, Bruce. Clarke's here to make sure I don't drift over the center line. Before I answer anything, I would like to know what's going on."

Lambert nodded. "Fair enough. About a year ago, Hassan Tarazi and Carl Jester left their positions at the NSA and Federal Reserve to work for a man known as Daemon. Last night, I made a deal with Tarazi in exchange for information on Daemon. Names, dates, places, etc. Some of it wasn't surprising, but most of it was, which is why I am here."

"And why would that be, Agent Lambert?" Clarke asked.

"Daemon's real name is Alec Janné. He used to be a member of the French General Directorate for External Security. The DGSE is the equivalent of our CIA."

Byrnes sniffed. "I'm not sure I would go that far."

Lambert ignored the comment. "The first I heard of Daemon was five years ago when FBI counterintelligence received information that he had cracked the Central Bank of the Russian Federation and was moving the funds through Wall Street. My former partner, Tyler Jackson, and I were assigned the case. During the investigation, Daemon shot Jackson. He fled the country and has been on the run ever since."

Clarke glanced at his Rolex. "That is a very interesting history lesson, Agent Lambert, but I fail to see how it relates to my client."

Lambert nodded. "Which is exactly my point, Mr. Clarke. None of this makes sense. Why would Janné come to the United States to hack the Russians? Especially when he could have stayed in France or in some backwater country where he wouldn't have had to look over his shoulder. The Bureau, as we all know, is very, very good at tracking financial fraud. Moving the money through New York before sending it overseas was a dangerous, stupid thing to do. Why take the extra risk when he didn't have to? The answer—and please feel free to contradict me at any time, Director—is that you recruited him into the CIA to steal the money from the Russians."

Byrnes dumped the last of his cocktail onto the brick. A bat flitted over the patio and acrobatically snagged a moth before disappearing into the darkness. The sound of croaking frogs came from the nearby lake.

"Why would my client recruit a French Intelligence agent to steal funds from the Russian government?" Clarke asked.

"I believe Director Byrnes recruited Alec Janné because Janné was young, bright, idealistic, and inexperienced. Janné had spent his brief career before all of this happened safely tucked away in a DGSE basement as a financial analyst. His first and only assignment for your client, I believe, was using his expertise in banking networks to gain access to the Russians. They were easy targets. They had cash from their oil reserves, and their financial systems were woefully out of date."

Byrnes, looking over at the pool, was picking his teeth. The man was brazen. Lambert was losing patience.

"Your plan, I believe, Director, was for Janné to crack the banks. Then you would leak his identity and have him permanently disappear. The Russians would complain to the French government while you go about your business with their billions in your pocket. Brilliant, really, except for one thing — Janné wasn't as ignorant or inexperienced as you thought. He realized he was being played, grabbed the money, and ran. You've been looking for him ever since."

"What are you implying by the phrase 'your business,' Agent Lambert?" Clarke asked.

Lambert met Byrnes' careful eyes. "That's a very good question. I've read your bio, Director, and there's not a black mark on it. Only the best of the best get to your level. That's why I can't figure out what the CIA would want with billions of untraceable dollars. The idea of you procuring outside financing opens up all kinds of deeply troubling questions."

Anger flashed across Byrnes' sunburnt face. He threw his toothpick into the grass.

"Are you formally charging my client with a crime?" the lawyer asked.

Lambert ignored the question. "Why did you send one of your contract killers to kill Suzanne Williams, Tyler Jackson, and myself?"

"My client has no comment on that," Clarke said.

"Are you going to hide behind him all night?" Lambert asked.

"I'm afraid you give me no choice, Bruce," Brynes said.

Lambert frowned then unbuttoned his shirt and unplugged the radio microphone.

"Actually, I lied earlier about why I came to see you. The real reason I'm here is to offer you a deal. Nothing happens in our line of work without an arrangement being struck. 'Dickering 101' should be a prerequisite for any kind of position in the government."

"We're listening," Clarke said.

Lambert turned towards the lawyer. "I know where Alec Janné is hiding. I know your client sent Joe Tresher to kill Jackson, his fiancée, and myself. I also know where the money from the Federal Reserve went and how Janné buried it. Your client can hide behind your skirts all night, Mr. Clarke. That's his right and, to tell you the truth, I would be the first to tell him to stay there."

"Who says I'm hiding?" Byrnes demanded.

"If you're not, then you should be. Tyler Jackson isn't happy about what's happened. Last time I talked to him, he had a very short list of people to see and places to go. You're the third name on his list — right behind Janné and Tresher. Of course, if I had a preference, I think I would go after you first because you're a lot easier to find. Tresher is a professional killer. Getting him won't be easy, even with my resources. Alec Janné is down in the Caribbean sipping cold drinks and checking out the latest in women's French bathing suits, or the lack thereof. Getting the cooperation of the French government means getting State involved, and we both know those guys pour cement in their shoes before they go anywhere. That leaves one last, convenient name on the list. Yours."

"Did I miss the deal, or are you trying to pad my bill, Agent Lambert?" Clarke asked.

"The deal is simple. I want to know everyone who's involved in this. What are all those billions going to be used for? Give me that and pending approval with all affected parties, I'll drop the accessory-to-murder charges against Mr. Byrnes."

"What about the rest?"

"Your client takes his chances under the Patriot Act."

"That's bullshit!" Byrnes exploded, his face purpling. "Only a fool would agree to that!"

All conversation abruptly stopped. The guests craned their heads to see what was going on. In the silence, Lambert heard Cecil clicking his metal barbecue tongs.

"A fool who wanted to live would agree to it," Lambert amended quietly. "You walk away from this, and you'll be looking over your shoulder the rest of your very short life. Your anonymity is blown, Director. You're a liability. If Jackson doesn't kill you, my personal bet is Joe Tresher or someone like him will. Now you can either give yourself a future by cooperating, or you can wait and see what comes along, but being alone out on the end of the limb isn't where I'd want to be."

Clarke chuckled humorlessly and flicked a bit of dust off the tips of his Cesare Paciottis. "That's a nice speech, Agent Lambert. However, I think we have no choice but to turn it down."

"You're making a mistake."

Clarke shrugged coolly. "The only time I make a deal is when someone has enough evidence to make a case. The information you supposedly obtained from Tarazi was acquired using drugs and is, therefore, inadmissible. The rest of your theories are conjecture at best. You parade Tarazi into a courtroom, and I'll run you over."

"Drugs? How did you —"

Byrnes smiled. "It's my job to know, Agent Lambert."

"Only Wilkens and I saw the report. Where did you get your information?"

"C'mon, now," Byrnes drawled, waving down a waiter for a

beer. When the man had gone, he said, "Don't tell me you're surprised the FBI has leaks?"

Lambert stared at him, mind spinning.

"Are you prepared to publicly point the finger at Wilkens?" Byrnes asked. "What do you think that'll do to your career?"

Lambert had heard the threat before. From Wilkens. "So that's why Hugh Dobrowski went to Tyler Jackson about Alec Janné in New York instead of going to Wilkens or myself. Dobrowski knew you had someone inside my office."

Byrnes shrugged. "I can't comment on that."

"Director, I see you have this well in hand," Clarke said, easing out of his chair. "If you'll excuse me, I need to see a man about a dog."

Lambert watched him retreat across the patio and open the sliding door. He expected Clarke to head to the bathroom. Instead, the lawyer stood with his back turned to the door. He was talking on the phone.

Just as well to have the lawyer out of the way. Lambert reached into his pocket, removed an envelope, and handed it to Byrnes. "Maybe you can comment on this, then."

Byrnes opened the envelope. Inside was an index card with a single name written on the front. He read the name and looked toward the house. The lawyer was nowhere in sight.

"There were three different reports," Lambert said quietly. "One had the truth and two didn't. Only I've seen the right copy. The other two were fabrications. As of this moment, three people have seen the report. Wilkens, his secretary, Laura Patterson, and myself. The report Wilkens saw stated that Tarazi agreed to testify in exchange for witness protection. The report Miss Patterson saw said he was coerced. Only I have seen the third—and true—report."

Lambert inspected Byrnes's pink ears. "By the way, have you ever been to a beach resort in New Jersey called Oyster Point? I've never been there, but Laura Patterson tells me it's very romantic. Her only complaint was she forgot her sunscreen and got sunburned."

Byrnes sagged.

Lambert opened his shirt to plug in the wire. "You're going to have to come with me, Director. You may be out tomorrow, and I'm probably wasting my time, but someone has to answer for all of this, and you're all I've got."

Byrnes scowled around the patio at his family and friends, then straightened defiantly.

"What have you done for the world, Bruce? Do you think anyone's going to care five years from now about what you're doing today? You can make your accusations and spin your pet theories all you want, but the truth is, you don't have a clue about what's really going on. Back when I was a kid, before all you pencil-pushers with your plastic badges figured out how to wipe your noses, McCarthy and Hoover had the world running scared from the communists. No one cared where this nickel or that dime went as long as the Russkies didn't take over the world.

"We went after entire governments and got them. We had so many puppets it was hard keeping all the strings from getting tangled up. Presidents, premiers, and prime ministers called us before they took a leak to see if yellow would go with the wallpaper. If they didn't, we printed up planeloads of their currency and paper-bombed their economy. We sent weapons and political consultants to their neighbors. We hired nasty men even the Mob wouldn't work with, and sent them south to kill their friends, cabinet ministers, and girlfriends. We've controlled three continents for the last fifty years. And for what, so Al-Qaeda could turn Texas into an Islamic caliphate?"

Lambert leaned forward. "Director, I wonder if you've maybe wandered too far into the deep end—"

Byrnes brushed him away. "When was the last time you looked at the news, Bruce? Do you like what you see? The world's going to hell, and the only thing you boys from Justice can do is hand out a few speeding tickets to keep it orderly. The Russians are rigging our elections. East Asia is a breeding ground for jihadists. They don't care about borders, they have no diplomats, and they're hard to find. They want to kill you, me, and everyone else. Who's going to protect your family? The bureaucrats in Washington? The President and Congress?" He snorted. "Please. The one thing I have learned after forty years of service is that *true* patriots of principle, men and women who are willing to give everything they have for their country, are exceedingly rare. Our way of life is at stake, Bruce. We're in a silent war, and wars require strong leaders who know what must be done and are not afraid to do it."

Quite the speech, Lambert thought.

The old warrior glared across the pool. A bit of smoke from the barbecue wafted past.

"And Tyler Jackson?"

Byrnes shrugged. "Your former partner was in the wrong place at the wrong time. We needed cover, and he was too good to pass up. A French operative shoots an FBI agent and bolts for parts unknown with the entire Russian economy in his pocket? You can't write fiction better than that."

"How far up does this go, Director? Who else is involved?"

Byrnes pushed out his lower lip. "You don't want to know, and you wouldn't live long enough to do anything about it if you did." He looked toward the house again.

The smoky night air split apart with a sizzling hiss. Blood splashed from Byrnes's chest. His head fell back, and he covered the wound with his hand.

Lambert leapt to his feet and kicked his chair out of the way.

An old man dressed in a dark suit stalked past and shot Byrnes in the knee. The bone shattered. Byrnes screamed.

"Nice party, Director," Hugh Dobrowski said, looking around at the guests. "The only thing it needs are some fireworks. Good thing I dropped by."

The pistol coughed three more times. The first bullet caught Byrnes in the neck. The second ripped into his chin. The third tunneled into his forehead.

Lambert pulled his Glock. "Drop it! Drop it now!"

Dobrowski turned towards Lambert. His pistol rose.

The Glock fired, hitting the man's shoulder.

Resignation solidified on the man's face, and he sited towards Lambert's chest.

"Drop the weapon!" Lambert screamed.

The pistol fired, but the shot went wide. Lambert returned fire.

Dobrowski crumpled. The patio turned crimson. His weapon fell from his hand.

Lambert kicked the revolver away and knelt. He grabbed the man by the lapels. "Why did you have to shoot him?"

"He's my ticket . . . ."

"What?"

"I have cancer." Dobrowski swallowed. "Arrangements have been made. I kill him . . . my family's taken care of."

"What you did was give him an easy way out!" Lambert said, releasing him. "You stupid, stupid fool!"

Blood bubbled from Dobrowski's lips. "Not to my little girl. Not ever."

He looked up at the sky, and a last breath escaped his ruined lungs.

46

JACKSON JOGGED towards the resort's faraway lights. The rain didn't bother him. It was time to deliver the hit, and he felt good. Cacti and dune grass grabbed at his legs, but even with his feet buried him up to the ankles in sand, the wind carried him forward. Now, he could see what he'd seen on the aerials. Hooking out into the ocean like a bent finger was the reef. Surf thundered against it, but the seaplane, safe inside the lagoon, bobbed against its ties on the beach. The resort was thirty feet above the beach and surrounded by dunes. From the top of one, they could look down on the compound.

Jackson held up a hand for the others to stop.

"Let me check the approach." Grabbing handfuls of dune grass, O'Connell scrambled to the top.

"I'll wait here," Dixie said.

Jackson took her elbow.

"No, I'm fine," she said, shooing him away. "Go."

By the time Jackson reached the top, O'Connell had taken out a scope and swept the area. He handed the scope to Jackson.

Jackson pushed up his goggles and focused the scope. A quarter mile away, security lights shone outside the resort's five buildings. Two of the poolside bungalows were on the side nearest them while the other two were on the far side. The clubhouse sat to their right, making a square with the pool in the middle. One of the bungalows had a light on. The others were dark.

"See anything?" Jackson said.

"Look near the foundation of the second building on the right," O'Connell said.

Jackson saw someone sleeping on the ground. The person's arm bent at an awkward angle.

Jackson swore. "I'm really getting tired of being late for the party."

"We may not be," O'Connell said. "Come on."

They slid down the dune.

"How's it look?" Dixie said.

"Not sure." Jackson grabbed Dixie's wrist. "Stay close."

Just ahead stood the border of the resort: a line of palm trees bending like ballerinas with their arms extended to the ground. The wind had stripped their fronds and left them naked. Beyond the palms were the two closest bungalows, the clubhouse, and a Bermuda grass lawn quickly being buried by blowing sand. A gate on the tennis court banged back and forth. Except for the light in the bungalow and the lights by the pool, the resort was dark and appeared to be deserted.

Jackson reached the back of the first bungalow and stopped next to the guard on the ground. The dead man wore khaki pants, a khaki T-shirt, and military-issue boots. Strapped around his chest was a bulletproof vest, but the vest hadn't saved him. A bullet had blown out the back of his skull. Only a large caliber bullet made that kind of wound.

Jackson looked past the buildings. Blowing sand. No sign of the killer. The shooter could be sitting on top of one of the surrounding dunes, watching them. Where could they hide?

O'Connell slid around the corner of the bungalow and headed toward the pool. Keeping to the shadows, Jackson and

Dixie followed. The wind-whipped power lines spun like jump ropes. The mercury security lights popped and hissed. Jackson reached the corner of the building. Lying next to the pool lay another dead guard. O'Connell motioned Dixie to stay back. He held up two fingers and slipped inside the second bungalow.

Jackson went into the first. His night vision goggles turned the interior a ghostly gray. Sweeping the shadows with his rifle, he moved noiselessly through the empty living room into the bedroom. A man and a woman lay on the bed under a light sheet. Both had been shot in the head.

He left the bungalow and rejoined Dixie and O'Connell by the wall.

"Two dead inside. Professional kills."

O'Connell pointed to the bungalow with the light on. "Look at the ground in front of the window."

Jackson saw something sparkle. "Glass fragments?"

"From the inside out. Some of the shards made it to the edge of the pool."

"The shooter didn't have a free ride, then."

"It looks that way. I don't like the mercury lights. Anybody inside would be blind."

"What do you suggest?"

"Let's check the other buildings before we decide."

Jackson led the way back to the dunes and approached the clubhouse from the rear. Parked behind the clubhouse sat an old Jeep. The building's back door wasn't locked, and they slipped inside. For the moment, the clubhouse would protect them from whomever had picked off the others, and it was a relief to be out of the wind.

The room wasn't large—just big enough for a grill, bar, and a few tables and chairs. The only illumination came through the window blinds from the mercury lights above the pool.

"With the storm, I guess nobody felt like eatin'," Dixie whispered.

O'Connell wiped his goggles and peeked out the window.

"You know what bothers me about this place?" Jackson said. "They haven't done a thing about the storm. Hurricanes are a big deal down here. At a minimum, they should have boarded up the windows."

"Maybe they knew it was goin' north," Dixie said.

"We didn't know that until an hour ago. They wouldn't have either. It doesn't make sense."

Jackson placed his carbine on the bar and took off his headset. The wire to his radio had gotten twisted. When he looked up, he saw wet footprints. He took a second look at the floor. What was he was seeing? Then he walked across the room and turned back toward the light. He walked back to the footprints. Crouching, he ran a finger over the tile. Damp and definitely lug sole. Two patterns. Heart pounding, he moved quickly behind the bar. Metal glinted, and he reached down to pick up an empty shell casing.

"What is it?" Dixie asked.

"Empty brass. At least an entire clip." Lowering his voice, he said, "There are wet footprints on the floor. Two sets."

Jackson fingered the brass then watched water drip into the floor drain behind the bar. Turning his head, he saw another drop fall off the corner of the refrigerator door. A second drop followed the first, then a third. A sense of foreboding filled him. Slowly, he reached out, took hold of the refrigerator door's handle, and opened it. Light spilled into his face, blinding him at the very instant he heard the whoosh of a body drop through the ceiling.

"Tyler!" Dixie shouted.

Pain exploded through his head. He fell to the floor. An automatic weapon bellowed. Glass shattered.

"The window!" a woman screamed. "The big one dove through the window! I had him and he disappeared!"

"That is twice, Sing! You're missing a lot lately!"

"There was no time! Maybe Tresher will get him!"

Janné put the muzzle of his pistol in Jackson's right eye.

"*Monsieur* Tyler Jackson," he said with a slight bow. "Last time I saw you, you were bleeding all over one of your white shirts in Chicago. I did not hit you that hard. Get to your feet."

Jackson reached for the bar. His head was on fire. The window to the left of the front door was shattered. The remains of the blinds lay scattered on the sill. Dixie stood in the middle of the floor with her hands above her head. An Asian woman held a MAC-10 assault pistol to Dixie's head.

Jackson kept hold of the bar with one hand. No time to pass out. He'd lose his chance to assess his opponent. Alec Janné was his height but outweighed him by thirty pounds. His arms and chest were thick with muscle. The rain had darkened his short blond hair. He wore running shorts and a black T-shirt, but no body armor.

Janné picked up Jackson's pistol. "Having you here is almost like Christmas. All we need in the palm trees are lights, yes?"

"What do you want?"

"*Ce qui je veulent?*" Janné barked out a laugh. "You come to kill me, and you want to know what I want? That is easy. One less Arizona cowboy, and the world would be a better place."

The humor left his face, and he raised his voice over the wind. "Sing, this way, please."

Sing motioned Dixie toward the bar.

"I hope y'all are organ donors," Dixie drawled, hands closing into fists.

Sing flashed a cold, psychotic smile. "Ooh, honey. You're right, Alec. She's exquisite. We are going to have so much fun."

Dixie swung at her, but Sing stepped out of reach. "Not so fast," she purred. "We haven't even had a chance to get to know one another yet. Do not make me do something we'll regret."

"Step into the light and face the windows," Janné ordered Jackson.

Jackson did as he was told. Janné stepped behind a support post.

"Tresher!" he shouted out the broken window. "I know why you are trying to kill me! It does not take much thought to figure out Byrnes's logic, but it will not work! I have an insurance policy! Do you hear me? If you kill me, Byrnes will fall! Tresher!"

He waited a few seconds then shouted again. "It does not have to be this way, *Monsieur!* There is a compromise where we both profit, yes? I have someone here you want! You get Jackson and I walk away free! Byrnes wins both ways! My insurance policy does not activate, and he gets the only link there is between me and him! What do you say, Tresher? Tresher!"

Jackson listened for a response. With whom would he stand a better chance? The devil within or the devil without? Wind gusted through the broken window.

"I don't think he's interested," Jackson said.

"He will listen given a chance. The extra time means you and I can finish our business. Where are the transfers you took in Chicago?"

"You should have asked me that before you broke my skull."

The Beretta barked, and the bullet passed so close to Jackson's head that he nearly fell.

"I want the names of the banks and the account numbers. You will give them to me now. If you do not, I will hurt you. Do not forget, you and Ms. Stevens are worth the same to me, alive or dead."

"Once you have the numbers, that is," Jackson corrected.

"You are gambling with cards you do not have." Janné motioned to Sing. "You want a demonstration, yes? Sing, show your guest why this is not a game."

An eager smile lit Sing's face. She shifted the MAC-10 to

her left hand and snapped open a straight razor with her right. The slender blade caught the light.

"Have you ever seen a pretty woman bleed?" she asked. "There's nothing like it. Even their tears are sweet."

She ran the edge of the knife lightly up Dixie's neck, then nicked the side of her neck. Dixie winced, but didn't cry out. A single droplet of blood welled free and slid down her skin. Sing touched her fingertip to the wound and licked it clean. Dixie trembled, but didn't move.

"You have excellent control," Sing whispered, her voice lilting and musical. "That's very, very nice. Now, do exactly as I tell you, and we'll have a wonderful time. You're very beautiful, and I wouldn't want to ruin your looks. Do you understand? Answer me."

Dixie swallowed. "Yes."

"You are quite a find. It's a shame we did not meet under better circumstances. Let's start with your hardware. Use your left hand and slowly take it off."

Dixie removed her goggles and radio.

"Now the suit. Careful now."

Dixie unbuttoned the desert suit and let it fall to the floor. Underneath the suit, she wore her vest, long sleeved camouflage T-shirt, black shorts, and boots.

Sing delicately moistened her lips. "Very nice, my lovely, very nice. Now slowly undo the vest's straps. Keep your right hand behind your head where I can see it."

"Leave her alone," Jackson said. "Hurt her, and there won't be enough of you for the gulls to carry off."

Janné laughed. "You had the money and the girl, and you could not simply walk away, yes? Did you pawn your fiancée's wedding ring after she left you?"

The window exploded. A bullet hissed past. Janné recoiled, the top half of his body snapping sideways, and he bolted for the back door.

Sing screamed and whirled toward Jackson, assault pistol

arcing fire. Jackson dove sideways onto one of the tables. The MAC barked, filling the room with light. The table gave way with a crack.

She stalked toward him. "First you will die, and then I will kill your friend outside the window!"

Knowing there was nothing he could do, but not willing to just lie there, Jackson rolled off the table. The MAC spat fire. A light exploded in the ceiling, spraying the floor with plastic, glass, and metal. Sing staggered to one side, a surprised look in her eyes. Blood spilled from her throat.

Swaying, she crumpled to the floor. "So...so very pretty...."

Dixie stood over Sing. The butterfly knife trembled in her hand, and blood streamed down the side of her head. She half fell, half sat on the floor. She looked at Jackson in confusion. "I'm sorry. I...she was faster than I...."

Kneeling beside her, Jackson took the knife and closed the blade. He checked Dixie's eyes and then brushed her hair aside The bullet had sliced open her scalp and exposed her skull. The wound was bleeding profusely. Supporting her shoulders, he helped her lie back on the floor. Wishing he knew more about first-aid, he grabbed a bar towel, rolled it up, and applied pressure. Her eyelids fluttered.

"Dixie, did she shoot you anywhere else?"

"I...I'm cold."

He spread her desert suit over her. It wasn't much, but he didn't want to leave her to find something better.

"D...did I get her?" she slurred.

"Yes."

"So we can go home?"

"As soon as you feel better."

He ripped open the Med-Tek kit, found a large square of gauze, and taped a bandage above her ear. Blood soaked it. He grabbed the towel. Where was O'Connell?

She clutched his hand. "I...I want to see my folks. Last

time I saw 'em was out in Vegas after...after New Year's. Remember? It was our first Christmas together."

He brushed the hair off her forehead. His fingers came away stained. "I'll never forget it."

"When I first saw you talkin' with them, I had to go into the ladies' room and cry." Her voice trailed away, forcing him to lean close. The look in her eyes scared him. "There was so much wrong with my life, but not a bit of it mattered when I saw the three of you there. It was the happiest moment of my life."

He tried to answer but couldn't.

Her fingers dug into his palm. "That was when I knew how much I loved you. I knew I shouldn't, but I couldn't help it." She swallowed. "Take me home. I want to sit on the front porch and talk about the weather. We'll eat my mama's apple pie. You can hold my hand. It'll be like a picture in a book."

He nodded. "I will."

She sighed, the air leaving her lungs. Her eyes fluttered like moth's wings. The wind moaned about the room, and one of the mercury lights over the pool exploded with a pop.

O'Connell climbed through the broken window. He had a cut on his face and limped.

"What happened?"

"Sing shot Dixie. You missed Janné."

"It wasn't me. It was the sniper who shot the guards. Move aside. Let me look at her."

Jackson got to his feet and retrieved his rifle.

"The shooter's name is Tresher," he said. "I don't know his first name. The man at the other end is somebody named Byrnes. Tresher is damage control. Byrnes pulls the strings."

O'Connell's head snapped up. "Marcus Byrnes of the CIA?"

"All I know is a last name. We'll talk about it when I get back."

"Wait a minute! You can't go after that kind of talent by

yourself! Byrnes runs covert ops for the Shop! If Tresher works for him, then we're lucky to be alive!"

Jackson ignored him and headed for the door.

"What do you want me to do when you don't come back?" O'Connell demanded.

Jackson paused, remembering Dixie sitting beside him on the beach, watching the windsurfers jump the waves. It was only a few hours ago, but it felt like a lifetime.

"Survive."

Lowering his head, he left.

47

JACKSON FOLLOWED THE BLOOD. The Jeep had been parked behind the community center. Now, tire tracks headed into the dunes.

"Janné!"

The wind ripped the words away. Anger, grief, and loss tore his heart. Why had he insisted that Dixie come with him? Was it simple arrogance, or plain old-fashioned stupidity? Lambert and the FBI could have handled this. If he'd let them, Dixie would still be alive.

Faraway in the distance, headlights knifed through the darkness. Shots rang out. The Jeep climbed a dune, stopped, and turned so that its lights faced back the way it had come. A figure got out and passed in front of the headlights.

Jackson ran without thinking. The wind was behind him, and he felt as if he were running on a cloud. Dune grass sliced his legs and more than once he tripped, but nothing could slow him down. If he took the time to think this through, Janné would get away.

He ran towards the Jeep and heard the blaring of its horn. He scrambled up the side of the dune and, heart blazing, fell against the Jeep's spare tire. A bullet had shattered the windshield and someone—either Janné or the shooter—had driven a screwdriver into the horn.

On the leeward side of the dune, the footprints and blood resumed. Jackson followed the trail to the ocean and saw the tracks disappear into the ebbing surf. Had Janné swum out to sea? Levitated into the air? Then he knew. Janné had made the trail obvious on purpose. He'd sent Jackson and Tresher on a wild goose chase. There was only one way off the island—the plane.

Jackson cursed himself for his stupidity and turned back in the opposite direction. The wind had changed direction. Blowing in directly in from offshore, it slammed into him head-on. Staggering, every step a battle, he fought his way forward. The scissor-sharp grass that he had leapt so easily on the way over tore at his legs, and blowing sand pinged his cheeks. Air came in ragged, gasping breaths.

Step by stumbling step, he fought his way through the dunes. Only the thought of losing Janné kept him upright. He heard the banging tennis court gate first, and then the hum of the power lines whipping back and forth. The clubhouse appeared. He found a last bit of strength and staggered past the buildings. An eternity later, his strength nearly gone, he reached the line of palm trees, bowing down. Shining from beneath the glowering clouds, pale light from the coming day lit the horizon. It wouldn't be long until dawn.

His legs had long since turned numb, and when a low, concrete-block wall appeared, his knees refused to lift. He threw himself over it and fell headlong down the thirty-foot embankment. His shoulder hit something hard and unyielding. Sand filled his eyes and mouth. He spat it out and looked up to see what he had crashed into. It was the sign from the postcard listing beach restrictions. He shook his head at the wonder of it all.

"The accounts you took from me are a lot of money to die over, *Monsieur*," Janné said from behind, Jackson's rifle held in his right hand. His left arm hung limply by his side. Blood streamed down his chest, but he still managed a smile. "If I do not kill you, Tresher will. I am not going to stay and debate the issue. You have the numbers, yes? I have a way off. You may have Byrnes while I take the transfers."

Jackson lay spreadeagled on the ground. He had never felt so tired, but he managed to raise his head. "Why do you care? What I got from you in Chicago is nothing compared with the billions you took from the Fed."

"My laptop is in my room. Tresher knows this. He is waiting for me to return for it. I will not leave with nothing."

"You want to buy your way off this rock? No way."

"What is it you want, *vous espèce d'Américain stupide!*" Janné demanded. "Wilkens terminated your employment! You owe your government nothing. What is worth dying over?"

Jackson clenched his fists. "Dixie's dead! The freak you ran around with killed her!"

Janné glanced behind him at the plane. "She knew the risks. You should have left her in the States."

"She *buried* the money!" Jackson snapped. "Even if I wanted to make a deal, I couldn't! The account numbers and banks were in her head!"

Janné stared. His mouth opened, but he didn't say anything. After a second, he unexpectedly turned and walked toward the coming dawn. A wave roared onto the reef.

"Fate must want you to die under an angry sky, *Monsieur* Jackson!" he called over his shoulder. "Give Tresher my regards! *Au revoir!*"

Jackson sprang to his feet and lunged across the sand. Janné snapped up the rifle and turned. The weapon barked. The bullet tore past. They went down in a tangle of limbs. Jackson landed a blow and tensed, expecting one in return, but Janné was not fighting back.

Then Jackson saw a red dot jumping towards him across the sand. He followed the laser to its source. Fifty yards past the plane and pointing a rifle at the beach, Tresher stood on the encircling reef. Waves taller than houses crashed behind him.

The dot jumped. Jackson dove away. The big, slow bullet rumbled past and smacked the ground. A second just missed to his left. A third clawed at his sleeve. Not knowing what else to do, he rolled away from Janné and toward the lagoon, but even if he managed to make it to the water and submerge, he wouldn't be safe for long. Tresher would find him: a duck in a shooting gallery. No one would know what had happened or why. Then Tresher would kill Pavak, O'Connell, and Morris, and that would be that. They would all follow Dixie into darkness.

Heart thundering in his ears, he belly-crawled back toward Janné. The injured man lay on his back, but turned on his side and clawed at the sand. Janné had been carrying Jackson's rifle. He must have dropped it when Tresher's bullet struck.

Jackson saw the gleam of metal. His fingers closed on the rifle's barrel. He staggered to his feet and spun around to face the distant reef. Knowing it wouldn't make a damn bit of difference, he squeezed off a desperate shot.

Maybe it was a trick of the rising sun, but Jackson thought he saw the bullet flash across the lagoon past the nose of the plane. Tresher recoiled and, stumbling backwards into the water, pinwheeled through the rocks. A wave slowly fell onto the reef and knocked him down. A long line of waves, each taller than an apartment building, marched steadily toward the reef.

Jackson cupped his hands. "Tresher!"

Tresher looked over his shoulder and shielded his face with his arm. A blue-black crest curled downward and crashed onto the reef so hard it shook the ground. Dozens more followed, each landing with a boom louder than thunder.

When the water finally receded, Tresher was gone.

Jackson stumbled over to Janné. The other man still

breathed, but Tresher's bullet had torn through his chest. Blood soaked his T-shirt.

"I should have killed Byrnes long ago," Janné whispered, dark eyes filling with the dawn's light. "At least he will fall. I will have that." Gritting his teeth, he drew in a breath. "Agent Lambert will get everything. In my room is my computer with the banks, accounts, and amounts."

"Encryption?"

Janné removed a small red-and-blue metal card from his pocket. Jackson glanced at the sixteen digits displayed in the card's narrow window, then picked up his AR-15, put a shell in the magazine, and dropped the weapon at Janné's feet.

"You always were soft," Janné whispered.

"Victory doesn't feel as good as I thought it would."

He turned to leave, but Janné grabbed his boot. "Wait, *Monsieur*, you must know something. *Directeur* Byrnes is only the start of this." He swallowed. "There are others...they are powerful, quiet." He coughed blood. His voice dropped to a rough whisper. "They think nothing of killing. Once they know you have the money, they will come for you. Lambert will not be able to protect you."

"Who are they?"

Janné grimaced, showing bloody teeth. When he answered, Jackson could barely hear him wheeze. His eyes were distant, focused on something only he could see. "I do not know. Money is their weakness. If you are to survive, you must find their funding."

"What do they want with the money?"

"What do those in power ever want?"

"More power."

Janné smiled slightly. "*Oui.*"

Jackson swore. "I don't believe this."

"You will."

Jackson pocketed the time-encryption card and let the wind push him back toward the resort. A bit of morning sun escaped the cloudy horizon. One by one, the remaining mercury lights switched off. He told himself that his mission wasn't over yet, but the words refused to register. All he could think about were quiet summer nights, front porches, and apple pies.

Stairs led from the beach to the resort. Shoes heavy with wet sand, he climbed the steps and had almost reached the pool when a lone gunshot cracked.

Inside the clubhouse, O'Connell waited. His pack, first aid kit, goggles, and electronics were piled on one of the tables. "I saw the end of it," he said. "What did you do with him?"

"There wasn't anything *to* do. I left him where he fell."

"I radioed Q and told him what happened. He and Morris are coming over with a stretcher."

"Good," Jackson said.

He looked at Dixie lying on the floor. What right had he had to put any of them at risk? Dixie was dead because of him. O'Connell had a wife and kids he'd barely seen in the two years since Jackson had hired him. What would he have told O'Connell's family if Sing had killed him? What was he going to say to Dixie's family when he saw them? That she had loved him, stuck with him to the end, and now was gone?

"Janné's laptop is in his room," Jackson said. "The accounts are on it."

"I'll go grab it," O'Connell said, heading for the door. "I imagine you'll want some time alone."

"Thanks, Doc."

Very slowly, Jackson knelt beside Dixie. It looked like O'Connell had shaved the hair from her wound and replaced the bloody bandage with a clean one. But why bother? She was dead. The first tear squeezed free.

"There was so much I wanted to tell you," he whispered. "Now the only word left is goodbye. I love you. I'm sorry I never told you before."

A bit of sunlight lit her in gold. He fixed her face deep in his mind and stood up. His pistol sat on the table next to O'Connell's pack. There was no one else left to kill, but he picked the gun up anyway.

A bit of glass rolled off the table and fell to the floor where it bounced with a click. He moved towards the door before he realized what he had seen and turned around. The glass caught the light, and he blinked at the table where O'Connell's equipment sat in a jumbled pile. He went over to pick up the empty vial of epinephrine off the floor. A roaring filled his ears, and for a second, he was lying in the back of the van in Chicago, looking at the van's ceiling while wildfire blazed across his face.

His hands started to shake, and then time seemed to stop as Dixie's eyes fluttered opened.

"I nearly die, and all I get is a lousy goodbye?" she said.

48

MORRIS FLEW them to a small Dominican hospital. The doctors said Dixie would need three days before she'd be well enough to travel. Jackson spent most of that time napping in the hospital's uncomfortable chairs. He had gotten Dixie a private room, but he piney scent of hospital disinfectant brought back bad memories of getting shot. The doctors and nurses were friendly, but during one of his naps, he had a nightmare where the head nurse held a running auction for his internal organs. After each organ sold, the doctor would cheerfully extract it, serve it up on a polished silver surgical tray, and call out the next item for sale.

Jackson fled outside into the bright sunshine. The wind picked up, and on a whim, he rented a sailboat and sailed until Dominica was nothing but a tiny dot behind him. A jagged purple cloud followed him east, turning the sky dark and heavy. Rain popped against the sail. A sudden squall kicked up, and the mainsail filled with a snap that nearly sent him tumbling overboard.

Trying to balance the side force of the sail against the lift of the keel, he forced the bow across the wind. The sail concentrated its force against the center of the boat, pushing it windward while the keel's hydrodynamic lift countered the sail's force and pushed it back leeward. The result between the two opposing forces was equilibrium, or speed. He knew the physics of sailing, but knowing and navigating in a squall were two different things. The nearest large land mass was Africa, a thousand miles away.

Eyes fixed on the sail's trim, he gave the sail more wind, until the mast turned into a hard, creaking line against the sky. The deck slowly heeled over, and the bow lifted out of the water. Finally, he was running flat out across the wind. Could he outrun fate?

Even the wind in his face did not blow away the questions. What did Bruce Lambert mean when he'd said Hugh Dobrowski killed Director Marcus Byrnes? Had Dobrowski known who was behind all this?

They will come for you.

He had better concentrate on sailing. He adjusted the rudder. Save the questions for another phone call or for when he saw Lambert in person.

The squall eventually moved on, leaving a hazy sky that turned the sun into a sinking, orange ball. He chased the storm northwest, a part of him wanting to just keep going, but the wind shifted, and he finally turned around.

By the time he returned, the sun had set. The television droned in Dixie's room. She was asleep, face peaceful.

He took a seat and watched a baseball game on one of the American stations. It was an election year, and the commercials were sound bites, lies, or a combination of both.

Dixie woke and gave him a sleepy smile.

"How are you feeling?" he asked.

"Tired. I've been watchin' the news all day to see if there's anythin' about us returning the government's missin' money. So far there's been a whole lot of nothin'."

"You're wasting your time. As far as the government is concerned, none of this happened. It was a hoax, nothing more. Even a rumor of this would send every grandma and hedge fund manager running from the market. It won't happen."

"They can't just bury it," she insisted. "That kind of money has to be missed."

"They can and they will. The closest you'll get to the truth is a technical glitch of some sort. Something where the computer accidentally gives someone a trillion dollars or makes everyone a millionaire. My bet is they won't even do that. Why cause problems when they don't have to? How's the head?"

She gave him a wan smile. "The light gives me headaches. It's hard to concentrate. But the stitches will come out in a week or so, and given time, the doctor says I should be as good as new."

"Except for your bald spot."

Her hand whipped out, and she grabbed hold of the fleshy part of his left arm with her fingers. He jerked free with a yelp.

"The hair will grow back, thank you very much, Mr. Jackson. Bring it up again, and I'll give you a lot more than a welt."

"You must really be feeling better," he said, rubbing his arm. "Your reflexes are almost back to normal. Has the doctor given you a parole date?"

"Tomorrow, and that's only because he had one of the nurses with him. Men will do anythin' if you smile and hike the sheet enough for them to see some leg."

He gave her a quizzical look. "You want out? For the last two years you've been whining for a vacation, and now that you've got one, all you want to do is leave?"

She swiped at him again, but he was ready this time and she missed.

"So where were you all day? A girl would almost think you were avoidin' her."

"I watched some baseball while you slept. One of the pitchers was so big, he should have been called Cy Gonna-Die Young."

She blinked.

"The only other time I saw a pitcher that big was when Fried Catfish Hunter played. Of course, Carlton Fisk gained so much weight after he retired from baseball that people started calling him Carl's Jr. Fisk."

Her gaze narrowed.

"After the baseball game, I watched some women's international gymnastics. If the Chinese team would have been any younger, they would have been sent back to China to work their factory jobs."

He waited for a reaction, didn't get one, and tapped on his cell phone like a microphone. "Hello? Is this thing on?"

She glared. "Unfortunately, yes."

He grinned and she smiled. It felt wonderful to see her happy.

"So where were you really?" she asked. "I kept waiting for you to visit."

"I rented a sailboat and went out to think."

"About?"

"I wish I knew," he said. "I just followed the sun until it went down, then called myself an idiot for sailing into the wild blue yonder without knowing where I was going. The only reason I'm here now is I saw the island's lights."

She laughed and winced. "It still feels strange just to lie here, you know. After all this time, I can't believe it's over."

They will come for you.

Her smile became a frown. "Tyler, what's goin' on? For two days you've been wearin' that grimace on your mug. What aren't you tellin' me?"

Reluctantly, he met her gaze and nearly told her what Janné had said.

"I just keep thinking about all the people who've died because of me. That isn't easy to live with. I shouldn't have brought you into this. I'm sorry."

"You did what you had to."

"I'm not sure I even know what happiness is anymore. You and my folks are all I have left. Everything else has been burned away. I feel like finding a lonely rock somewhere and waiting for lightning to strike."

"Tyler, it's over! We're the ones walkin' away! It could have been a lot worse. It's o-v-e-r." She spelled out the word.

He exhaled and let her have the moment. "You're right, Dixie. I worry too much. The most important thing is getting you out of here so we can have that victory party."

"Don't be countin' on a wild time. I'll have to take it easy. O'Connell's still limpin' around from twisting his ankle. He came in earlier and wanted to know if I was up for some wheelchair racin'. Did you talk with Lambert yet?"

Jackson withdrew a slip of paper and handed it across. "The deal's done. He's agreed to everything."

She took the paper and frowned. "He'd be a fool not to. He'll get a corner office after this. Did he leave us any crumbs, or does he just want us to disappear?"

"I didn't want to mention it before because I didn't want to get your hopes up, but when I said everything, I meant everything."

"My head hurts too much to think, Tyler. What are you tryin' to say?"

"The terms are immunity for everyone involved. Bruce is taking care of the details right now. As of an hour or so ago, Genesis never happened. You're a free woman, Dixie."

She stared for a second, then started to cry. He gave her a tissue, but she wanted his shoulder instead. He bent over and she raised her arms. He held her for a long, long time.

"Thank you," she finally said, wiping her eyes. "I don't know what else to say but thank you."

"The only reason I'm here today is because of you. I owe you everything, Dixie."

She released him and he moved to the foot of the bed. "You have your life back, Dixie. You can do anything you want."

She smiled. Happiness looked good on her.

"There's one more thing," he said. "Bruce says he's willing to go to bat for me if I want to get back into the FBI."

Her eyes widened. "Are you sure you want to do that?"

"I don't know. I told him I'm thinking about it."

"How much did he give us for returnin' the money?"

"He said he would buy us lunch next time we're in New York."

The tears vanished. "What!"

Jackson kept his expression neutral. "He released the funds that Wilkens had locked down. We have Janné's laptop. With a bit of work, I'm sure we could track down the rest of the money he took from the Russians. Twenty percent of billions is more money than I can count."

"That could take years!"

The door opened and one of the nurses tapped her watch.

Jackson bent over and gave Dixie a kiss. "I'm going back to hotel. You get some rest."

HE PUSHED a chair to the small table in his room. Could he just walk away from the money, or should he give it back? A few keystrokes and the billions of transactions would disappear forever.

The thought cheered him up as he unzipped his overnight bag and withdrew Janné's computer from its case.

They will come for you.

From his wallet, he took a list of anonymous gateway servers and chose one at random. He started up a secure shell client on the machine and jumped through a series of routers across the United States to log into the public IMAP server Lambert kept for personal use. Finger poised over the DELETE key, he stared at the banks and the millions of account numbers Janné had stolen from the Chicago Federal Reserve. Then he dropped the list into Lambert's e-mail account. Thirty seconds later, he bounced backward through the routers and disappeared.

He'd officially saved the world.

He went down to the atrium, a .22 caliber pocket automatic hidden under his shirt, and tossed alfalfa pellets to the Japanese carp. O'Connell and Pavak came through the entry doors. Both men wore Hawaiian shirts, shorts, sandals, and matching sunburns. Pavak had a six-pack of Jamaican Red Stripe beer. They were obviously in good spirits. Giving Jackson a wink, O'Connell removed a check from his shirt pocket and handed it across.

"What's this?" Jackson asked.

"Your half of the lottery ticket I bought up in Chicago. Fifty bucks."

"Lottery ticket? You mean you won?"

"Not the whole thing. But yeah, we'll get a check."

Jackson read the amount on the check. "Two hundred for a buck? We're in the wrong line of work." He made a paper airplane out of the check and sailed it back across the table.

The blood drained from O'Connell's face. "Now why did you have to do that?"

"It was your dollar, Doc. Keep it."

O'Connell gave the check to Pavak and pushed another check Jackson's way. This one had five zeros. "Don't blow it all in one place, you conscientious freak."

Jackson picked up the check. "What's going on?"

Pavak folded the first check into his pocket. "I bet Doc you would give it back to him."

Jackson started to make another paper airplane, but stopped when Pavak licked his lips. Once a sleaze, always a sleaze.

"Do us both a favor and keep the money," O'Connell whispered.

Jackson looked at both of his friends, and then tore the check in half and gave each of them a piece.

"Call it an investment in your PI business. Next year at this time, I'll visit, and you can write me a dividend check. It'll be like old times."

Pavak sneered. "So we kill ourselves, and you get all the money?"

"Like I said, it'll be just like old times."

They laughed.

He told them about Lambert's offer of returning to the FBI. They asked him what he wanted to do, and he told them he honestly didn't know. He was thinking it over.

O'Connell wanted to call it a night. "Coming, Pavak?"

"Might as well."

"Me, too." Jackson picked up two glasses and a chilled bottle of champagne from the bar. Back in his room, he poured the champagne and was about to take a drink when a hesitant knock sounded on his door. He checked the peephole. Dixie stood in the hallway. She wore her camouflage shorts, boots, and a garish tourist T-shirt. She had removed the bandage from her head and combed her hair over the stitches. Her eyes were moist, and she looked as jumpy as an alley cat during an electrical storm.

He opened the door. "Dixie! I thought you were supposed to be in the hospital until tomorrow!"

She looked from him to the carpet and back again.

"I am. I mean, I'm supposed to be. I, well, I sort of snuck out." She shook her head. "I keep havin' these nightmares. I couldn't sleep, so I decided I didn't want to spend another night in the hospital. But when I got here, I realized I didn't have a room. I don't have my wallet, and I spent all my cash on a cab and this stupid T-shirt so I wouldn't have to wear somethin' with blood all over it. Do you know how hard it is to buy a shirt this time of night? I'm sorry, but I don't have anywhere else to go."

"Dixie —"

"I know your feelings are all screwed up, but a girl can really only say so much. If you want me to leave, then I will. Just get me a room until I can find my wallet." She wiped away a tear. "I just hope I didn't lose it. For some reason I can't remember where I put it, and I'm really exhausted. Maybe I shouldn't have left the hospital, but I just —"

Jackson stepped forward and put a finger to her lips. "Will you stop for a second? Geez, how is a guy supposed to tell you how he feels if you won't let him get a word in edgewise?" He took a breath. "I know my feelings are a mess, but I don't know where I would be without you. I love you, Dixie."

She started to cry and melted against him. She felt wonderful in his arms. Then he felt her pull away. She was looking past him at the two glasses and the champagne.

"Who is that for!"

He shrugged. "I got to thinking about our victory party, so I picked up some champagne."

"Oh, don't even tell me!" she protested. "There is absolutely no way on earth you could have known I was comin'! I didn't even know myself until a half hour ago."

He handed her a glass. "Here's to you, me, and walking away at the end."

"But how did you know?"

He gave her his best, most dazzling grin. "I had a hunch."

AFTERWORD

Thank you for reading *Satan's Gold*. I hope you enjoyed meeting Tyler Jackson, Dixie, and crew. If you did, I would greatly appreciate you leaving a review in the online bookstore of your choice. Reviews are crucial for any author, and a line or two about your experience can make a huge difference. If you're part of the Goodreads community, comments there are especially valuable.

www.goodreads.com

ACKNOWLEDGMENTS

To all the writers' groups in Chicago, Phoenix, Tempe, and online, this book wouldn't have happened without your friendship, suggestions, guidance and priceless critiques. But most especially to Donna Hoagkemp — who has read almost every word I've ever written and hasn't killed me or herself after doing so. Also, thanks to Kelly McWilliams for her astute proofreading and editorial assistance.

No book is ever "written" by the author alone, nor is any book complete without a reader at the other end.

ABOUT THE AUTHOR

Michael Ray Ewing has spent his career working as a High-Performance Computing engineer. His workflow automation software, Rhapsody, is the winner of two awards from *NetWorld* and *Lotus Magazine*.

Characters, like the writers who create them, need a deep and tangled past. Because of the ups and downs in his industry, he writes about people whose lives are roller coasters. *Satan's Gold* won the Emerging Writers Gateway award for best crime thriller.

www.michaelrayewing.com